Big Man and the Little Men

ALSO BY CLIFFORD THOMPSON

What It Is: Race, Family, and One Thinking Black Man's Blues

Twin of Blackness: A Memoir

Love for Sale and Other Essays

Signifying Nothing: A Novel

BIG MAN

-and the-

LITTLE MEN

~a graphic novel~
written and illustrated by

CLIFFORD THOMPSON

Other Press New York

Production editor: Yvonne E. Cárdenas

10 9 8 7 6 5 4 3 2 1

Library of Congress Cataloging-in-Publication Data
Names: Thompson, Clifford, writer, illustrator.
Title: Big man and the little men : a graphic novel / written and illustrated
    by Clifford Thompson.
Description: New York : Other Press, [2022]
Identifiers: LCCN 2022018854 (print) | LCCN 2022018855 (ebook) |
    ISBN 9781635422009 (hardcover) | ISBN 9781635422016 (ebook)
Subjects: LCGFT: Graphic novels
Classification: LCC PN6727.T457 B54 2022 (print) | LCC PN6727.T457 (ebook) |
    DDC 741.5/973—dc23/eng/20220610
LC record available at https://lccn.loc.gov/2022018854
LC ebook record available at https://lccn.loc.gov/2022018855

Publisher's Note
This is a work of fiction. Names, characters, places, and incidents either are the product of the author's imagination or are used fictitiously, and any resemblance to actual persons, living or dead, events, or locales is entirely coincidental.

for my two
FABULOUS
SISTERS

PROLOGUE

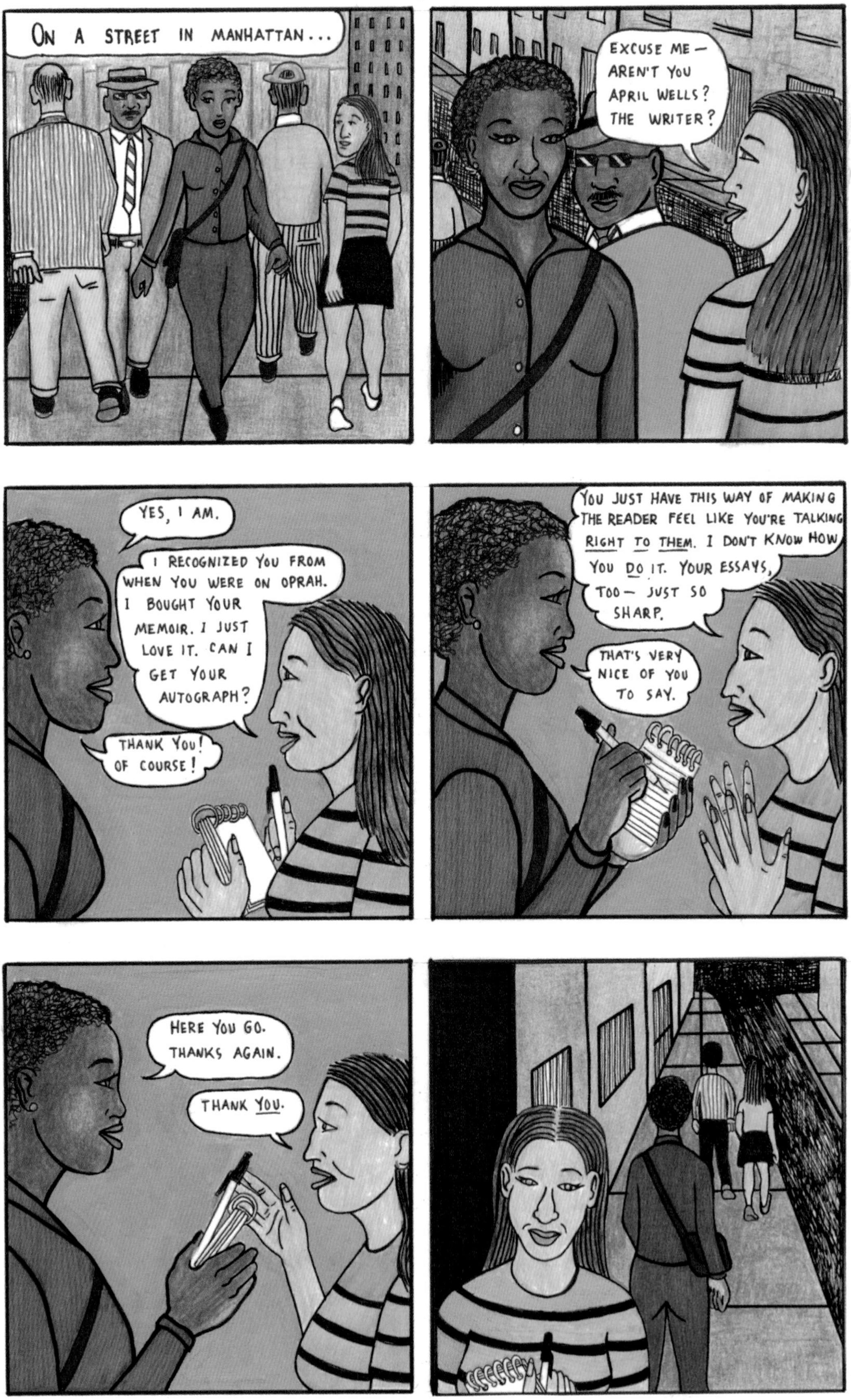
ON A STREET IN MANHATTAN...
EXCUSE ME— AREN'T YOU APRIL WELLS? THE WRITER?
YES, I AM.
I RECOGNIZED YOU FROM WHEN YOU WERE ON OPRAH. I BOUGHT YOUR MEMOIR. I JUST LOVE IT. CAN I GET YOUR AUTOGRAPH?
THANK YOU! OF COURSE!
YOU JUST HAVE THIS WAY OF MAKING THE READER FEEL LIKE YOU'RE TALKING RIGHT TO THEM. I DON'T KNOW HOW YOU DO IT. YOUR ESSAYS, TOO— JUST SO SHARP.
THAT'S VERY NICE OF YOU TO SAY.
HERE YOU GO. THANKS AGAIN.
THANK YOU.

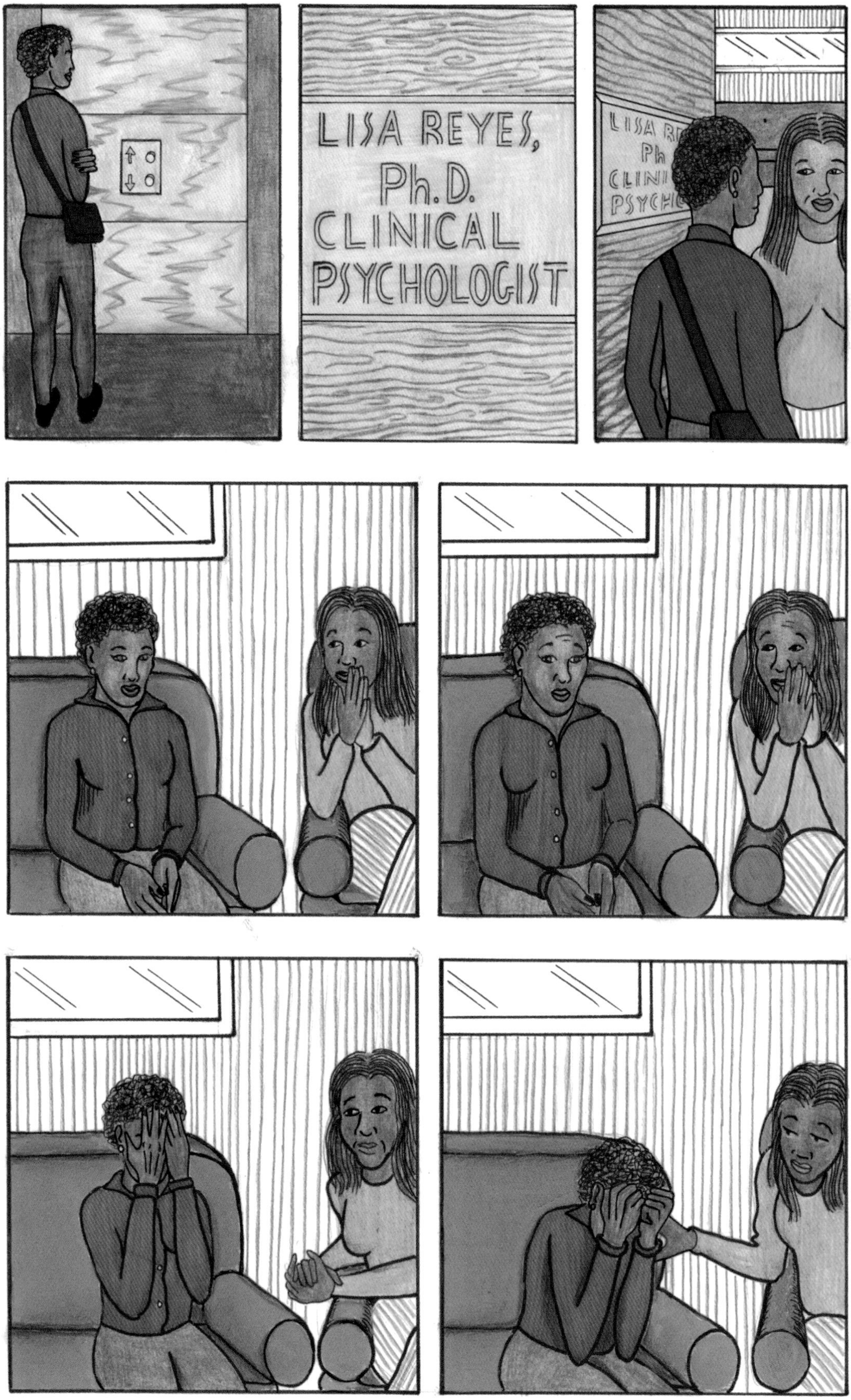
LISA REYES,
Ph.D.
CLINICAL
PSYCHOLOGIST

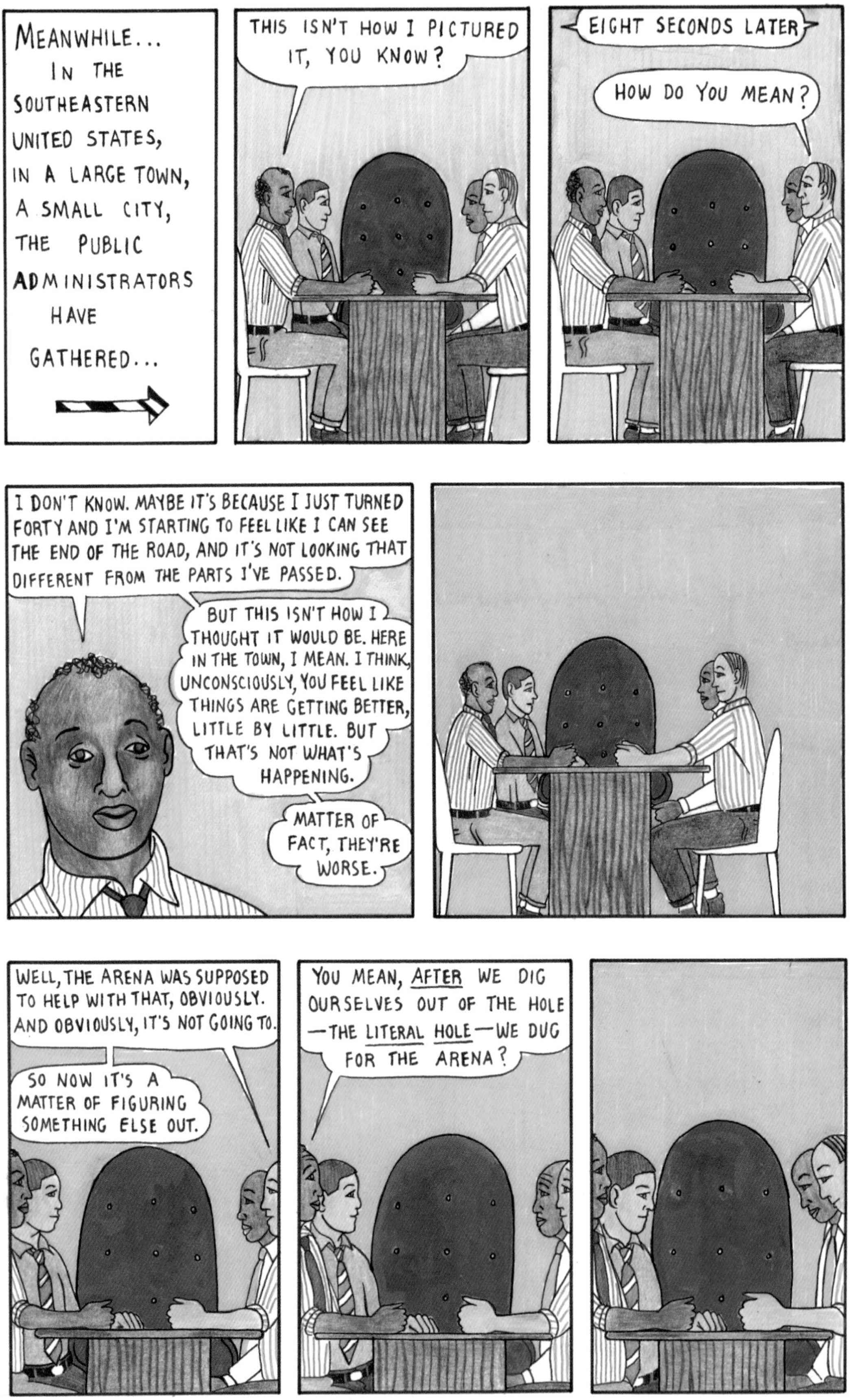
MEANWHILE... IN THE SOUTHEASTERN UNITED STATES, IN A LARGE TOWN, A SMALL CITY, THE PUBLIC ADMINISTRATORS HAVE GATHERED...
THIS ISN'T HOW I PICTURED IT, YOU KNOW?
EIGHT SECONDS LATER
HOW DO YOU MEAN?
I DON'T KNOW. MAYBE IT'S BECAUSE I JUST TURNED FORTY AND I'M STARTING TO FEEL LIKE I CAN SEE THE END OF THE ROAD, AND IT'S NOT LOOKING THAT DIFFERENT FROM THE PARTS I'VE PASSED.
BUT THIS ISN'T HOW I THOUGHT IT WOULD BE. HERE IN THE TOWN, I MEAN. I THINK, UNCONSCIOUSLY, YOU FEEL LIKE THINGS ARE GETTING BETTER, LITTLE BY LITTLE. BUT THAT'S NOT WHAT'S HAPPENING.
MATTER OF FACT, THEY'RE WORSE.
WELL, THE ARENA WAS SUPPOSED TO HELP WITH THAT, OBVIOUSLY. AND OBVIOUSLY, IT'S NOT GOING TO.
SO NOW IT'S A MATTER OF FIGURING SOMETHING ELSE OUT.
YOU MEAN, AFTER WE DIG OURSELVES OUT OF THE HOLE —THE LITERAL HOLE—WE DUG FOR THE ARENA?

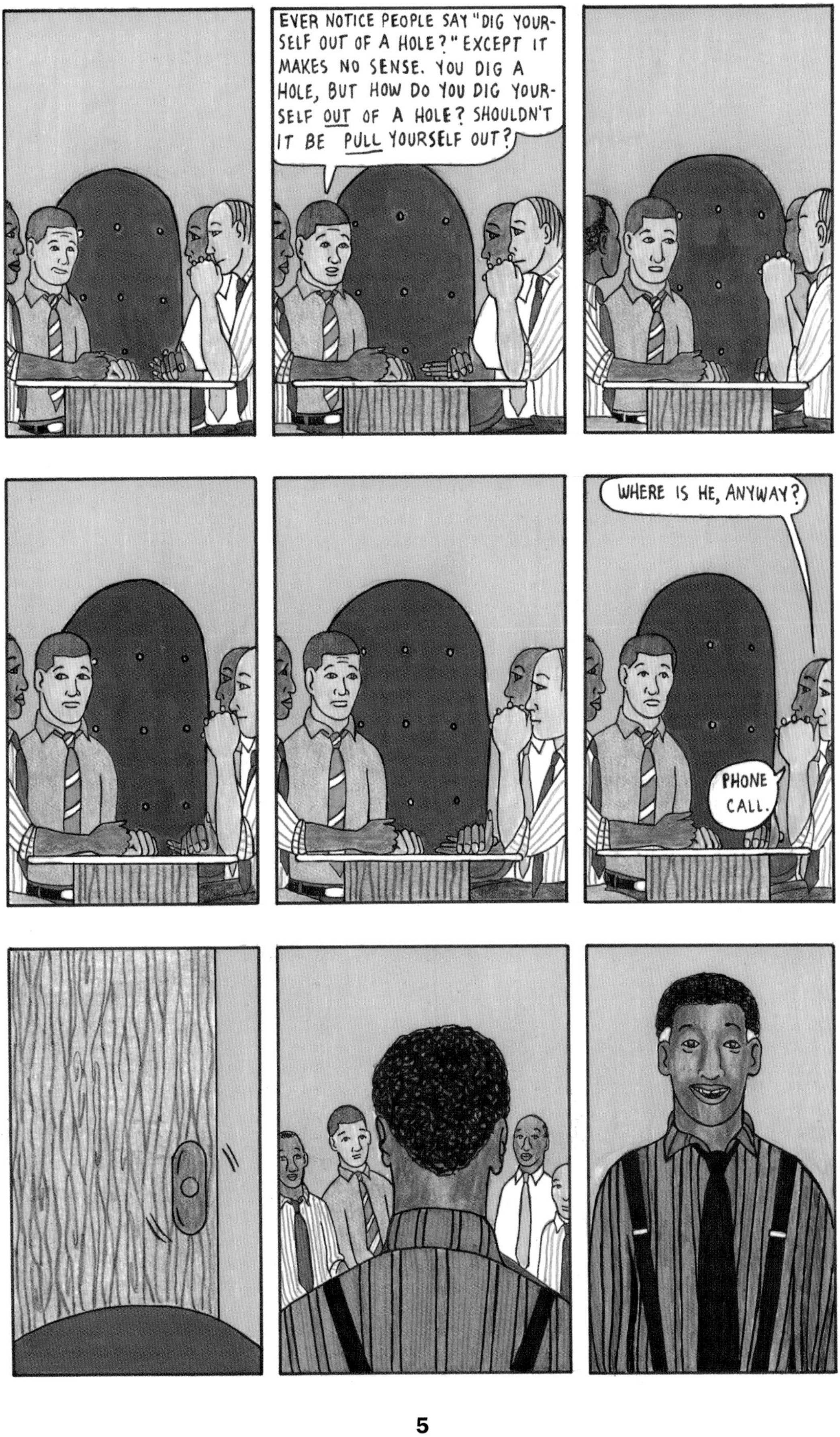
EVER NOTICE PEOPLE SAY "DIG YOURSELF OUT OF A HOLE?" EXCEPT IT MAKES NO SENSE. YOU DIG A HOLE, BUT HOW DO YOU DIG YOURSELF OUT OF A HOLE? SHOULDN'T IT BE PULL YOURSELF OUT?
WHERE IS HE, ANYWAY?
PHONE CALL.

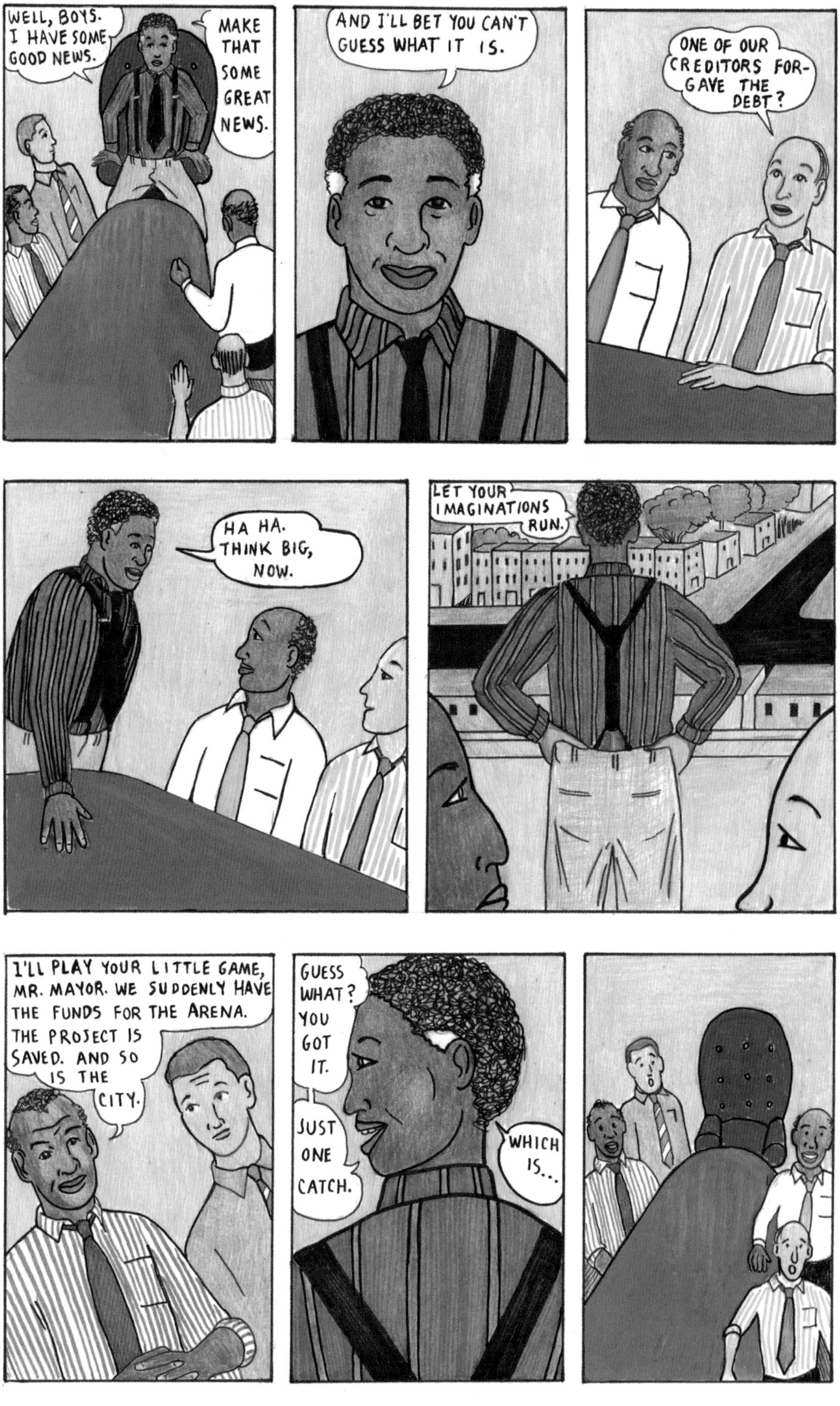
WELL, BOYS. I HAVE SOME GOOD NEWS.
MAKE THAT SOME GREAT NEWS.
AND I'LL BET YOU CAN'T GUESS WHAT IT IS.
ONE OF OUR CREDITORS FOR-GAVE THE DEBT?
HA HA. THINK BIG, NOW.
LET YOUR IMAGINATIONS RUN.
I'LL PLAY YOUR LITTLE GAME, MR. MAYOR. WE SUDDENLY HAVE THE FUNDS FOR THE ARENA. THE PROJECT IS SAVED. AND SO IS THE CITY.
GUESS WHAT? YOU GOT IT.
JUST ONE CATCH.
WHICH IS...

PART ONE

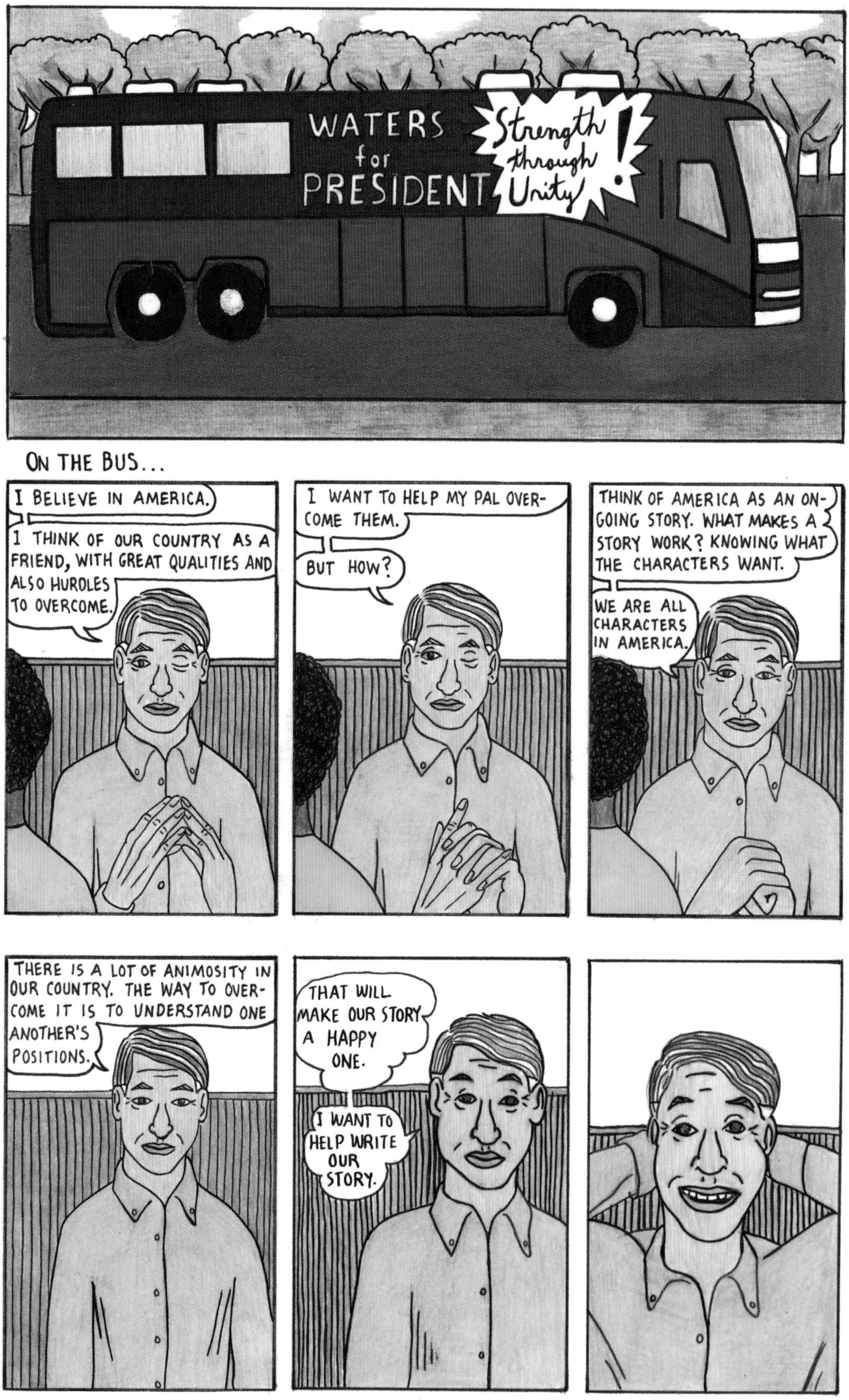
WATERS for PRESIDENT
Strength through Unity!
ON THE BUS...
I BELIEVE IN AMERICA.
I THINK OF OUR COUNTRY AS A FRIEND, WITH GREAT QUALITIES AND ALSO HURDLES TO OVERCOME.
I WANT TO HELP MY PAL OVERCOME THEM.
BUT HOW?
THINK OF AMERICA AS AN ONGOING STORY. WHAT MAKES A STORY WORK? KNOWING WHAT THE CHARACTERS WANT.
WE ARE ALL CHARACTERS IN AMERICA.
THERE IS A LOT OF ANIMOSITY IN OUR COUNTRY. THE WAY TO OVERCOME IT IS TO UNDERSTAND ONE ANOTHER'S POSITIONS.
THAT WILL MAKE OUR STORY A HAPPY ONE.
I WANT TO HELP WRITE OUR STORY.

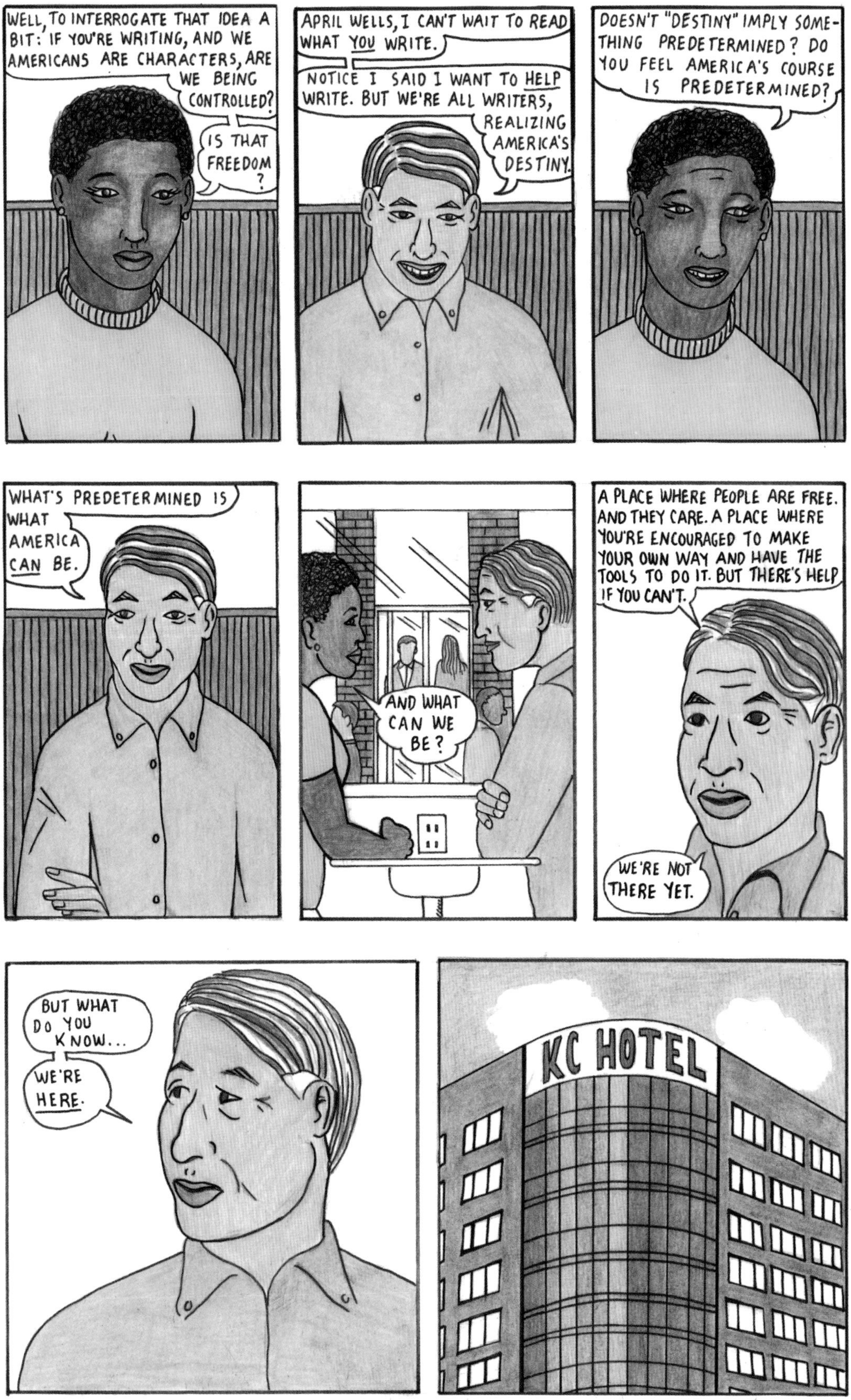
WELL, TO INTERROGATE THAT IDEA A BIT: IF YOU'RE WRITING, AND WE AMERICANS ARE CHARACTERS, ARE WE BEING CONTROLLED?
IS THAT FREEDOM?
APRIL WELLS, I CAN'T WAIT TO READ WHAT YOU WRITE.
NOTICE I SAID I WANT TO HELP WRITE. BUT WE'RE ALL WRITERS, REALIZING AMERICA'S DESTINY.
DOESN'T "DESTINY" IMPLY SOMETHING PREDETERMINED? DO YOU FEEL AMERICA'S COURSE IS PREDETERMINED?
WHAT'S PREDETERMINED IS WHAT AMERICA CAN BE.
AND WHAT CAN WE BE?
A PLACE WHERE PEOPLE ARE FREE. AND THEY CARE. A PLACE WHERE YOU'RE ENCOURAGED TO MAKE YOUR OWN WAY AND HAVE THE TOOLS TO DO IT. BUT THERE'S HELP IF YOU CAN'T.
WE'RE NOT THERE YET.
BUT WHAT DO YOU KNOW...
WE'RE HERE.
KC HOTEL

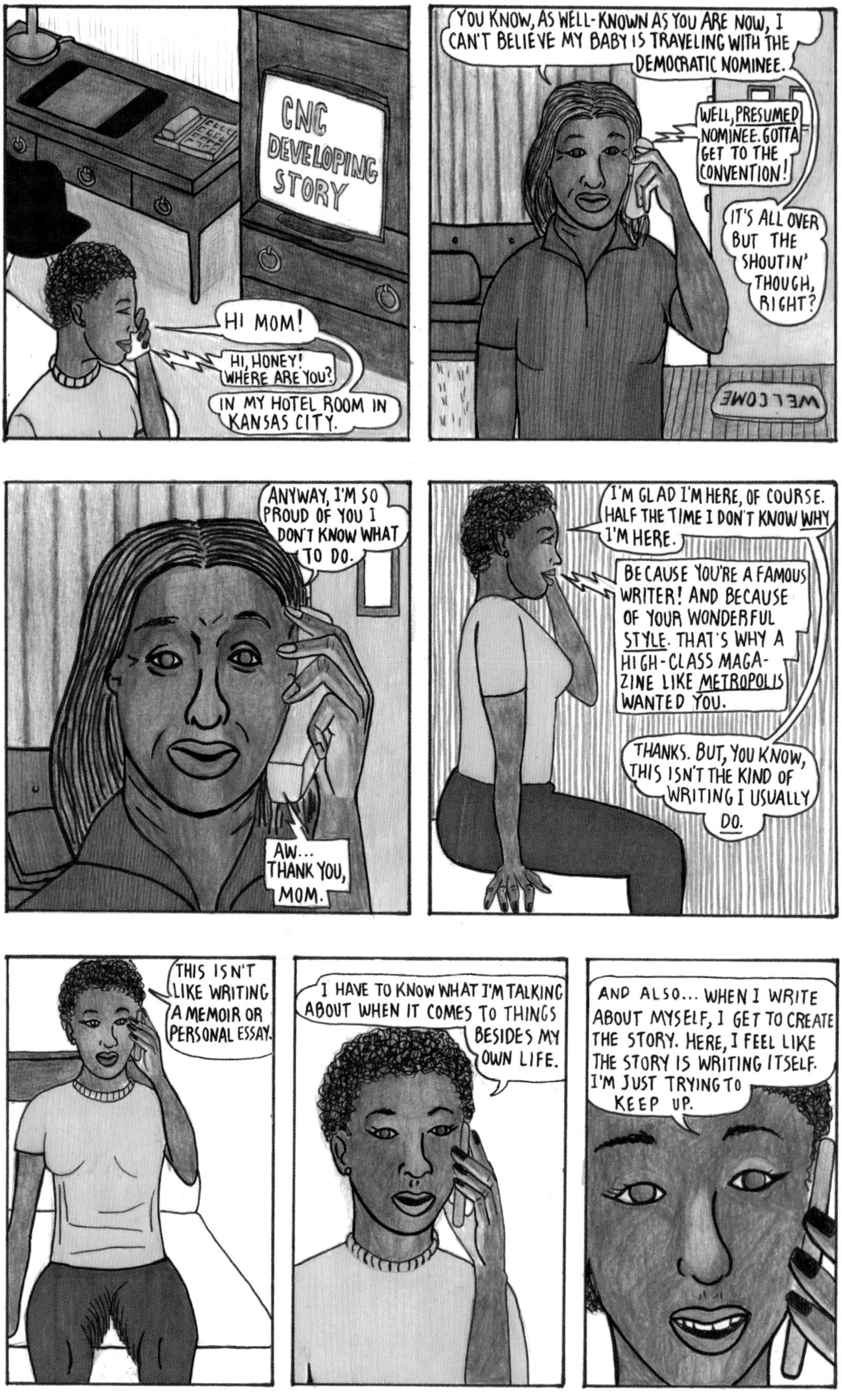
CNC
DEVELOPING
STORY
HI MOM!
HI, HONEY! WHERE ARE YOU?
IN MY HOTEL ROOM IN KANSAS CITY.
YOU KNOW, AS WELL-KNOWN AS YOU ARE NOW, I CAN'T BELIEVE MY BABY IS TRAVELING WITH THE DEMOCRATIC NOMINEE.
WELL, PRESUMED NOMINEE. GOTTA GET TO THE CONVENTION!
IT'S ALL OVER BUT THE SHOUTIN' THOUGH, RIGHT?
WELCOME
ANYWAY, I'M SO PROUD OF YOU I DON'T KNOW WHAT TO DO.
AW... THANK YOU, MOM.
I'M GLAD I'M HERE, OF COURSE. HALF THE TIME I DON'T KNOW WHY I'M HERE.
BECAUSE YOU'RE A FAMOUS WRITER! AND BECAUSE OF YOUR WONDERFUL STYLE. THAT'S WHY A HIGH-CLASS MAGAZINE LIKE METROPOLIS WANTED YOU.
THANKS. BUT, YOU KNOW, THIS ISN'T THE KIND OF WRITING I USUALLY DO.
THIS ISN'T LIKE WRITING A MEMOIR OR PERSONAL ESSAY.
I HAVE TO KNOW WHAT I'M TALKING ABOUT WHEN IT COMES TO THINGS BESIDES MY OWN LIFE.
AND ALSO... WHEN I WRITE ABOUT MYSELF, I GET TO CREATE THE STORY. HERE, I FEEL LIKE THE STORY IS WRITING ITSELF. I'M JUST TRYING TO KEEP UP.

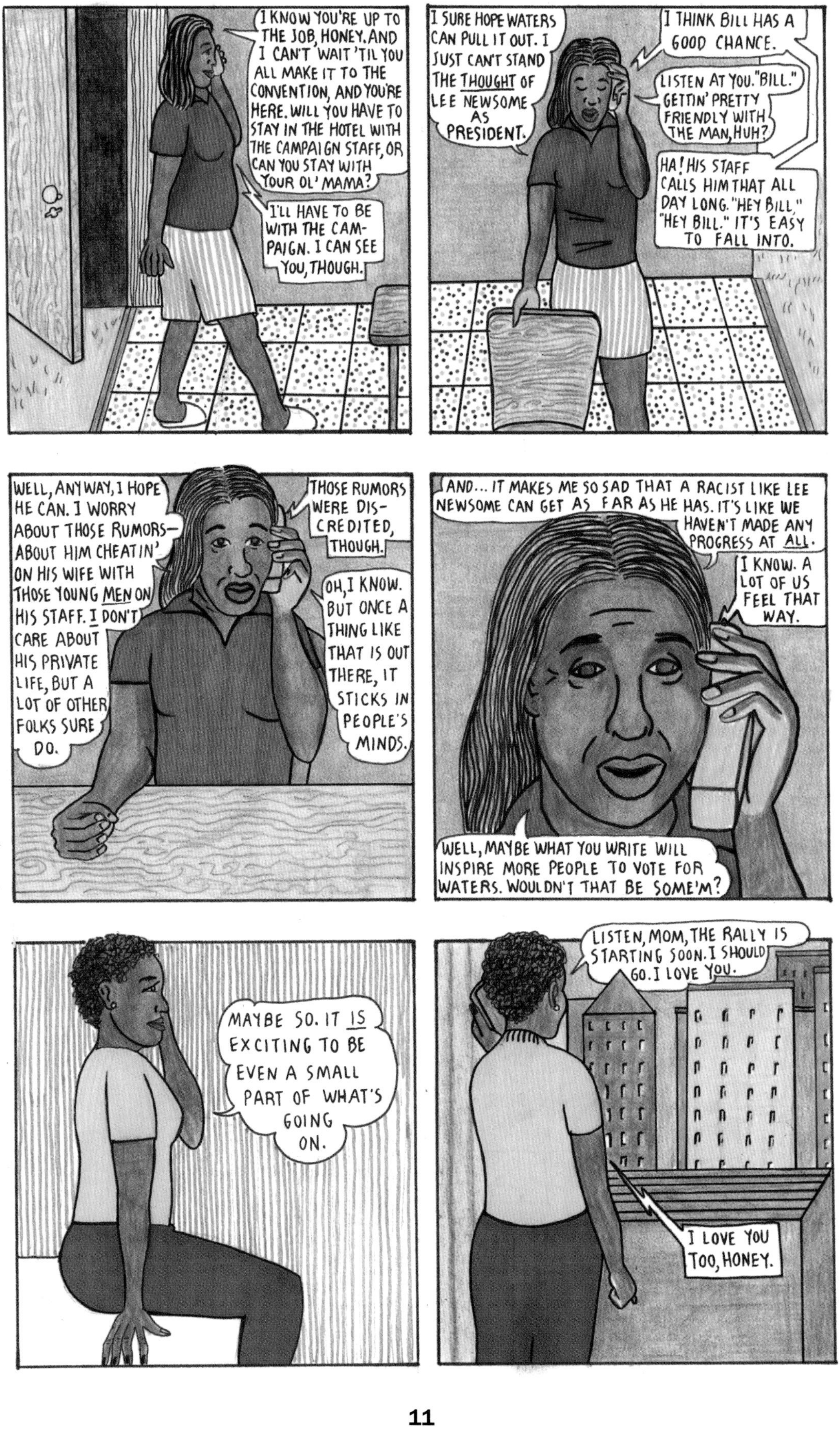
I KNOW YOU'RE UP TO THE JOB, HONEY. AND I CAN'T WAIT 'TIL YOU ALL MAKE IT TO THE CONVENTION, AND YOU'RE HERE. WILL YOU HAVE TO STAY IN THE HOTEL WITH THE CAMPAIGN STAFF, OR CAN YOU STAY WITH YOUR OL' MAMA?
I'LL HAVE TO BE WITH THE CAMPAIGN. I CAN SEE YOU, THOUGH.
I SURE HOPE WATERS CAN PULL IT OUT. I JUST CAN'T STAND THE THOUGHT OF LEE NEWSOME AS PRESIDENT.
I THINK BILL HAS A GOOD CHANCE.
LISTEN AT YOU. "BILL." GETTIN' PRETTY FRIENDLY WITH THE MAN, HUH?
HA! HIS STAFF CALLS HIM THAT ALL DAY LONG. "HEY BILL," "HEY BILL." IT'S EASY TO FALL INTO.
WELL, ANYWAY, I HOPE HE CAN. I WORRY ABOUT THOSE RUMORS— ABOUT HIM CHEATIN' ON HIS WIFE WITH THOSE YOUNG MEN ON HIS STAFF. I DON'T CARE ABOUT HIS PRIVATE LIFE, BUT A LOT OF OTHER FOLKS SURE DO.
THOSE RUMORS WERE DISCREDITED, THOUGH.
OH, I KNOW. BUT ONCE A THING LIKE THAT IS OUT THERE, IT STICKS IN PEOPLE'S MINDS.
AND... IT MAKES ME SO SAD THAT A RACIST LIKE LEE NEWSOME CAN GET AS FAR AS HE HAS. IT'S LIKE WE HAVEN'T MADE ANY PROGRESS AT ALL.
I KNOW. A LOT OF US FEEL THAT WAY.
WELL, MAYBE WHAT YOU WRITE WILL INSPIRE MORE PEOPLE TO VOTE FOR WATERS. WOULDN'T THAT BE SOME'M?
MAYBE SO. IT IS EXCITING TO BE EVEN A SMALL PART OF WHAT'S GOING ON.
LISTEN, MOM, THE RALLY IS STARTING SOON. I SHOULD GO. I LOVE YOU.
I LOVE YOU TOO, HONEY.

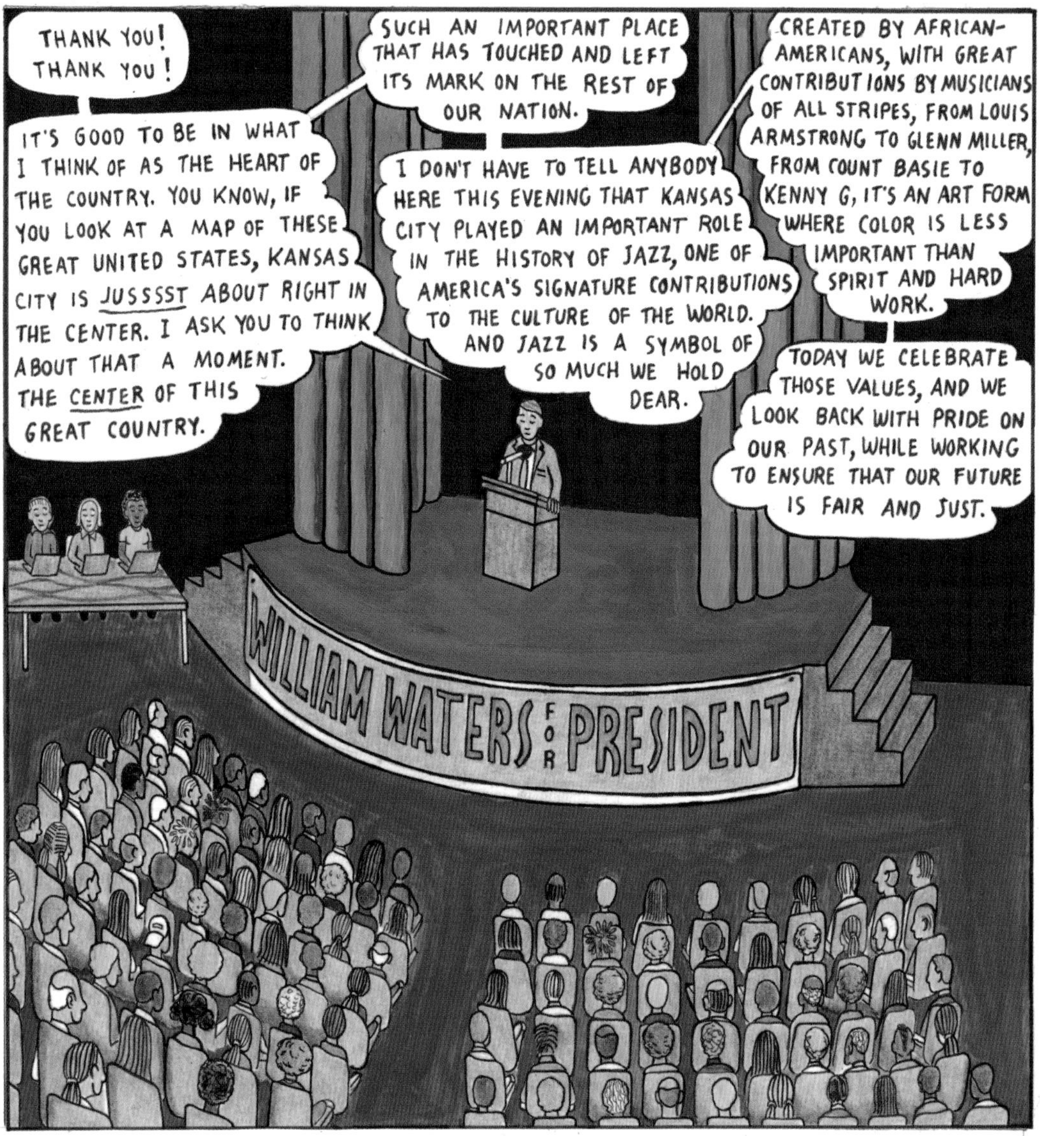
THANK YOU! THANK YOU!
IT'S GOOD TO BE IN WHAT I THINK OF AS THE HEART OF THE COUNTRY. YOU KNOW, IF YOU LOOK AT A MAP OF THESE GREAT UNITED STATES, KANSAS CITY IS JUSSSST ABOUT RIGHT IN THE CENTER. I ASK YOU TO THINK ABOUT THAT A MOMENT. THE CENTER OF THIS GREAT COUNTRY.
SUCH AN IMPORTANT PLACE THAT HAS TOUCHED AND LEFT ITS MARK ON THE REST OF OUR NATION.
I DON'T HAVE TO TELL ANYBODY HERE THIS EVENING THAT KANSAS CITY PLAYED AN IMPORTANT ROLE IN THE HISTORY OF JAZZ, ONE OF AMERICA'S SIGNATURE CONTRIBUTIONS TO THE CULTURE OF THE WORLD. AND JAZZ IS A SYMBOL OF SO MUCH WE HOLD DEAR.
CREATED BY AFRICAN-AMERICANS, WITH GREAT CONTRIBUTIONS BY MUSICIANS OF ALL STRIPES, FROM LOUIS ARMSTRONG TO GLENN MILLER, FROM COUNT BASIE TO KENNY G, IT'S AN ART FORM WHERE COLOR IS LESS IMPORTANT THAN SPIRIT AND HARD WORK.
TODAY WE CELEBRATE THOSE VALUES, AND WE LOOK BACK WITH PRIDE ON OUR PAST, WHILE WORKING TO ENSURE THAT OUR FUTURE IS FAIR AND JUST.
WILLIAM WATERS FOR PRESIDENT

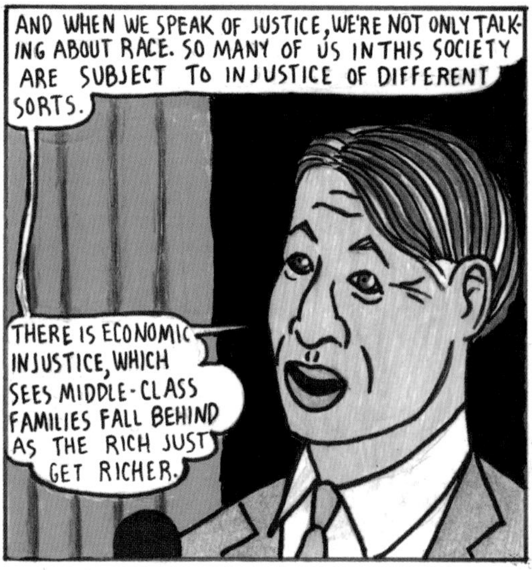
AND WHEN WE SPEAK OF JUSTICE, WE'RE NOT ONLY TALKING ABOUT RACE. SO MANY OF US IN THIS SOCIETY ARE SUBJECT TO INJUSTICE OF DIFFERENT SORTS.
THERE IS ECONOMIC INJUSTICE, WHICH SEES MIDDLE-CLASS FAMILIES FALL BEHIND AS THE RICH JUST GET RICHER.

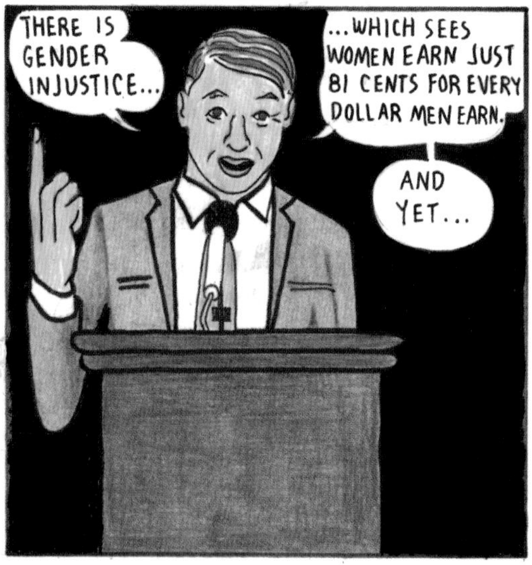
THERE IS GENDER INJUSTICE...
...WHICH SEES WOMEN EARN JUST 81 CENTS FOR EVERY DOLLAR MEN EARN.
AND YET...

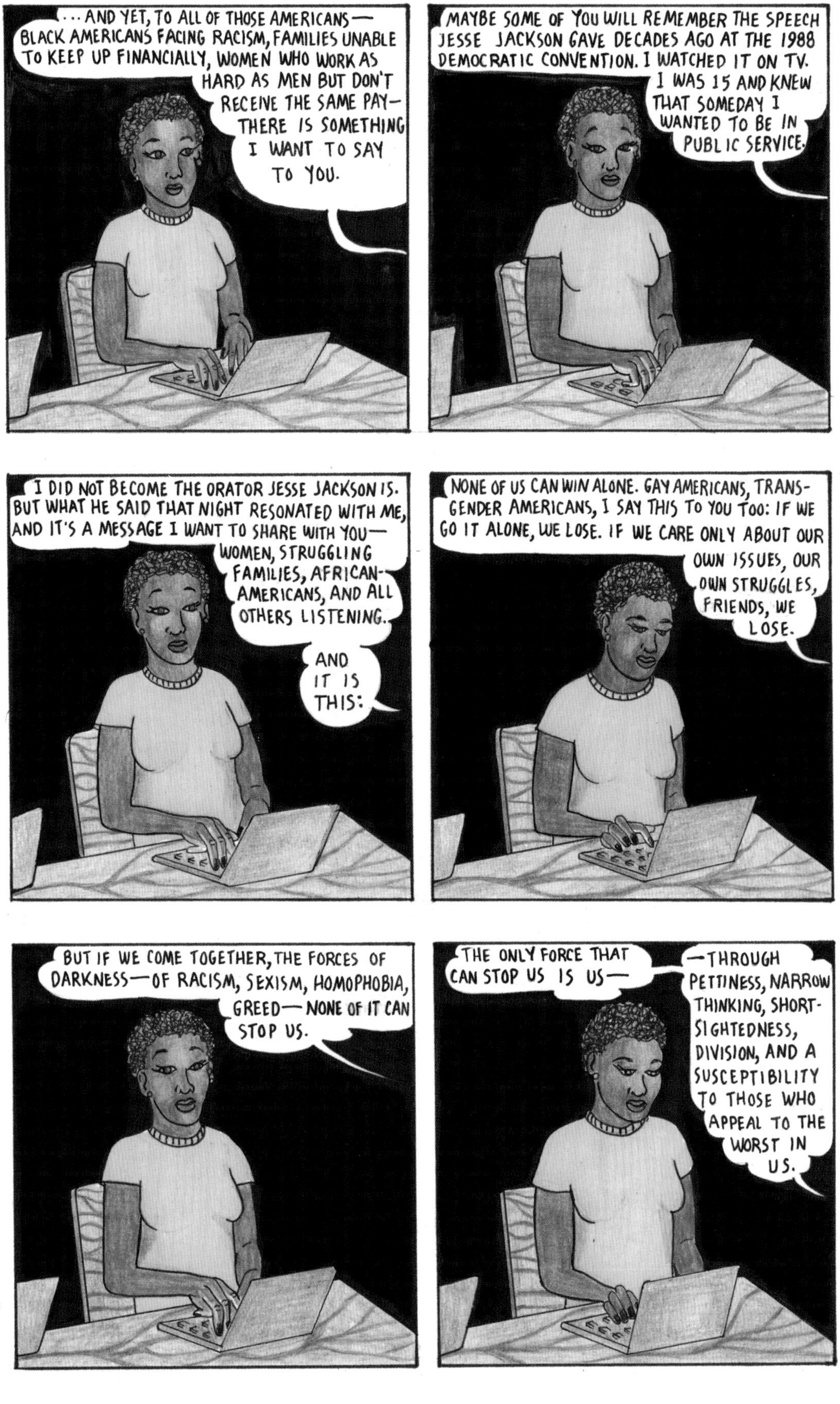
...AND YET, TO ALL OF THOSE AMERICANS— BLACK AMERICANS FACING RACISM, FAMILIES UNABLE TO KEEP UP FINANCIALLY, WOMEN WHO WORK AS HARD AS MEN BUT DON'T RECEIVE THE SAME PAY— THERE IS SOMETHING I WANT TO SAY TO YOU.
MAYBE SOME OF YOU WILL REMEMBER THE SPEECH JESSE JACKSON GAVE DECADES AGO AT THE 1988 DEMOCRATIC CONVENTION. I WATCHED IT ON TV. I WAS 15 AND KNEW THAT SOMEDAY I WANTED TO BE IN PUBLIC SERVICE.
I DID NOT BECOME THE ORATOR JESSE JACKSON IS. BUT WHAT HE SAID THAT NIGHT RESONATED WITH ME, AND IT'S A MESSAGE I WANT TO SHARE WITH YOU— WOMEN, STRUGGLING FAMILIES, AFRICAN-AMERICANS, AND ALL OTHERS LISTENING.
AND IT IS THIS:
NONE OF US CAN WIN ALONE. GAY AMERICANS, TRANS-GENDER AMERICANS, I SAY THIS TO YOU TOO: IF WE GO IT ALONE, WE LOSE. IF WE CARE ONLY ABOUT OUR OWN ISSUES, OUR OWN STRUGGLES, FRIENDS, WE LOSE.
BUT IF WE COME TOGETHER, THE FORCES OF DARKNESS—OF RACISM, SEXISM, HOMOPHOBIA, GREED—NONE OF IT CAN STOP US.
THE ONLY FORCE THAT CAN STOP US IS US—
—THROUGH PETTINESS, NARROW THINKING, SHORT-SIGHTEDNESS, DIVISION, AND A SUSCEPTIBILITY TO THOSE WHO APPEAL TO THE WORST IN US.

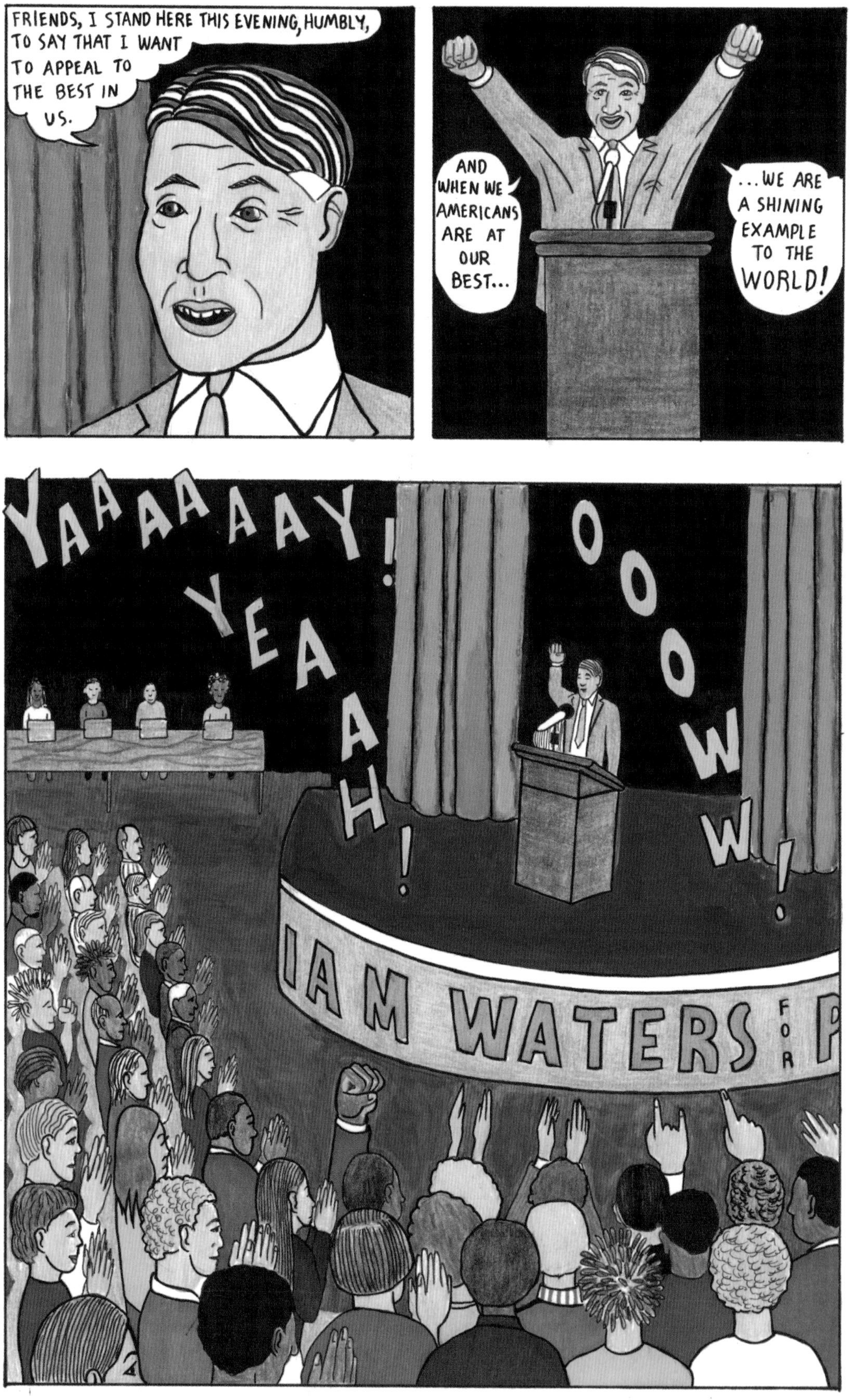
FRIENDS, I STAND HERE THIS EVENING, HUMBLY, TO SAY THAT I WANT TO APPEAL TO THE BEST IN US.
AND WHEN WE AMERICANS ARE AT OUR BEST...
...WE ARE A SHINING EXAMPLE TO THE WORLD!
YAAAAAY!
YEAAAH!
OOOWW!
IAM WATERS FOR P

THAT NIGHT IN APRIL'S ROOM: THE WRITING PROCESS...

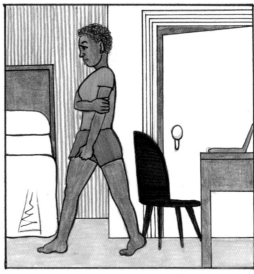

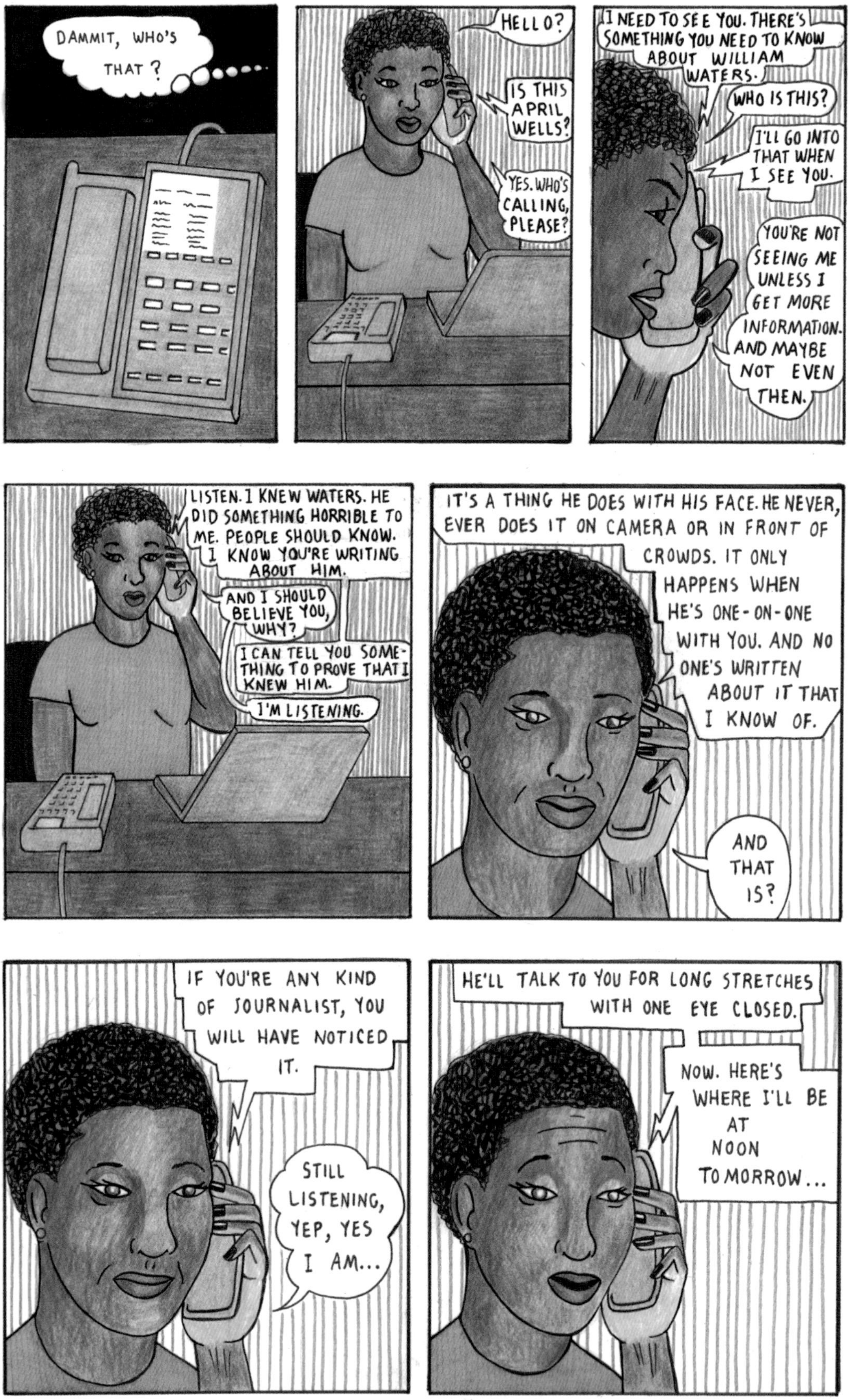
DAMMIT, WHO'S THAT?
HELLO?
IS THIS APRIL WELLS?
YES. WHO'S CALLING, PLEASE?
I NEED TO SEE YOU. THERE'S SOMETHING YOU NEED TO KNOW ABOUT WILLIAM WATERS.
WHO IS THIS?
I'LL GO INTO THAT WHEN I SEE YOU.
YOU'RE NOT SEEING ME UNLESS I GET MORE INFORMATION. AND MAYBE NOT EVEN THEN.
LISTEN. I KNEW WATERS. HE DID SOMETHING HORRIBLE TO ME. PEOPLE SHOULD KNOW. I KNOW YOU'RE WRITING ABOUT HIM.
AND I SHOULD BELIEVE YOU, WHY?
I CAN TELL YOU SOMETHING TO PROVE THAT I KNEW HIM.
I'M LISTENING.
IT'S A THING HE DOES WITH HIS FACE. HE NEVER, EVER DOES IT ON CAMERA OR IN FRONT OF CROWDS. IT ONLY HAPPENS WHEN HE'S ONE-ON-ONE WITH YOU. AND NO ONE'S WRITTEN ABOUT IT THAT I KNOW OF.
AND THAT IS?
IF YOU'RE ANY KIND OF JOURNALIST, YOU WILL HAVE NOTICED IT.
STILL LISTENING, YEP, YES I AM...
HE'LL TALK TO YOU FOR LONG STRETCHES WITH ONE EYE CLOSED.
NOW. HERE'S WHERE I'LL BE AT NOON TOMORROW...

THE NEXT DAY...

DIZZY'S DINER

INSIDE THE DINER...

YOU PICKED THE MOST CROWDED TIME OF DAY. WHY?

SO OUR CONVERSATION WILL BLEND IN WITH THE OTHERS AND OUR WORDS WON'T ECHO.

BUT I DID TAKE THIS PRECAUTION...

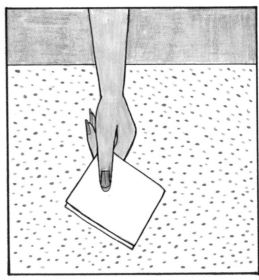

AND YOU WOULD LIKE ME TO DO WHAT WITH THIS?

LET ME BACK UP. WHO ARE YOU? WHERE AND WHEN IS THIS SUPPOSED TO HAVE HAPPENED?

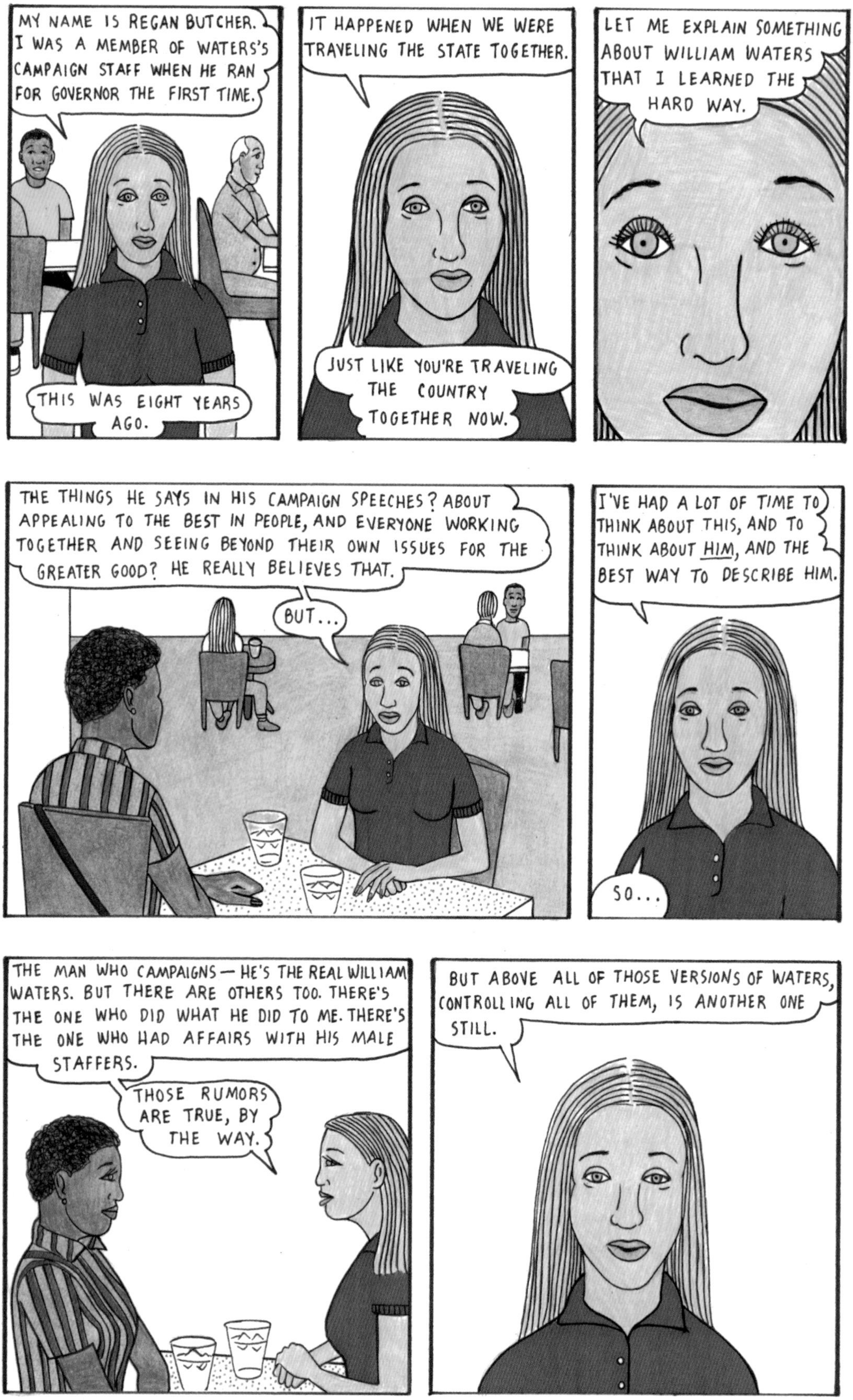
MY NAME IS REGAN BUTCHER. I WAS A MEMBER OF WATERS'S CAMPAIGN STAFF WHEN HE RAN FOR GOVERNOR THE FIRST TIME.
THIS WAS EIGHT YEARS AGO.
IT HAPPENED WHEN WE WERE TRAVELING THE STATE TOGETHER.
JUST LIKE YOU'RE TRAVELING THE COUNTRY TOGETHER NOW.
LET ME EXPLAIN SOMETHING ABOUT WILLIAM WATERS THAT I LEARNED THE HARD WAY.
THE THINGS HE SAYS IN HIS CAMPAIGN SPEECHES? ABOUT APPEALING TO THE BEST IN PEOPLE, AND EVERYONE WORKING TOGETHER AND SEEING BEYOND THEIR OWN ISSUES FOR THE GREATER GOOD? HE REALLY BELIEVES THAT.
BUT...
I'VE HAD A LOT OF TIME TO THINK ABOUT THIS, AND TO THINK ABOUT HIM, AND THE BEST WAY TO DESCRIBE HIM.
SO...
THE MAN WHO CAMPAIGNS — HE'S THE REAL WILLIAM WATERS. BUT THERE ARE OTHERS TOO. THERE'S THE ONE WHO DID WHAT HE DID TO ME. THERE'S THE ONE WHO HAD AFFAIRS WITH HIS MALE STAFFERS.
THOSE RUMORS ARE TRUE, BY THE WAY.
BUT ABOVE ALL OF THOSE VERSIONS OF WATERS, CONTROLLING ALL OF THEM, IS ANOTHER ONE STILL.

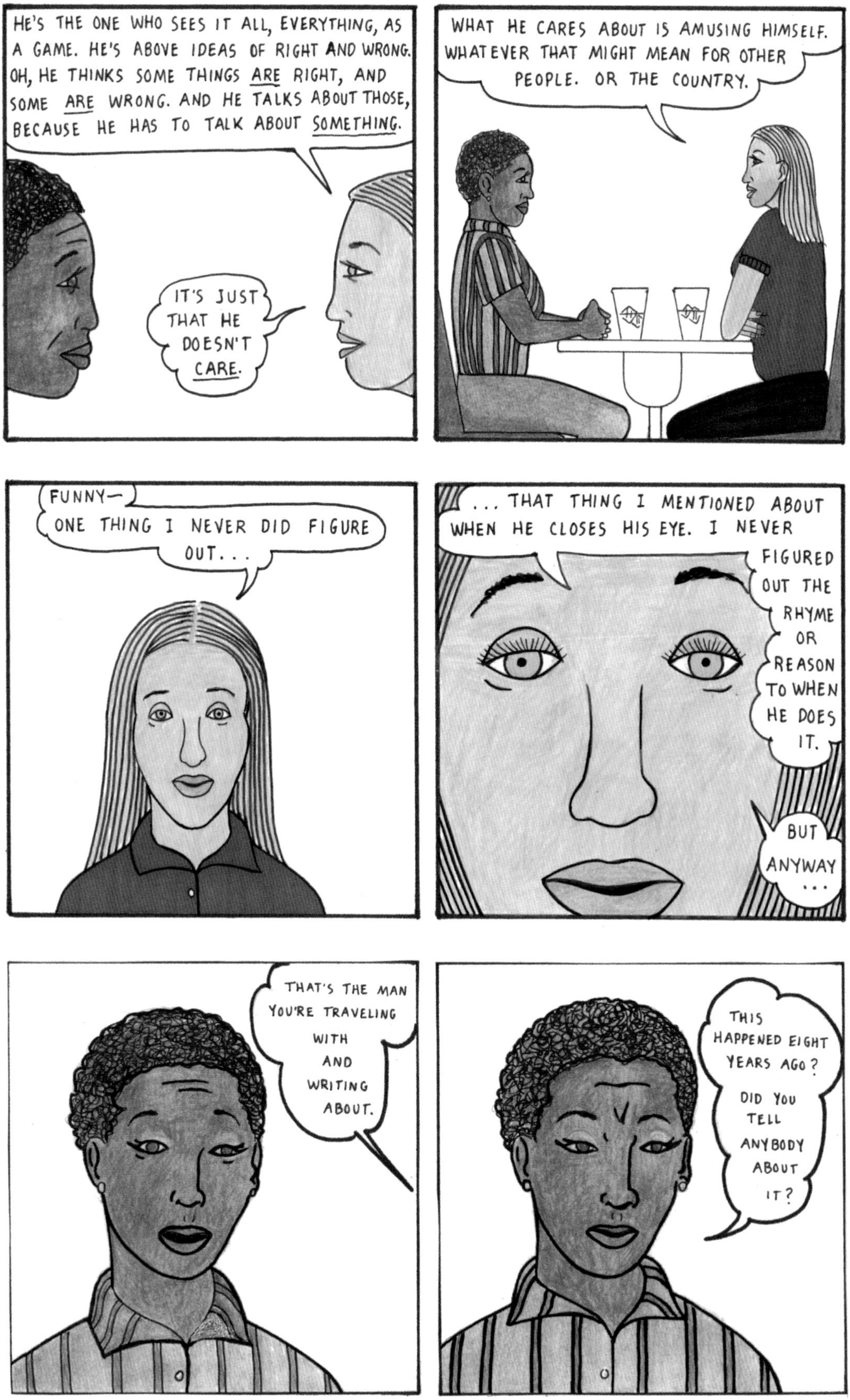
HE'S THE ONE WHO SEES IT ALL, EVERYTHING, AS A GAME. HE'S ABOVE IDEAS OF RIGHT AND WRONG. OH, HE THINKS SOME THINGS ARE RIGHT, AND SOME ARE WRONG. AND HE TALKS ABOUT THOSE, BECAUSE HE HAS TO TALK ABOUT SOMETHING.
IT'S JUST THAT HE DOESN'T CARE.
WHAT HE CARES ABOUT IS AMUSING HIMSELF. WHATEVER THAT MIGHT MEAN FOR OTHER PEOPLE. OR THE COUNTRY.
FUNNY— ONE THING I NEVER DID FIGURE OUT...
... THAT THING I MENTIONED ABOUT WHEN HE CLOSES HIS EYE. I NEVER FIGURED OUT THE RHYME OR REASON TO WHEN HE DOES IT.
BUT ANYWAY...
THAT'S THE MAN YOU'RE TRAVELING WITH AND WRITING ABOUT.
THIS HAPPENED EIGHT YEARS AGO?
DID YOU TELL ANYBODY ABOUT IT?

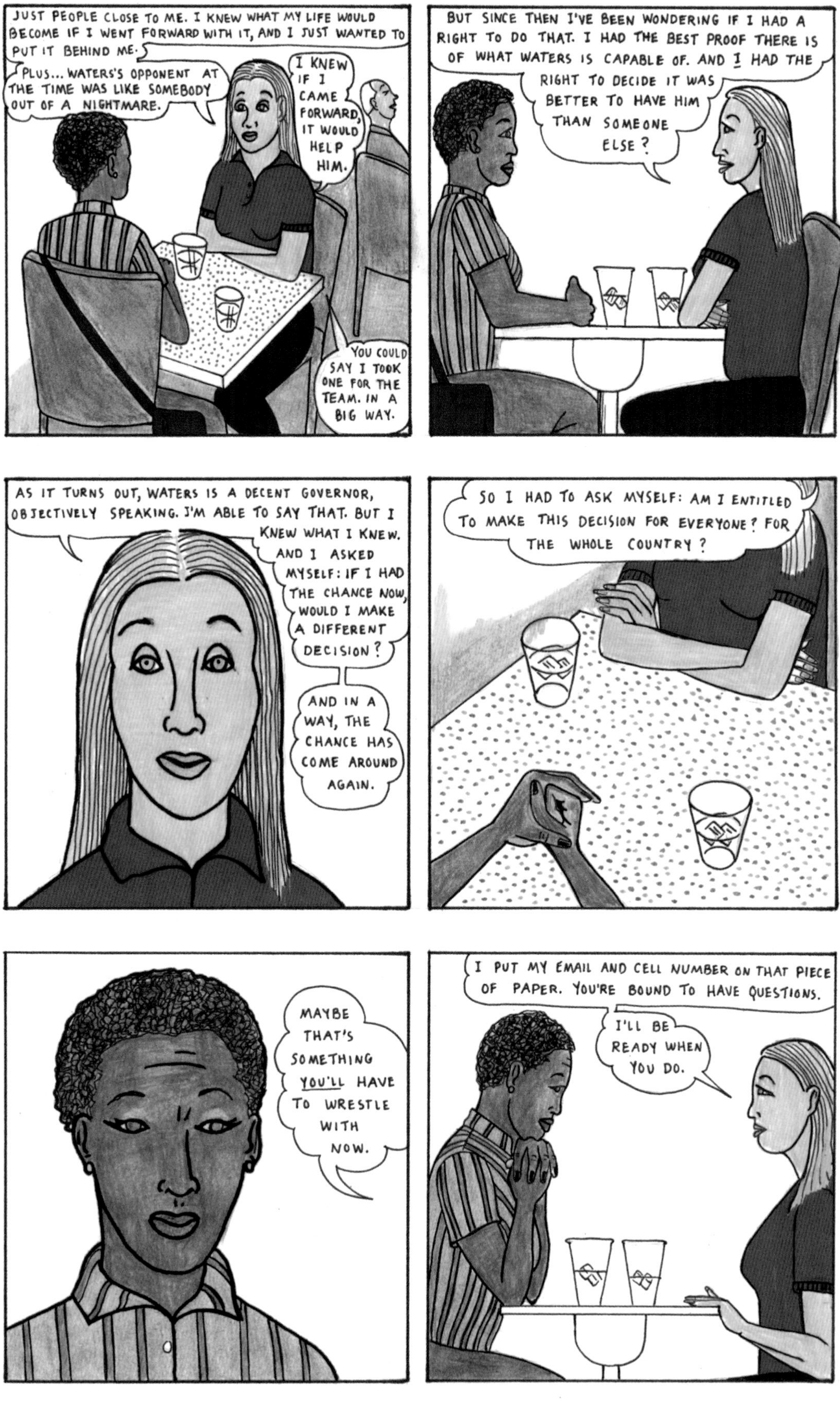
JUST PEOPLE CLOSE TO ME. I KNEW WHAT MY LIFE WOULD BECOME IF I WENT FORWARD WITH IT, AND I JUST WANTED TO PUT IT BEHIND ME.
PLUS... WATERS'S OPPONENT AT THE TIME WAS LIKE SOMEBODY OUT OF A NIGHTMARE.
I KNEW IF I CAME FORWARD, IT WOULD HELP HIM.
YOU COULD SAY I TOOK ONE FOR THE TEAM. IN A BIG WAY.
BUT SINCE THEN I'VE BEEN WONDERING IF I HAD A RIGHT TO DO THAT. I HAD THE BEST PROOF THERE IS OF WHAT WATERS IS CAPABLE OF. AND I HAD THE
RIGHT TO DECIDE IT WAS BETTER TO HAVE HIM THAN SOMEONE ELSE?
AS IT TURNS OUT, WATERS IS A DECENT GOVERNOR, OBJECTIVELY SPEAKING. I'M ABLE TO SAY THAT. BUT I KNEW WHAT I KNEW.
AND I ASKED MYSELF: IF I HAD THE CHANCE NOW, WOULD I MAKE A DIFFERENT DECISION?
AND IN A WAY, THE CHANCE HAS COME AROUND AGAIN.
SO I HAD TO ASK MYSELF: AM I ENTITLED TO MAKE THIS DECISION FOR EVERYONE? FOR THE WHOLE COUNTRY?
MAYBE THAT'S SOMETHING YOU'LL HAVE TO WRESTLE WITH NOW.
I PUT MY EMAIL AND CELL NUMBER ON THAT PIECE OF PAPER. YOU'RE BOUND TO HAVE QUESTIONS.
I'LL BE READY WHEN YOU DO.

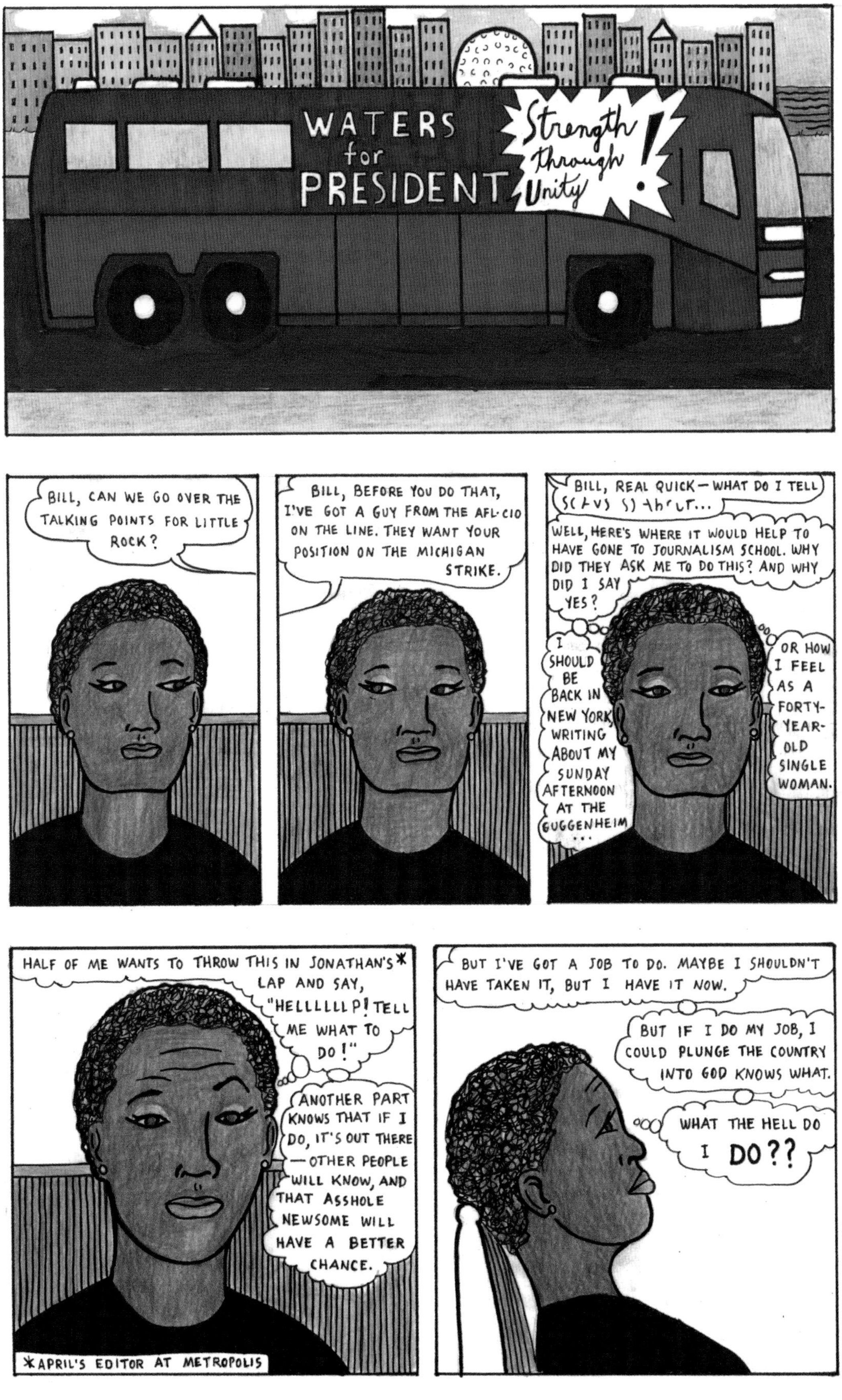
WATERS for PRESIDENT
Strength through Unity!
BILL, CAN WE GO OVER THE TALKING POINTS FOR LITTLE ROCK?
BILL, BEFORE YOU DO THAT, I'VE GOT A GUY FROM THE AFL-CIO ON THE LINE. THEY WANT YOUR POSITION ON THE MICHIGAN STRIKE.
BILL, REAL QUICK—WHAT DO I TELL
WELL, HERE'S WHERE IT WOULD HELP TO HAVE GONE TO JOURNALISM SCHOOL. WHY DID THEY ASK ME TO DO THIS? AND WHY DID I SAY YES?
I SHOULD BE BACK IN NEW YORK WRITING ABOUT MY SUNDAY AFTERNOON AT THE GUGGENHEIM . . .
OR HOW I FEEL AS A FORTY-YEAR-OLD SINGLE WOMAN.
HALF OF ME WANTS TO THROW THIS IN JONATHAN'S* LAP AND SAY, "HELLLLLLP! TELL ME WHAT TO DO!"
ANOTHER PART KNOWS THAT IF I DO, IT'S OUT THERE—OTHER PEOPLE WILL KNOW, AND THAT ASSHOLE NEWSOME WILL HAVE A BETTER CHANCE.
*APRIL'S EDITOR AT METROPOLIS
BUT I'VE GOT A JOB TO DO. MAYBE I SHOULDN'T HAVE TAKEN IT, BUT I HAVE IT NOW.
BUT IF I DO MY JOB, I COULD PLUNGE THE COUNTRY INTO GOD KNOWS WHAT.
WHAT THE HELL DO I DO??

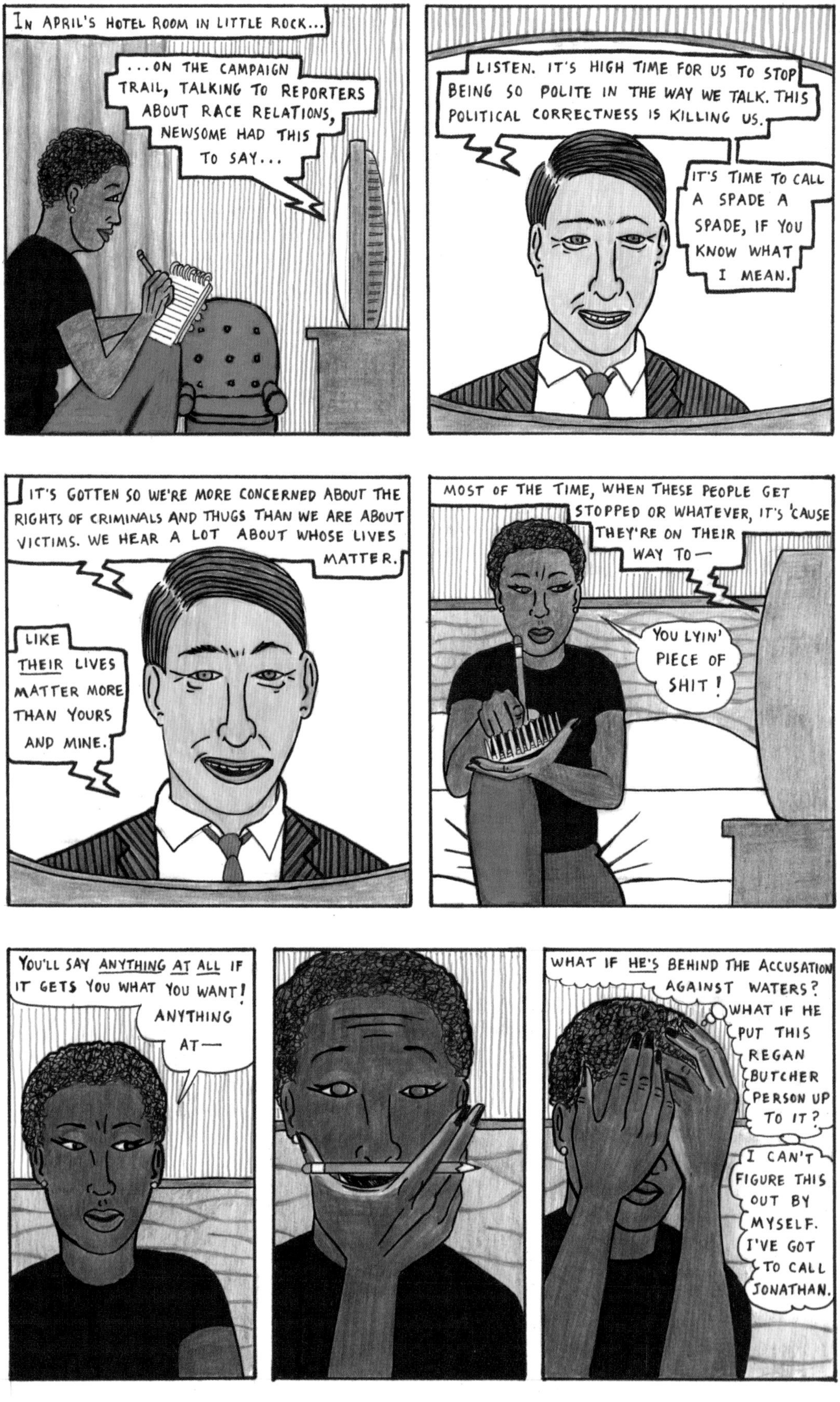

In April's Hotel Room in Little Rock...
...On the campaign trail, talking to reporters about race relations, Newsome had this to say...
Listen. It's high time for us to stop being so polite in the way we talk. This political correctness is killing us.
It's time to call a spade a spade, if you know what I mean.
It's gotten so we're more concerned about the rights of criminals and thugs than we are about victims. We hear a lot about whose lives matter.
Like their lives matter more than yours and mine.
Most of the time, when these people get stopped or whatever, it's 'cause they're on their way to—
You lyin' piece of shit!
You'll say anything at all if it gets you what you want!
Anything at—
What if he's behind the accusation against Waters?
What if he put this Regan Butcher person up to it?
I can't figure this out by myself. I've got to call Jonathan.

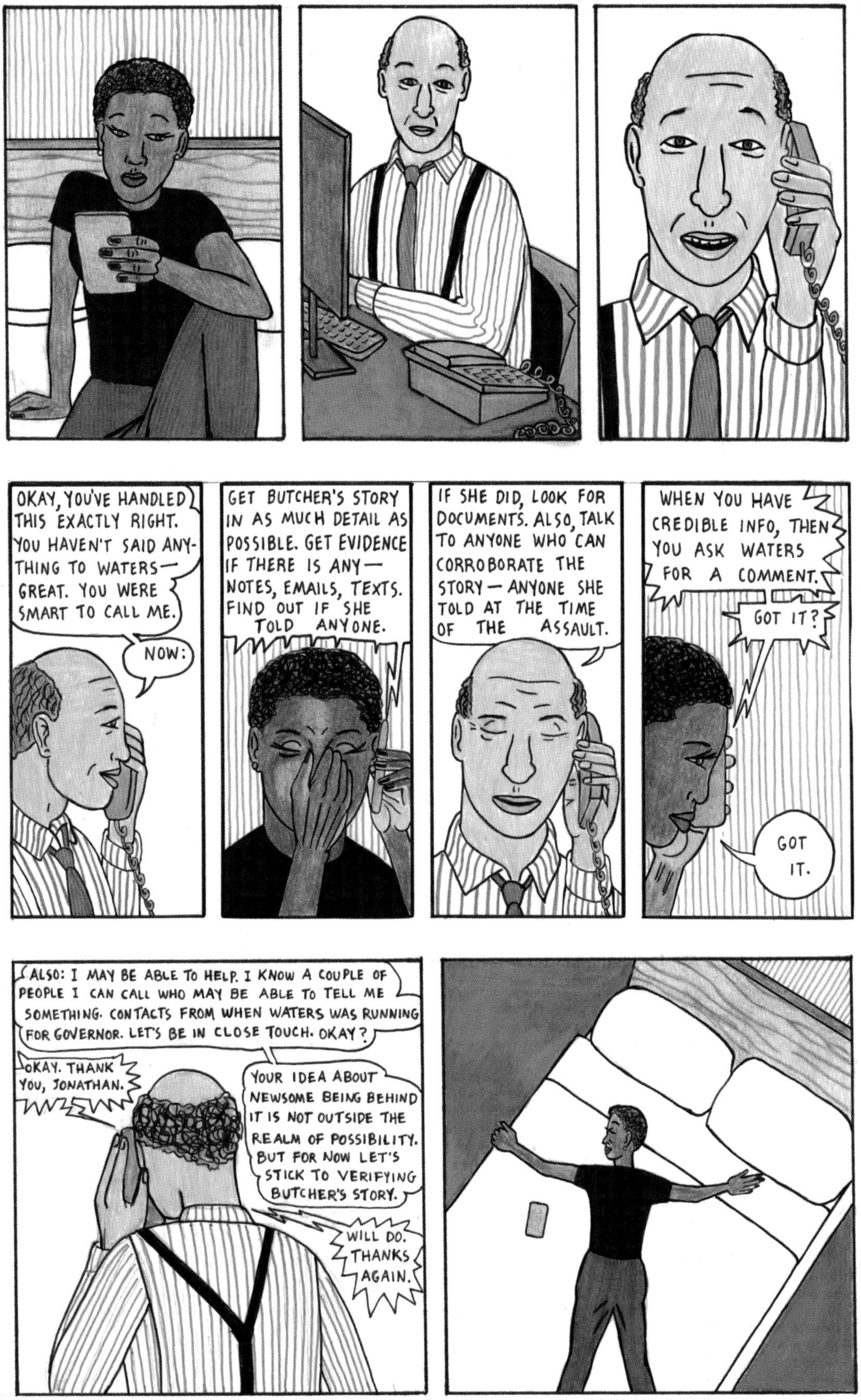
OKAY, YOU'VE HANDLED THIS EXACTLY RIGHT. YOU HAVEN'T SAID ANYTHING TO WATERS— GREAT. YOU WERE SMART TO CALL ME.
NOW:
GET BUTCHER'S STORY IN AS MUCH DETAIL AS POSSIBLE. GET EVIDENCE IF THERE IS ANY— NOTES, EMAILS, TEXTS. FIND OUT IF SHE TOLD ANYONE.
IF SHE DID, LOOK FOR DOCUMENTS. ALSO, TALK TO ANYONE WHO CAN CORROBORATE THE STORY— ANYONE SHE TOLD AT THE TIME OF THE ASSAULT.
WHEN YOU HAVE CREDIBLE INFO, THEN YOU ASK WATERS FOR A COMMENT.
GOT IT?
GOT IT.
ALSO: I MAY BE ABLE TO HELP. I KNOW A COUPLE OF PEOPLE I CAN CALL WHO MAY BE ABLE TO TELL ME SOMETHING. CONTACTS FROM WHEN WATERS WAS RUNNING FOR GOVERNOR. LET'S BE IN CLOSE TOUCH. OKAY?
OKAY. THANK YOU, JONATHAN.
YOUR IDEA ABOUT NEWSOME BEING BEHIND IT IS NOT OUTSIDE THE REALM OF POSSIBILITY. BUT FOR NOW LET'S STICK TO VERIFYING BUTCHER'S STORY.
WILL DO. THANKS AGAIN.

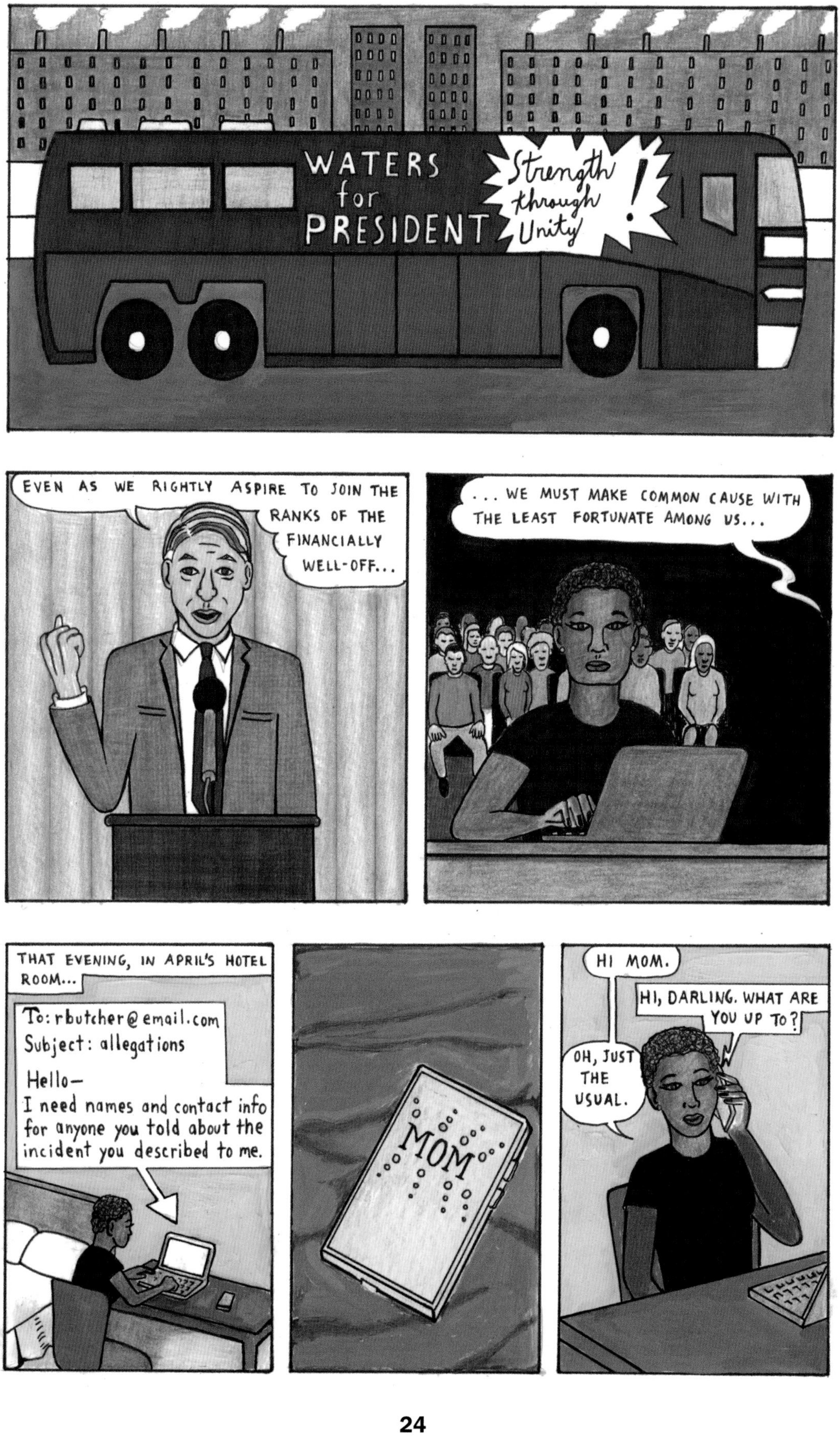
WATERS for PRESIDENT
Strength through Unity!
EVEN AS WE RIGHTLY ASPIRE TO JOIN THE RANKS OF THE FINANCIALLY WELL-OFF...
...WE MUST MAKE COMMON CAUSE WITH THE LEAST FORTUNATE AMONG US...
THAT EVENING, IN APRIL'S HOTEL ROOM...
To: rbutcher@email.com
Subject: allegations
Hello—
I need names and contact info for anyone you told about the incident you described to me.
MOM
HI MOM.
HI, DARLING. WHAT ARE YOU UP TO?
OH, JUST THE USUAL.

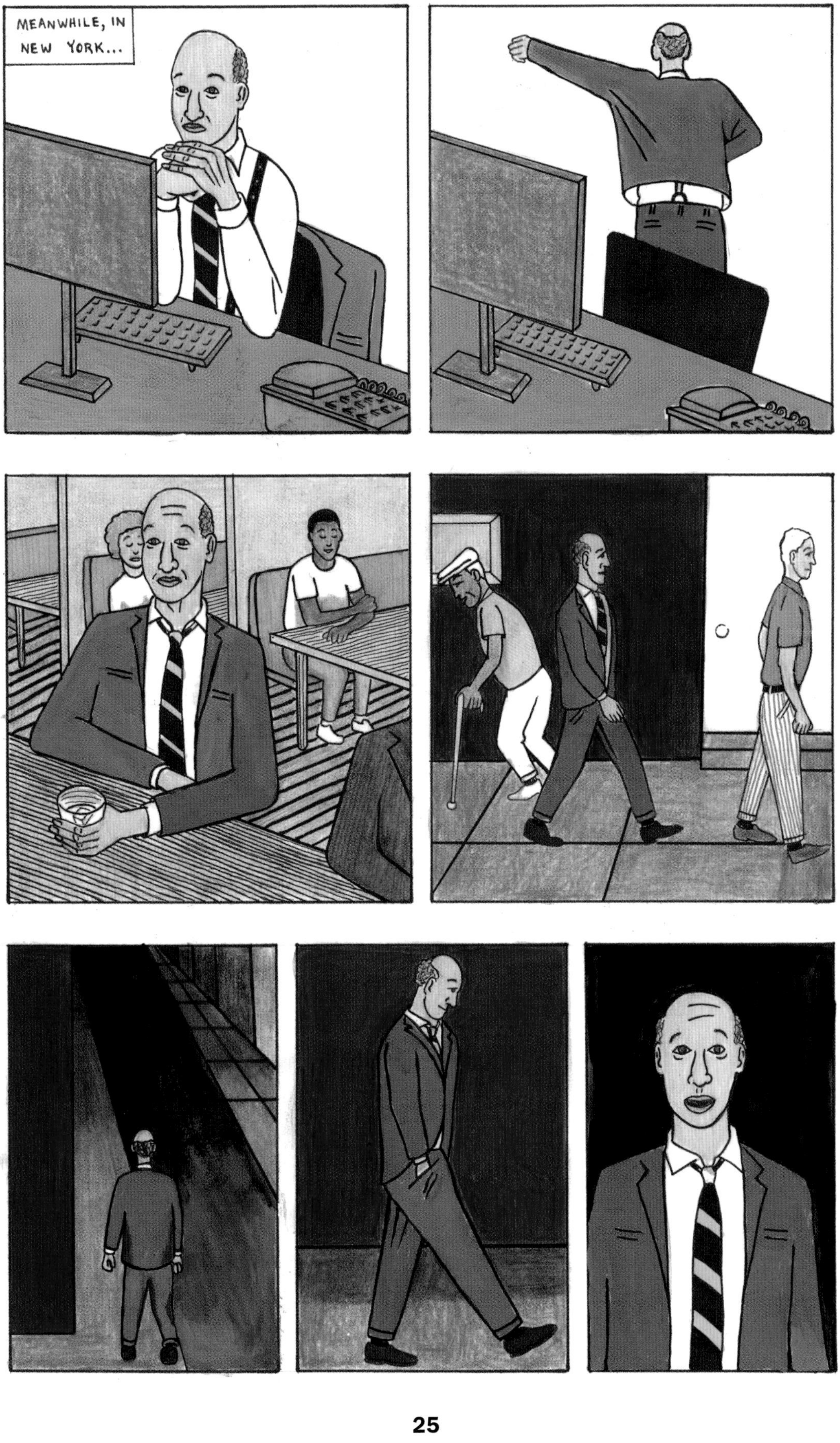
MEANWHILE, IN NEW YORK...

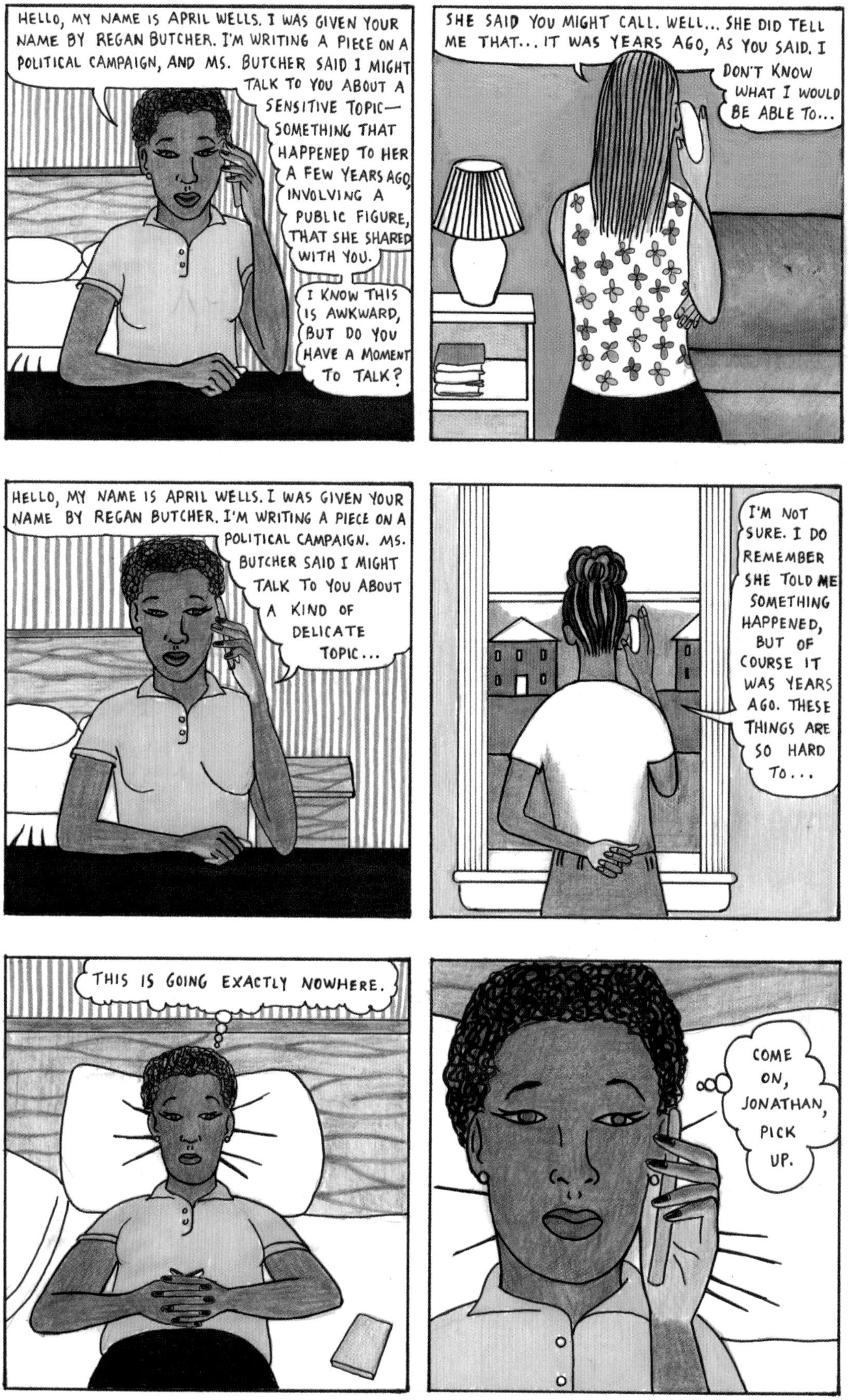
HELLO, MY NAME IS APRIL WELLS. I WAS GIVEN YOUR NAME BY REGAN BUTCHER. I'M WRITING A PIECE ON A POLITICAL CAMPAIGN, AND MS. BUTCHER SAID I MIGHT TALK TO YOU ABOUT A SENSITIVE TOPIC— SOMETHING THAT HAPPENED TO HER A FEW YEARS AGO, INVOLVING A PUBLIC FIGURE, THAT SHE SHARED WITH YOU.
I KNOW THIS IS AWKWARD, BUT DO YOU HAVE A MOMENT TO TALK?
SHE SAID YOU MIGHT CALL. WELL... SHE DID TELL ME THAT... IT WAS YEARS AGO, AS YOU SAID. I
DON'T KNOW WHAT I WOULD BE ABLE TO...
HELLO, MY NAME IS APRIL WELLS. I WAS GIVEN YOUR NAME BY REGAN BUTCHER. I'M WRITING A PIECE ON A POLITICAL CAMPAIGN. MS. BUTCHER SAID I MIGHT TALK TO YOU ABOUT A KIND OF DELICATE TOPIC...
I'M NOT SURE. I DO REMEMBER SHE TOLD ME SOMETHING HAPPENED, BUT OF COURSE IT WAS YEARS AGO. THESE THINGS ARE SO HARD TO...
THIS IS GOING EXACTLY NOWHERE.
COME ON, JONATHAN, PICK UP.

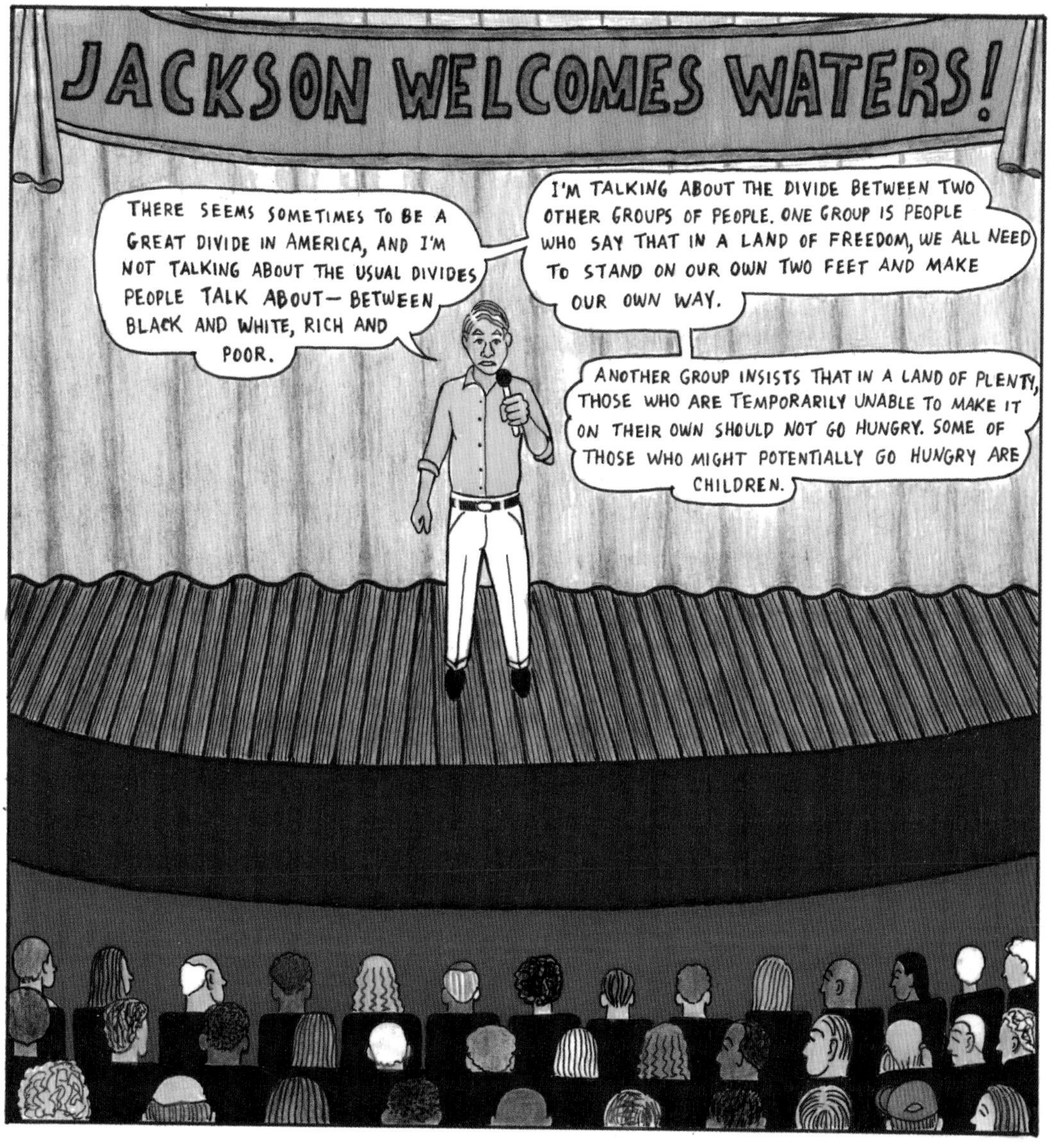
JACKSON WELCOMES WATERS!
THERE SEEMS SOMETIMES TO BE A GREAT DIVIDE IN AMERICA, AND I'M NOT TALKING ABOUT THE USUAL DIVIDES PEOPLE TALK ABOUT— BETWEEN BLACK AND WHITE, RICH AND POOR.
I'M TALKING ABOUT THE DIVIDE BETWEEN TWO OTHER GROUPS OF PEOPLE. ONE GROUP IS PEOPLE WHO SAY THAT IN A LAND OF FREEDOM, WE ALL NEED TO STAND ON OUR OWN TWO FEET AND MAKE OUR OWN WAY.
ANOTHER GROUP INSISTS THAT IN A LAND OF PLENTY, THOSE WHO ARE TEMPORARILY UNABLE TO MAKE IT ON THEIR OWN SHOULD NOT GO HUNGRY. SOME OF THOSE WHO MIGHT POTENTIALLY GO HUNGRY ARE CHILDREN.

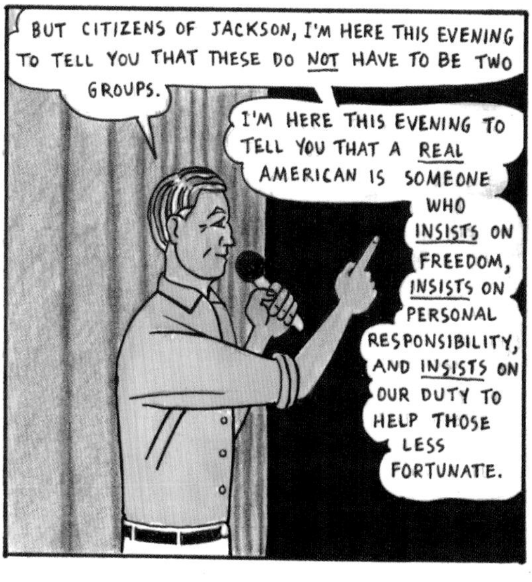
BUT CITIZENS OF JACKSON, I'M HERE THIS EVENING TO TELL YOU THAT THESE DO NOT HAVE TO BE TWO GROUPS.
I'M HERE THIS EVENING TO TELL YOU THAT A REAL AMERICAN IS SOMEONE WHO INSISTS ON FREEDOM, INSISTS ON PERSONAL RESPONSIBILITY, AND INSISTS ON OUR DUTY TO HELP THOSE LESS FORTUNATE.

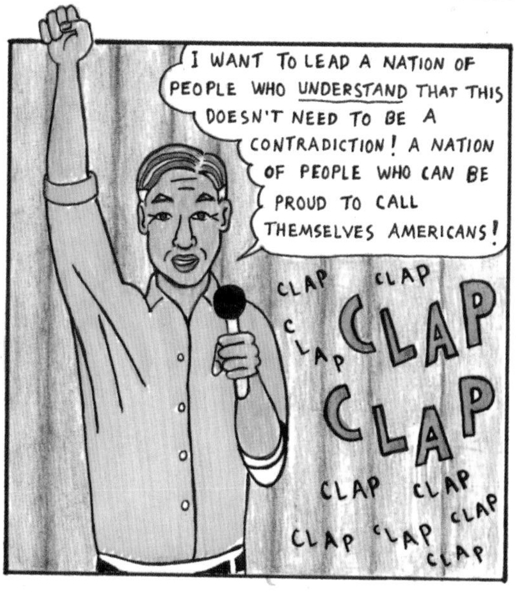
I WANT TO LEAD A NATION OF PEOPLE WHO UNDERSTAND THAT THIS DOESN'T NEED TO BE A CONTRADICTION! A NATION OF PEOPLE WHO CAN BE PROUD TO CALL THEMSELVES AMERICANS!
CLAP CLAP CLAP CLAP CLAP
CLAP CLAP CLAP CLAP CLAP CLAP

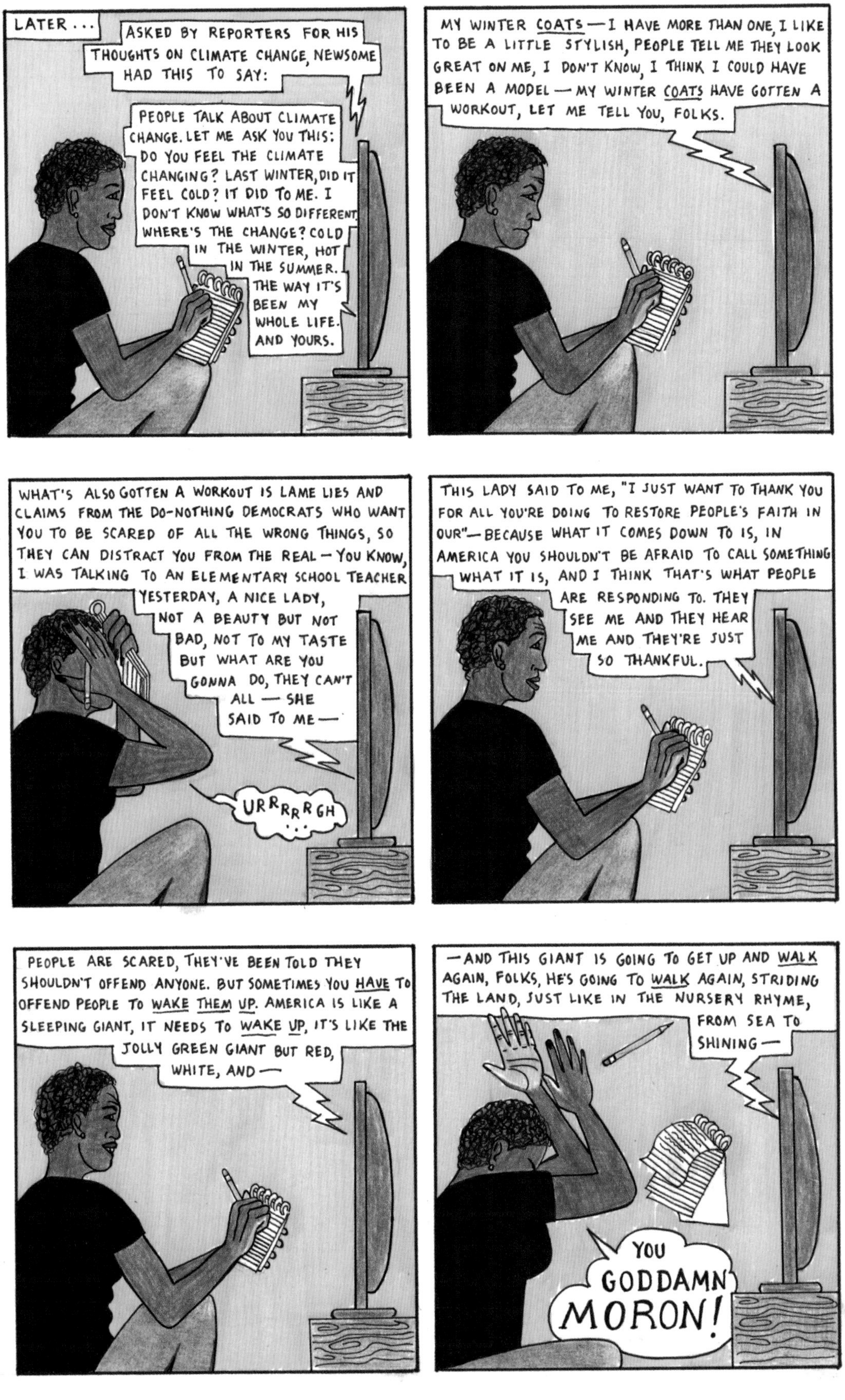
LATER...
ASKED BY REPORTERS FOR HIS THOUGHTS ON CLIMATE CHANGE, NEWSOME HAD THIS TO SAY:
PEOPLE TALK ABOUT CLIMATE CHANGE. LET ME ASK YOU THIS: DO YOU FEEL THE CLIMATE CHANGING? LAST WINTER, DID IT FEEL COLD? IT DID TO ME. I DON'T KNOW WHAT'S SO DIFFERENT. WHERE'S THE CHANGE? COLD IN THE WINTER, HOT IN THE SUMMER. THE WAY IT'S BEEN MY WHOLE LIFE. AND YOURS.
MY WINTER COATS — I HAVE MORE THAN ONE, I LIKE TO BE A LITTLE STYLISH, PEOPLE TELL ME THEY LOOK GREAT ON ME, I DON'T KNOW, I THINK I COULD HAVE BEEN A MODEL — MY WINTER COATS HAVE GOTTEN A WORKOUT, LET ME TELL YOU, FOLKS.
WHAT'S ALSO GOTTEN A WORKOUT IS LAME LIES AND CLAIMS FROM THE DO-NOTHING DEMOCRATS WHO WANT YOU TO BE SCARED OF ALL THE WRONG THINGS, SO THEY CAN DISTRACT YOU FROM THE REAL — YOU KNOW, I WAS TALKING TO AN ELEMENTARY SCHOOL TEACHER YESTERDAY, A NICE LADY, NOT A BEAUTY BUT NOT BAD, NOT TO MY TASTE BUT WHAT ARE YOU GONNA DO, THEY CAN'T ALL — SHE SAID TO ME —
URRRRRGH...
THIS LADY SAID TO ME, "I JUST WANT TO THANK YOU FOR ALL YOU'RE DOING TO RESTORE PEOPLE'S FAITH IN OUR" — BECAUSE WHAT IT COMES DOWN TO IS, IN AMERICA YOU SHOULDN'T BE AFRAID TO CALL SOMETHING WHAT IT IS, AND I THINK THAT'S WHAT PEOPLE ARE RESPONDING TO. THEY SEE ME AND THEY HEAR ME AND THEY'RE JUST SO THANKFUL.
PEOPLE ARE SCARED, THEY'VE BEEN TOLD THEY SHOULDN'T OFFEND ANYONE. BUT SOMETIMES YOU HAVE TO OFFEND PEOPLE TO WAKE THEM UP. AMERICA IS LIKE A SLEEPING GIANT, IT NEEDS TO WAKE UP, IT'S LIKE THE JOLLY GREEN GIANT BUT RED, WHITE, AND —
— AND THIS GIANT IS GOING TO GET UP AND WALK AGAIN, FOLKS, HE'S GOING TO WALK AGAIN, STRIDING THE LAND, JUST LIKE IN THE NURSERY RHYME, FROM SEA TO SHINING —
YOU GODDAMN MORON!

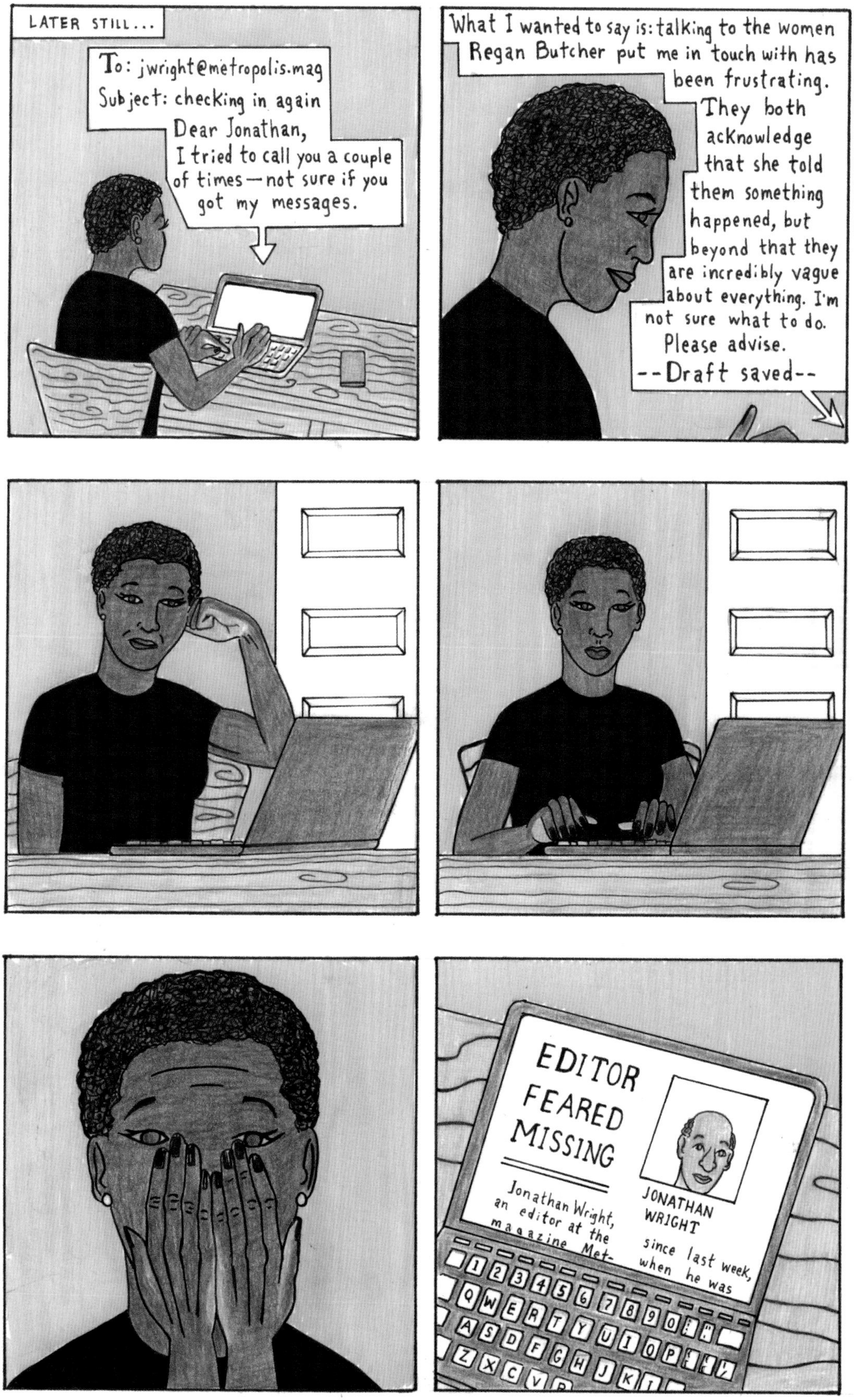
LATER STILL...
To: jwright@metropolis.mag
Subject: checking in again
Dear Jonathan,
I tried to call you a couple of times—not sure if you got my messages.
What I wanted to say is: talking to the women Regan Butcher put me in touch with has been frustrating. They both acknowledge that she told them something happened, but beyond that they are incredibly vague about everything. I'm not sure what to do. Please advise.
--Draft saved--
EDITOR FEARED MISSING
JONATHAN WRIGHT
Jonathan Wright, an editor at the magazine Met-
since last week, when he was

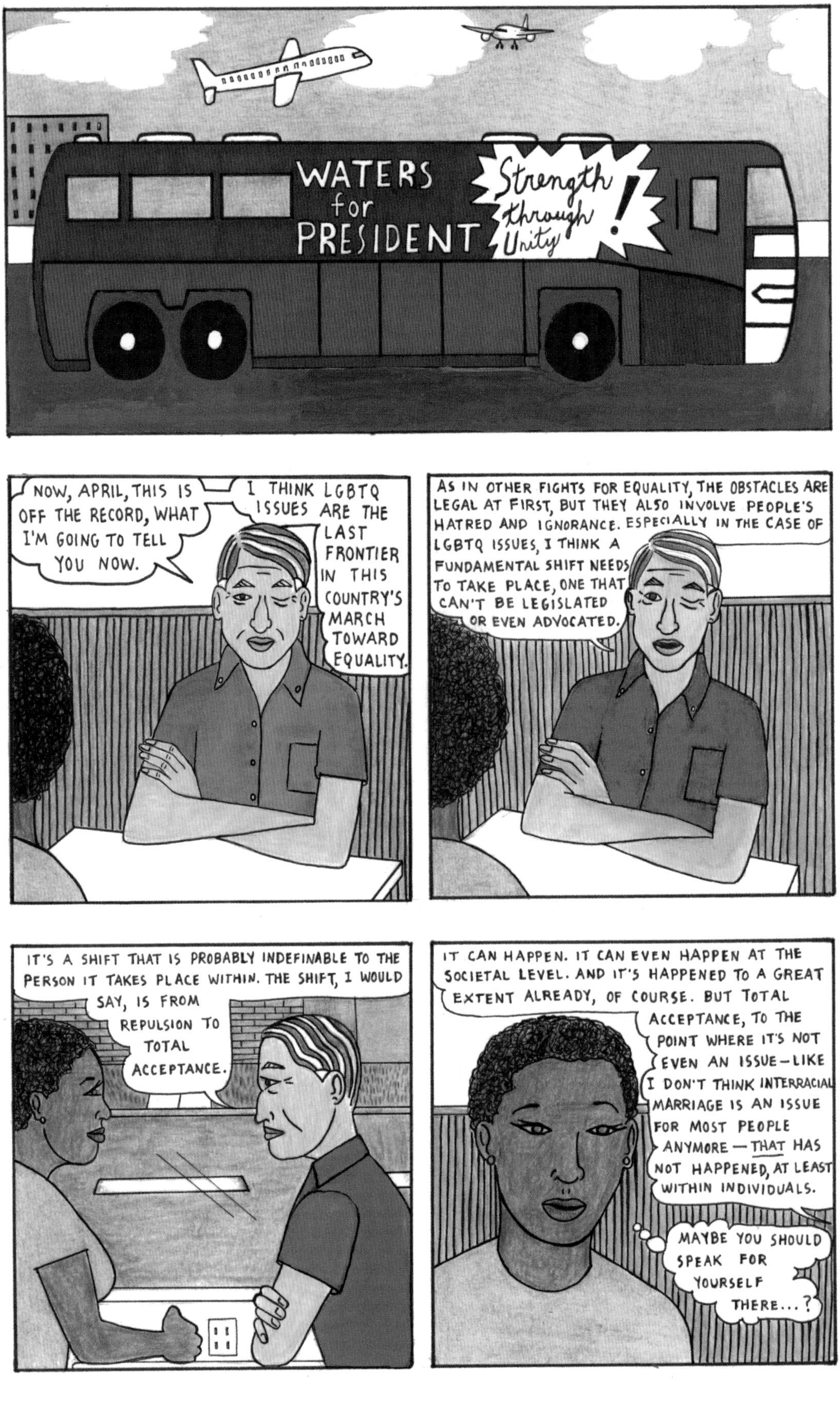
WATERS for PRESIDENT
Strength through Unity!
NOW, APRIL, THIS IS OFF THE RECORD, WHAT I'M GOING TO TELL YOU NOW.
I THINK LGBTQ ISSUES ARE THE LAST FRONTIER IN THIS COUNTRY'S MARCH TOWARD EQUALITY.
AS IN OTHER FIGHTS FOR EQUALITY, THE OBSTACLES ARE LEGAL AT FIRST, BUT THEY ALSO INVOLVE PEOPLE'S HATRED AND IGNORANCE. ESPECIALLY IN THE CASE OF LGBTQ ISSUES, I THINK A FUNDAMENTAL SHIFT NEEDS TO TAKE PLACE, ONE THAT CAN'T BE LEGISLATED OR EVEN ADVOCATED.
IT'S A SHIFT THAT IS PROBABLY INDEFINABLE TO THE PERSON IT TAKES PLACE WITHIN. THE SHIFT, I WOULD SAY, IS FROM REPULSION TO TOTAL ACCEPTANCE.
IT CAN HAPPEN. IT CAN EVEN HAPPEN AT THE SOCIETAL LEVEL. AND IT'S HAPPENED TO A GREAT EXTENT ALREADY, OF COURSE. BUT TOTAL ACCEPTANCE, TO THE POINT WHERE IT'S NOT EVEN AN ISSUE—LIKE I DON'T THINK INTERRACIAL MARRIAGE IS AN ISSUE FOR MOST PEOPLE ANYMORE—THAT HAS NOT HAPPENED, AT LEAST WITHIN INDIVIDUALS.
MAYBE YOU SHOULD SPEAK FOR YOURSELF THERE...?

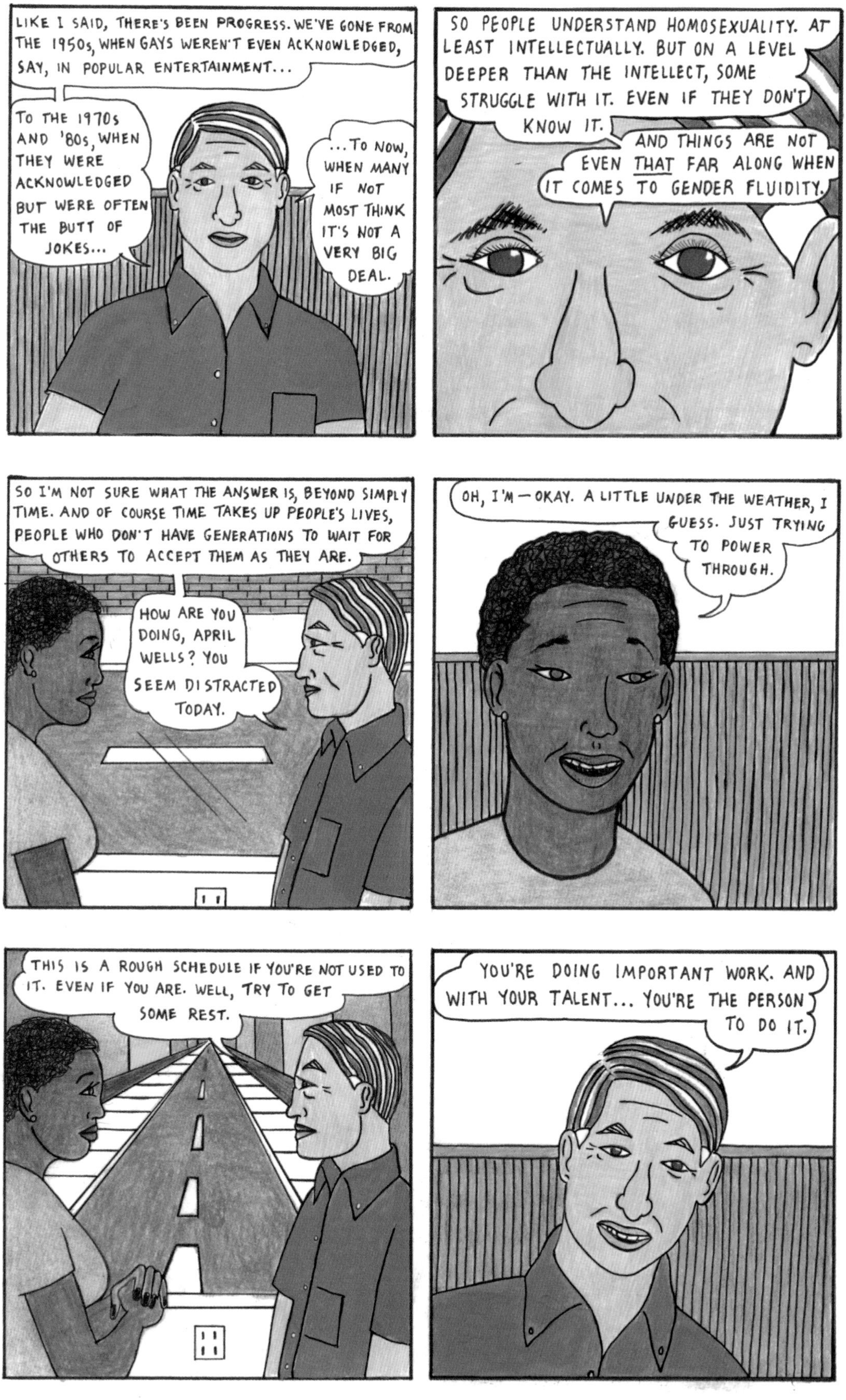
LIKE I SAID, THERE'S BEEN PROGRESS. WE'VE GONE FROM THE 1950s, WHEN GAYS WEREN'T EVEN ACKNOWLEDGED, SAY, IN POPULAR ENTERTAINMENT...
TO THE 1970s AND '80s, WHEN THEY WERE ACKNOWLEDGED BUT WERE OFTEN THE BUTT OF JOKES...
...TO NOW, WHEN MANY IF NOT MOST THINK IT'S NOT A VERY BIG DEAL.
SO PEOPLE UNDERSTAND HOMOSEXUALITY. AT LEAST INTELLECTUALLY. BUT ON A LEVEL DEEPER THAN THE INTELLECT, SOME STRUGGLE WITH IT. EVEN IF THEY DON'T KNOW IT.
AND THINGS ARE NOT EVEN THAT FAR ALONG WHEN IT COMES TO GENDER FLUIDITY.
SO I'M NOT SURE WHAT THE ANSWER IS, BEYOND SIMPLY TIME. AND OF COURSE TIME TAKES UP PEOPLE'S LIVES, PEOPLE WHO DON'T HAVE GENERATIONS TO WAIT FOR OTHERS TO ACCEPT THEM AS THEY ARE.
HOW ARE YOU DOING, APRIL WELLS? YOU SEEM DISTRACTED TODAY.
OH, I'M—OKAY. A LITTLE UNDER THE WEATHER, I GUESS. JUST TRYING TO POWER THROUGH.
THIS IS A ROUGH SCHEDULE IF YOU'RE NOT USED TO IT. EVEN IF YOU ARE. WELL, TRY TO GET SOME REST.
YOU'RE DOING IMPORTANT WORK. AND WITH YOUR TALENT... YOU'RE THE PERSON TO DO IT.

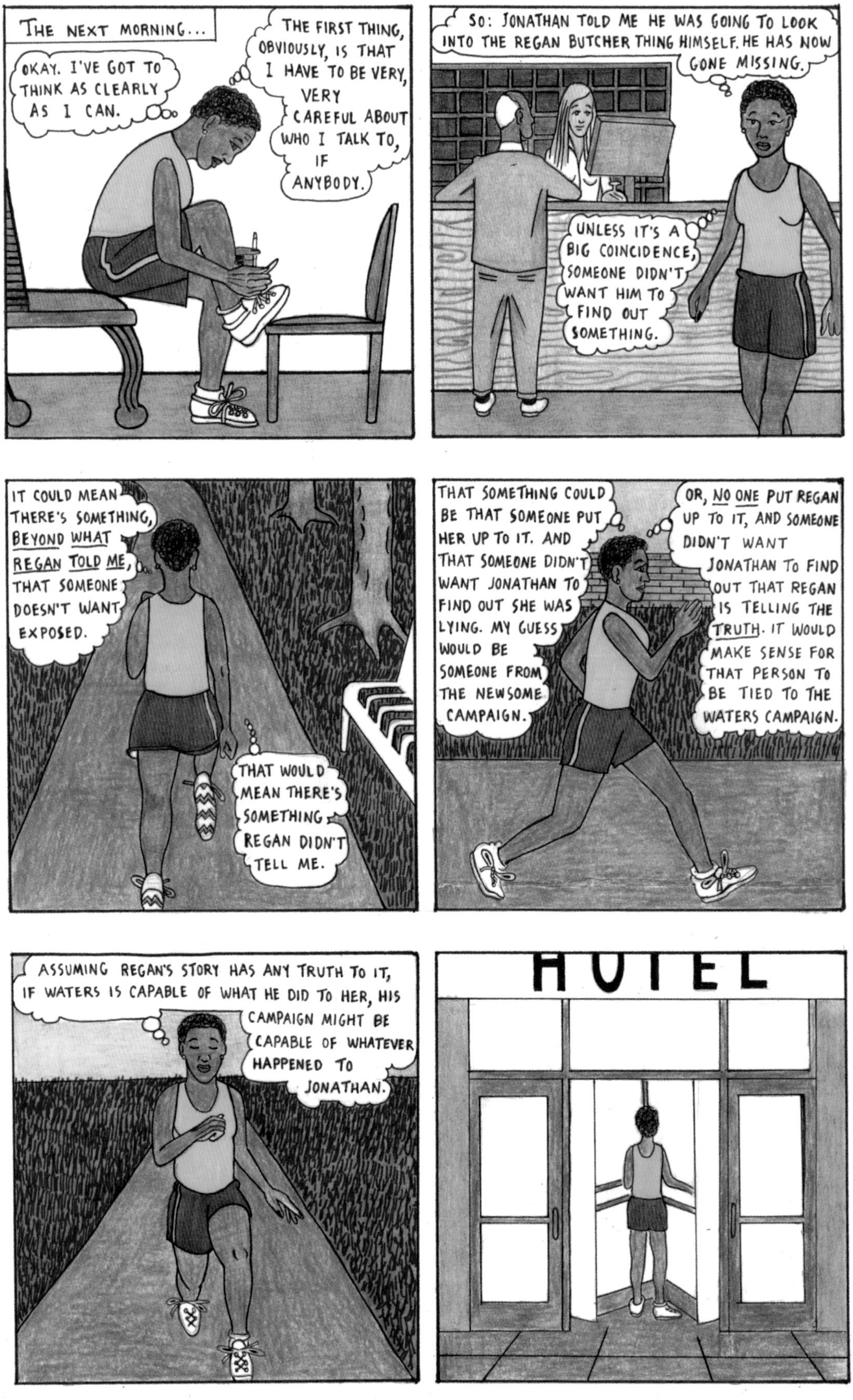
THE NEXT MORNING...
OKAY. I'VE GOT TO THINK AS CLEARLY AS I CAN.
THE FIRST THING, OBVIOUSLY, IS THAT I HAVE TO BE VERY, VERY CAREFUL ABOUT WHO I TALK TO, IF ANYBODY.
SO: JONATHAN TOLD ME HE WAS GOING TO LOOK INTO THE REGAN BUTCHER THING HIMSELF. HE HAS NOW GONE MISSING.
UNLESS IT'S A BIG COINCIDENCE, SOMEONE DIDN'T WANT HIM TO FIND OUT SOMETHING.
IT COULD MEAN THERE'S SOMETHING, BEYOND WHAT REGAN TOLD ME, THAT SOMEONE DOESN'T WANT EXPOSED.
THAT WOULD MEAN THERE'S SOMETHING REGAN DIDN'T TELL ME.
THAT SOMETHING COULD BE THAT SOMEONE PUT HER UP TO IT. AND THAT SOMEONE DIDN'T WANT JONATHAN TO FIND OUT SHE WAS LYING. MY GUESS WOULD BE SOMEONE FROM THE NEWSOME CAMPAIGN.
OR, NO ONE PUT REGAN UP TO IT, AND SOMEONE DIDN'T WANT JONATHAN TO FIND OUT THAT REGAN IS TELLING THE TRUTH. IT WOULD MAKE SENSE FOR THAT PERSON TO BE TIED TO THE WATERS CAMPAIGN.
ASSUMING REGAN'S STORY HAS ANY TRUTH TO IT, IF WATERS IS CAPABLE OF WHAT HE DID TO HER, HIS CAMPAIGN MIGHT BE CAPABLE OF WHATEVER HAPPENED TO JONATHAN.
HOTEL

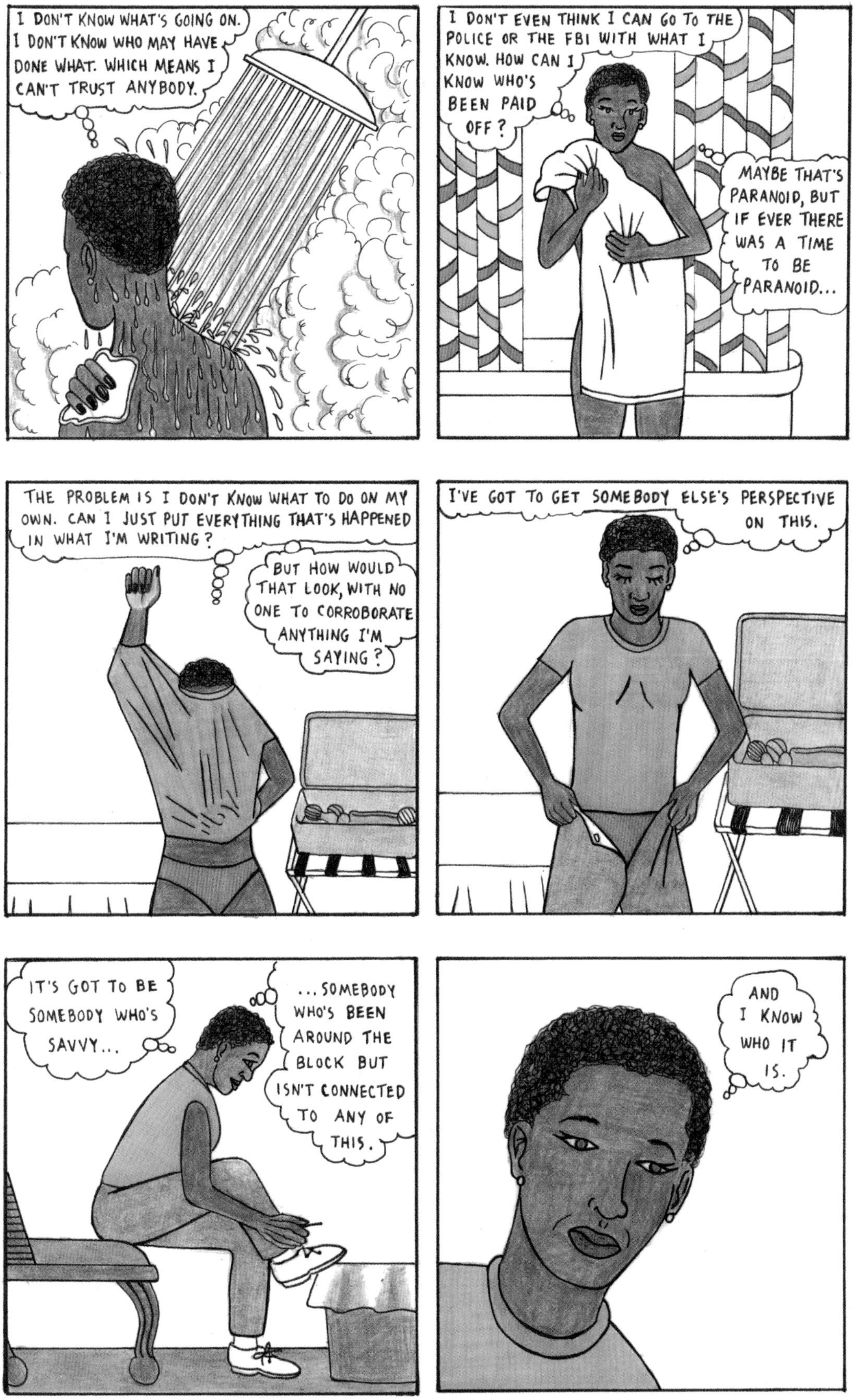
I DON'T KNOW WHAT'S GOING ON. I DON'T KNOW WHO MAY HAVE DONE WHAT. WHICH MEANS I CAN'T TRUST ANYBODY.
I DON'T EVEN THINK I CAN GO TO THE POLICE OR THE FBI WITH WHAT I KNOW. HOW CAN I KNOW WHO'S BEEN PAID OFF?
MAYBE THAT'S PARANOID, BUT IF EVER THERE WAS A TIME TO BE PARANOID...
THE PROBLEM IS I DON'T KNOW WHAT TO DO ON MY OWN. CAN I JUST PUT EVERYTHING THAT'S HAPPENED IN WHAT I'M WRITING?
BUT HOW WOULD THAT LOOK, WITH NO ONE TO CORROBORATE ANYTHING I'M SAYING?
I'VE GOT TO GET SOMEBODY ELSE'S PERSPECTIVE ON THIS.
IT'S GOT TO BE SOMEBODY WHO'S SAVVY...
...SOMEBODY WHO'S BEEN AROUND THE BLOCK BUT ISN'T CONNECTED TO ANY OF THIS.
AND I KNOW WHO IT IS.

PART TWO

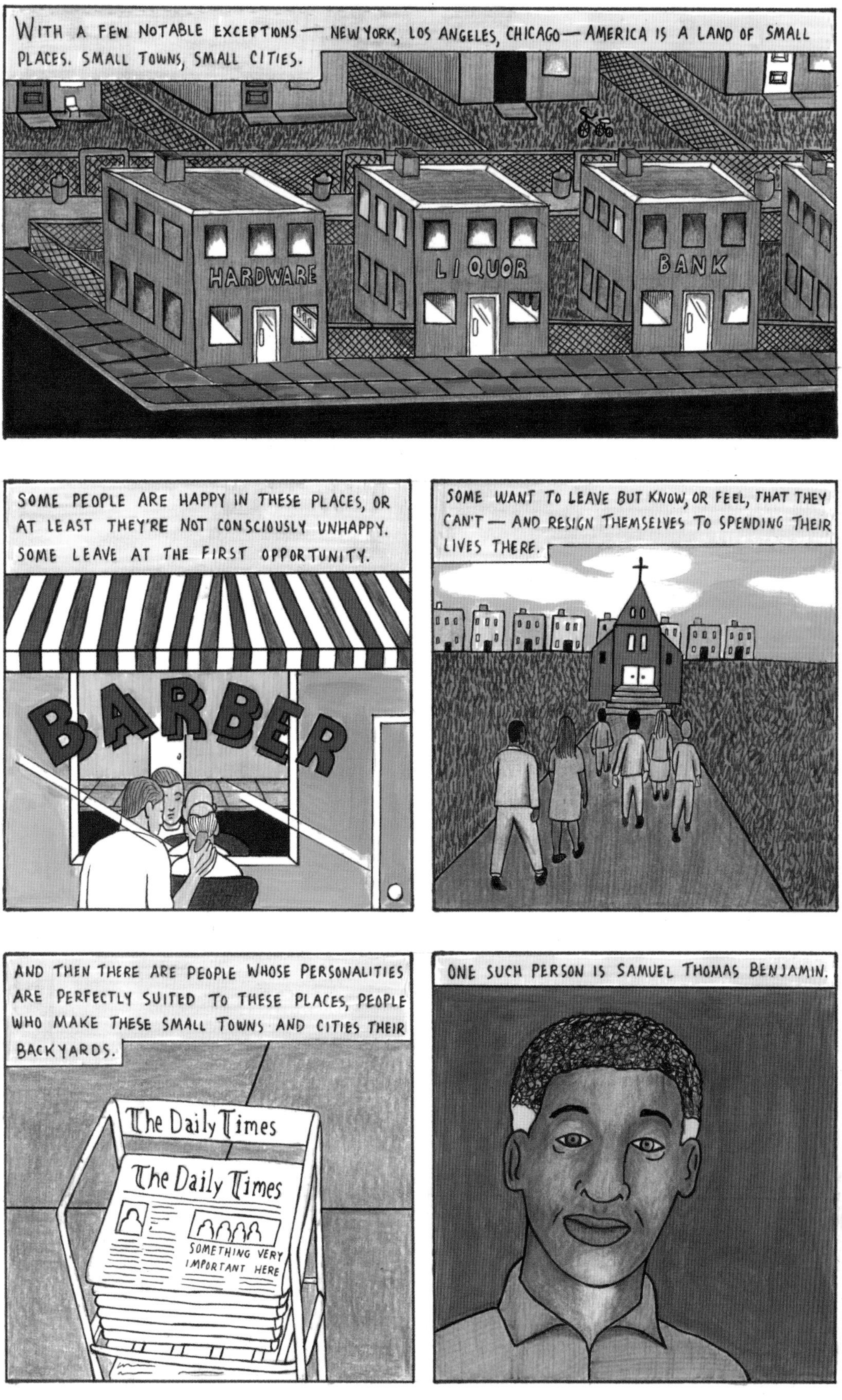
WITH A FEW NOTABLE EXCEPTIONS — NEW YORK, LOS ANGELES, CHICAGO — AMERICA IS A LAND OF SMALL PLACES. SMALL TOWNS, SMALL CITIES.
HARDWARE
LIQUOR
BANK
SOME PEOPLE ARE HAPPY IN THESE PLACES, OR AT LEAST THEY'RE NOT CONSCIOUSLY UNHAPPY. SOME LEAVE AT THE FIRST OPPORTUNITY.
BARBER
SOME WANT TO LEAVE BUT KNOW, OR FEEL, THAT THEY CAN'T — AND RESIGN THEMSELVES TO SPENDING THEIR LIVES THERE.
AND THEN THERE ARE PEOPLE WHOSE PERSONALITIES ARE PERFECTLY SUITED TO THESE PLACES, PEOPLE WHO MAKE THESE SMALL TOWNS AND CITIES THEIR BACKYARDS.
The Daily Times
The Daily Times
SOMETHING VERY IMPORTANT HERE
ONE SUCH PERSON IS SAMUEL THOMAS BENJAMIN.

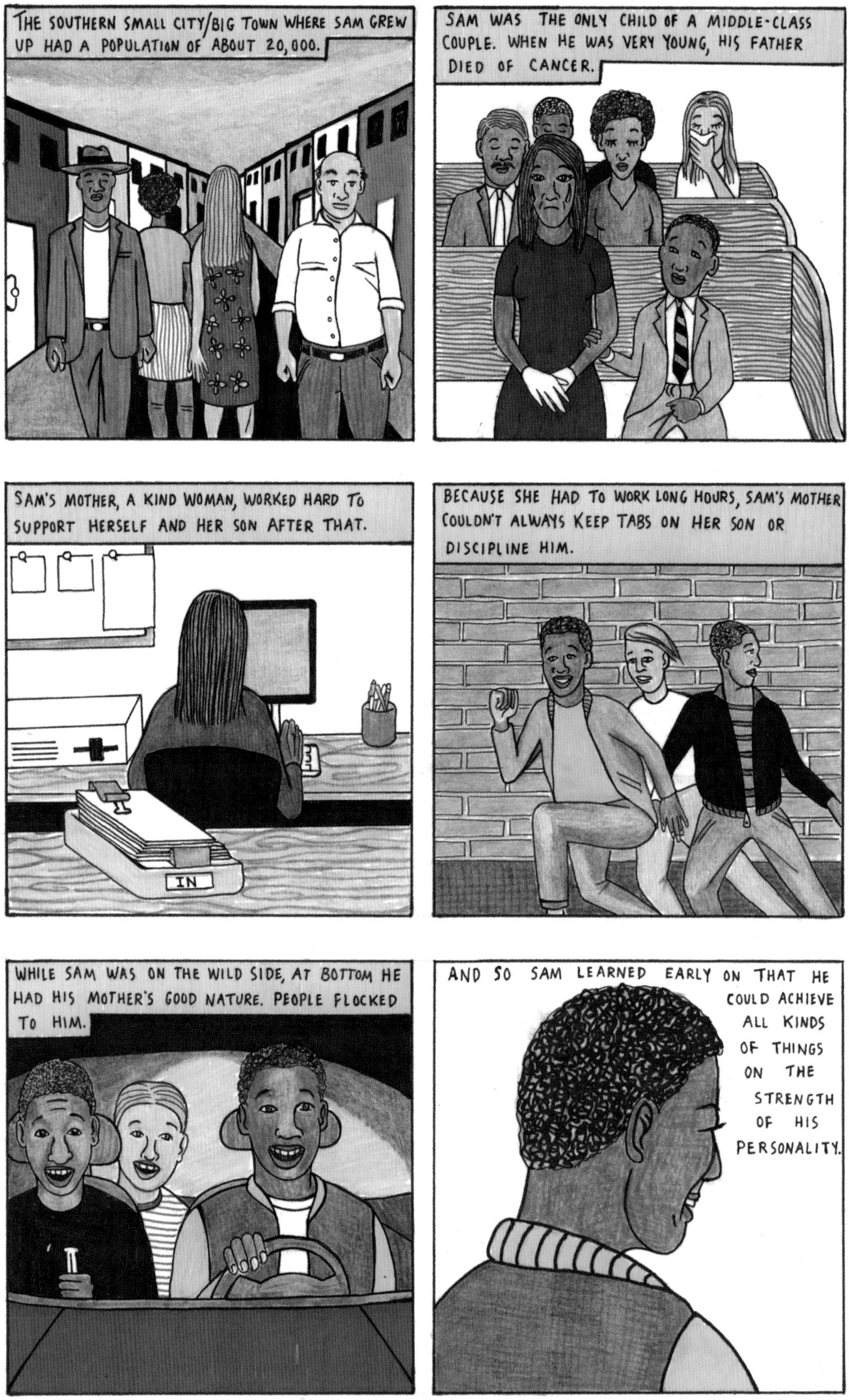
THE SOUTHERN SMALL CITY/BIG TOWN WHERE SAM GREW UP HAD A POPULATION OF ABOUT 20,000.
SAM WAS THE ONLY CHILD OF A MIDDLE-CLASS COUPLE. WHEN HE WAS VERY YOUNG, HIS FATHER DIED OF CANCER.
SAM'S MOTHER, A KIND WOMAN, WORKED HARD TO SUPPORT HERSELF AND HER SON AFTER THAT.
IN
BECAUSE SHE HAD TO WORK LONG HOURS, SAM'S MOTHER COULDN'T ALWAYS KEEP TABS ON HER SON OR DISCIPLINE HIM.
WHILE SAM WAS ON THE WILD SIDE, AT BOTTOM HE HAD HIS MOTHER'S GOOD NATURE. PEOPLE FLOCKED TO HIM.
AND SO SAM LEARNED EARLY ON THAT HE COULD ACHIEVE ALL KINDS OF THINGS ON THE STRENGTH OF HIS PERSONALITY.

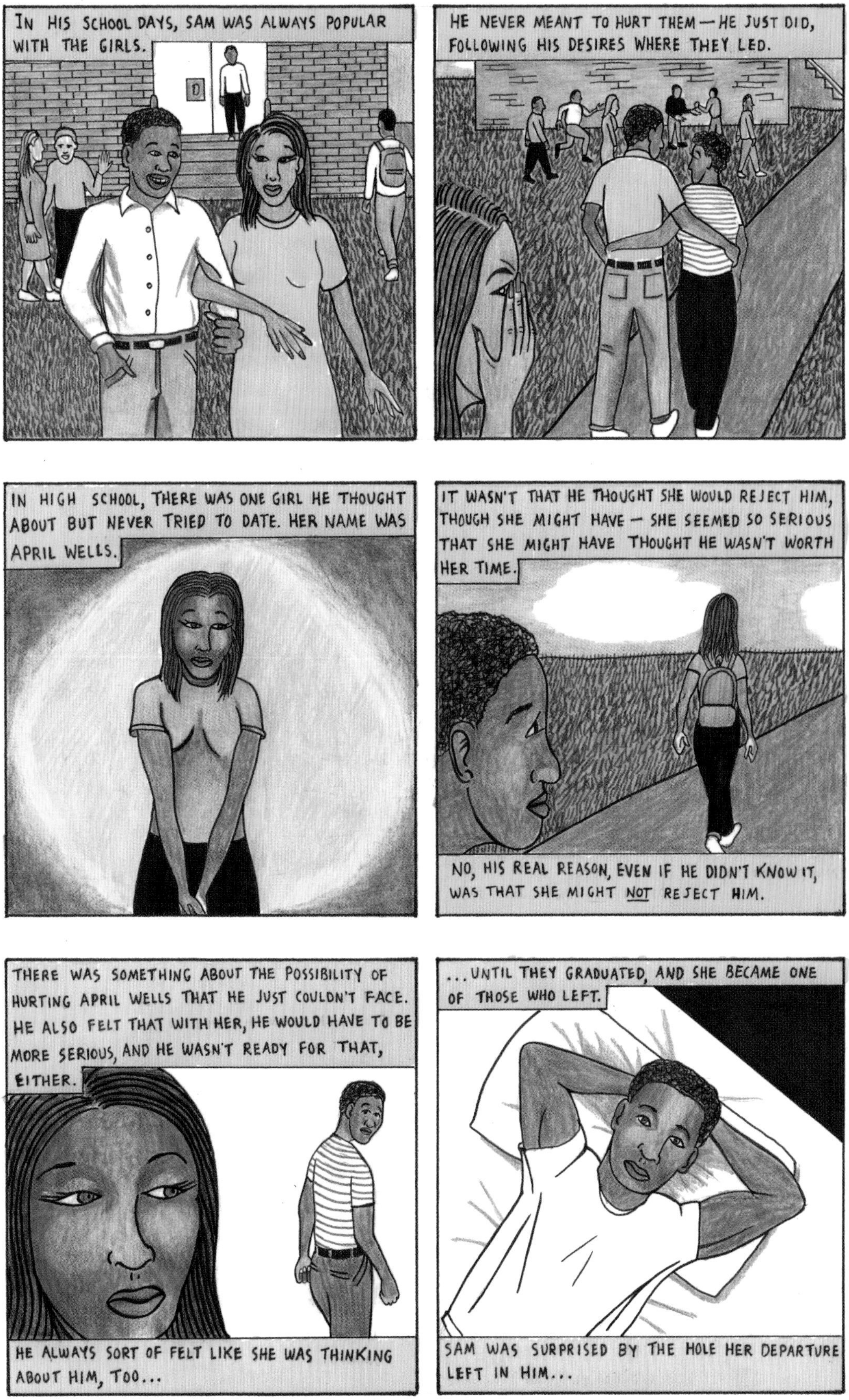
IN HIS SCHOOL DAYS, SAM WAS ALWAYS POPULAR WITH THE GIRLS.
D
HE NEVER MEANT TO HURT THEM—HE JUST DID, FOLLOWING HIS DESIRES WHERE THEY LED.
IN HIGH SCHOOL, THERE WAS ONE GIRL HE THOUGHT ABOUT BUT NEVER TRIED TO DATE. HER NAME WAS APRIL WELLS.
IT WASN'T THAT HE THOUGHT SHE WOULD REJECT HIM, THOUGH SHE MIGHT HAVE — SHE SEEMED SO SERIOUS THAT SHE MIGHT HAVE THOUGHT HE WASN'T WORTH HER TIME.
NO, HIS REAL REASON, EVEN IF HE DIDN'T KNOW IT, WAS THAT SHE MIGHT NOT REJECT HIM.
THERE WAS SOMETHING ABOUT THE POSSIBILITY OF HURTING APRIL WELLS THAT HE JUST COULDN'T FACE. HE ALSO FELT THAT WITH HER, HE WOULD HAVE TO BE MORE SERIOUS, AND HE WASN'T READY FOR THAT, EITHER.
HE ALWAYS SORT OF FELT LIKE SHE WAS THINKING ABOUT HIM, TOO...
...UNTIL THEY GRADUATED, AND SHE BECAME ONE OF THOSE WHO LEFT.
SAM WAS SURPRISED BY THE HOLE HER DEPARTURE LEFT IN HIM...

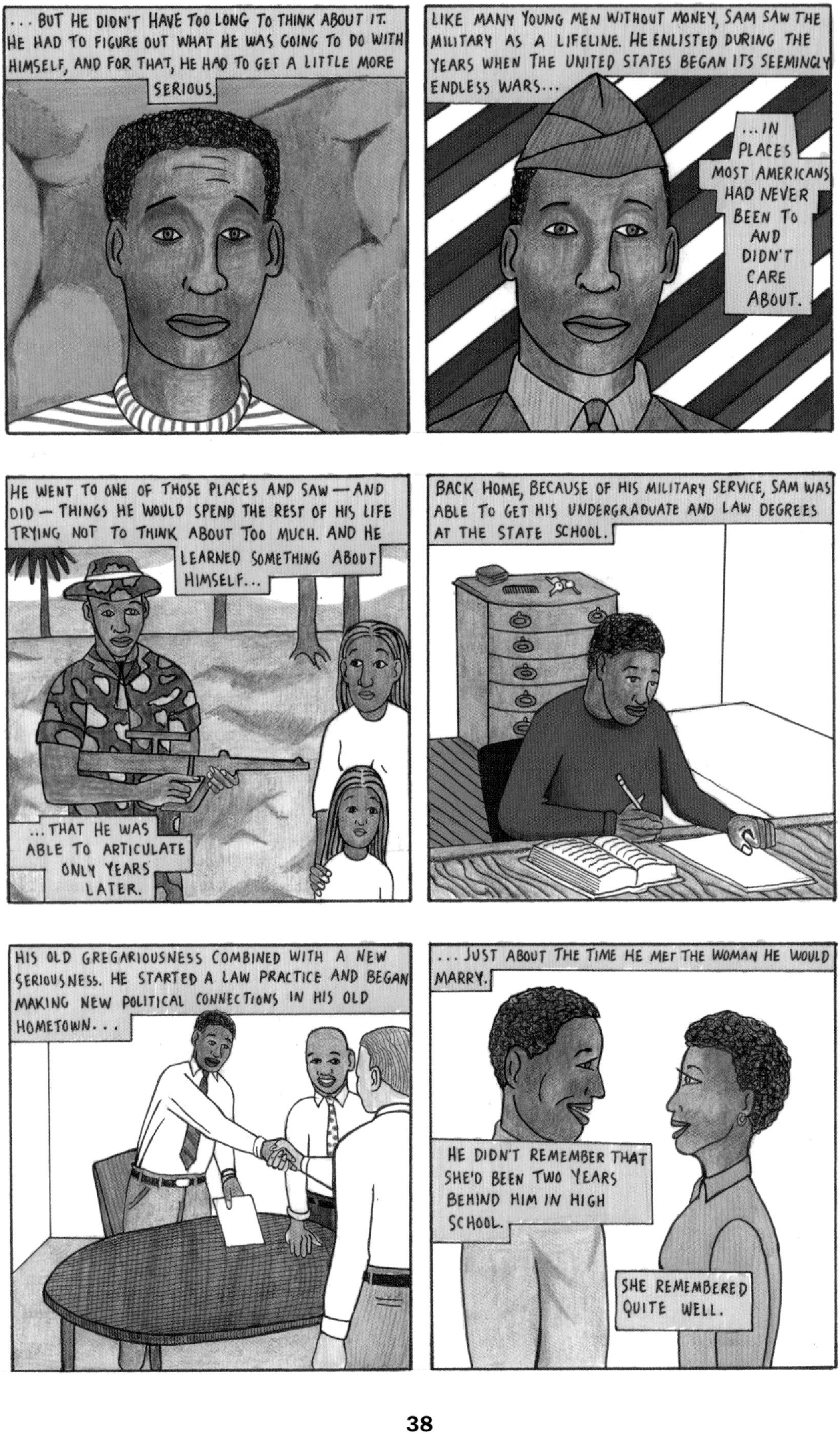
... BUT HE DIDN'T HAVE TOO LONG TO THINK ABOUT IT. HE HAD TO FIGURE OUT WHAT HE WAS GOING TO DO WITH HIMSELF, AND FOR THAT, HE HAD TO GET A LITTLE MORE SERIOUS.
LIKE MANY YOUNG MEN WITHOUT MONEY, SAM SAW THE MILITARY AS A LIFELINE. HE ENLISTED DURING THE YEARS WHEN THE UNITED STATES BEGAN ITS SEEMINGLY ENDLESS WARS...
... IN PLACES MOST AMERICANS HAD NEVER BEEN TO AND DIDN'T CARE ABOUT.
HE WENT TO ONE OF THOSE PLACES AND SAW—AND DID—THINGS HE WOULD SPEND THE REST OF HIS LIFE TRYING NOT TO THINK ABOUT TOO MUCH. AND HE LEARNED SOMETHING ABOUT HIMSELF...
... THAT HE WAS ABLE TO ARTICULATE ONLY YEARS LATER.
BACK HOME, BECAUSE OF HIS MILITARY SERVICE, SAM WAS ABLE TO GET HIS UNDERGRADUATE AND LAW DEGREES AT THE STATE SCHOOL.
HIS OLD GREGARIOUSNESS COMBINED WITH A NEW SERIOUSNESS. HE STARTED A LAW PRACTICE AND BEGAN MAKING NEW POLITICAL CONNECTIONS IN HIS OLD HOMETOWN...
... JUST ABOUT THE TIME HE MET THE WOMAN HE WOULD MARRY.
HE DIDN'T REMEMBER THAT SHE'D BEEN TWO YEARS BEHIND HIM IN HIGH SCHOOL.
SHE REMEMBERED QUITE WELL.

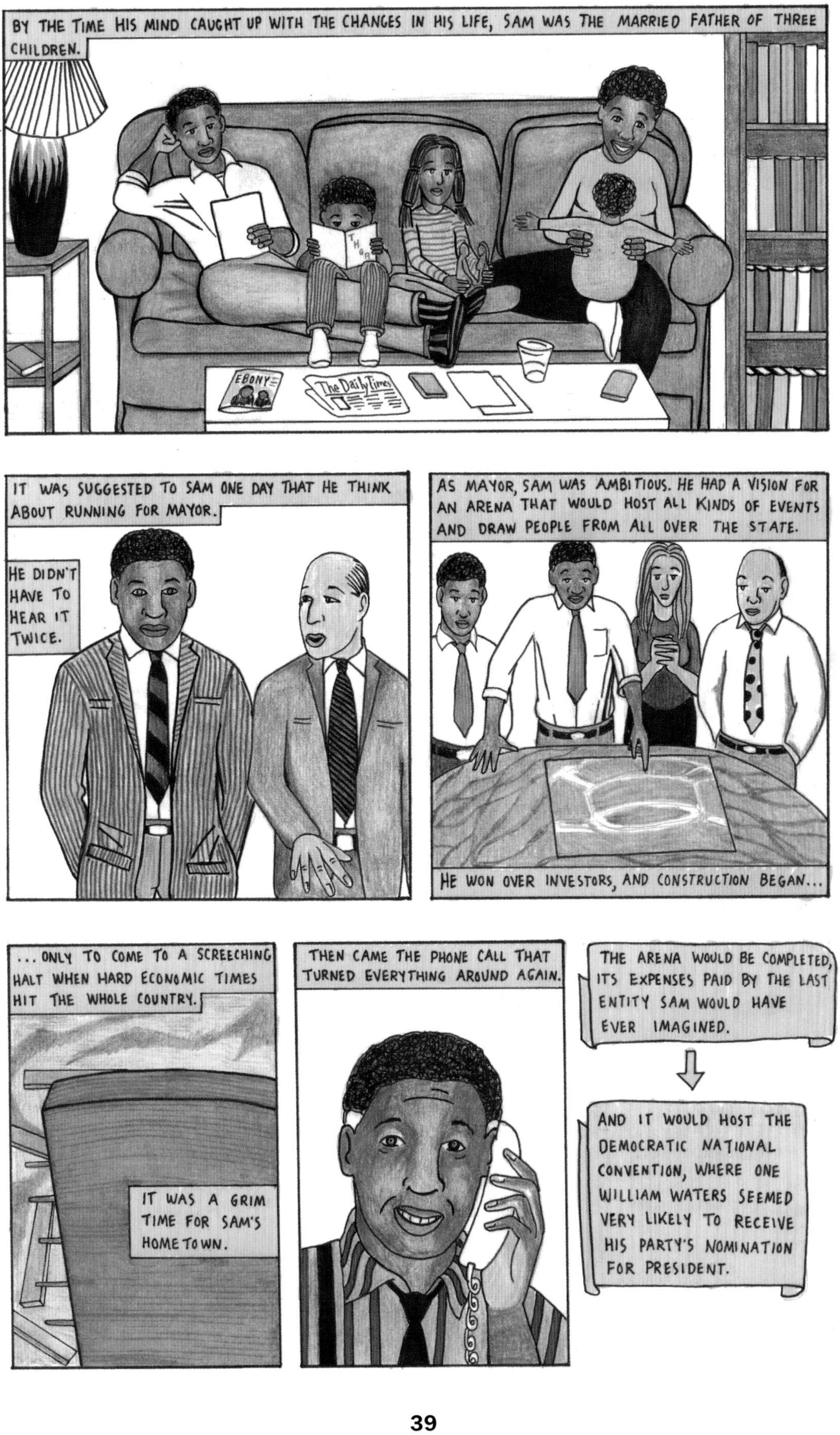
BY THE TIME HIS MIND CAUGHT UP WITH THE CHANGES IN HIS LIFE, SAM WAS THE MARRIED FATHER OF THREE CHILDREN.
EBONY
The Daily Times
IT WAS SUGGESTED TO SAM ONE DAY THAT HE THINK ABOUT RUNNING FOR MAYOR.
HE DIDN'T HAVE TO HEAR IT TWICE.
AS MAYOR, SAM WAS AMBITIOUS. HE HAD A VISION FOR AN ARENA THAT WOULD HOST ALL KINDS OF EVENTS AND DRAW PEOPLE FROM ALL OVER THE STATE.
HE WON OVER INVESTORS, AND CONSTRUCTION BEGAN...
...ONLY TO COME TO A SCREECHING HALT WHEN HARD ECONOMIC TIMES HIT THE WHOLE COUNTRY.
IT WAS A GRIM TIME FOR SAM'S HOMETOWN.
THEN CAME THE PHONE CALL THAT TURNED EVERYTHING AROUND AGAIN.
THE ARENA WOULD BE COMPLETED, ITS EXPENSES PAID BY THE LAST ENTITY SAM WOULD HAVE EVER IMAGINED.
AND IT WOULD HOST THE DEMOCRATIC NATIONAL CONVENTION, WHERE ONE WILLIAM WATERS SEEMED VERY LIKELY TO RECEIVE HIS PARTY'S NOMINATION FOR PRESIDENT.

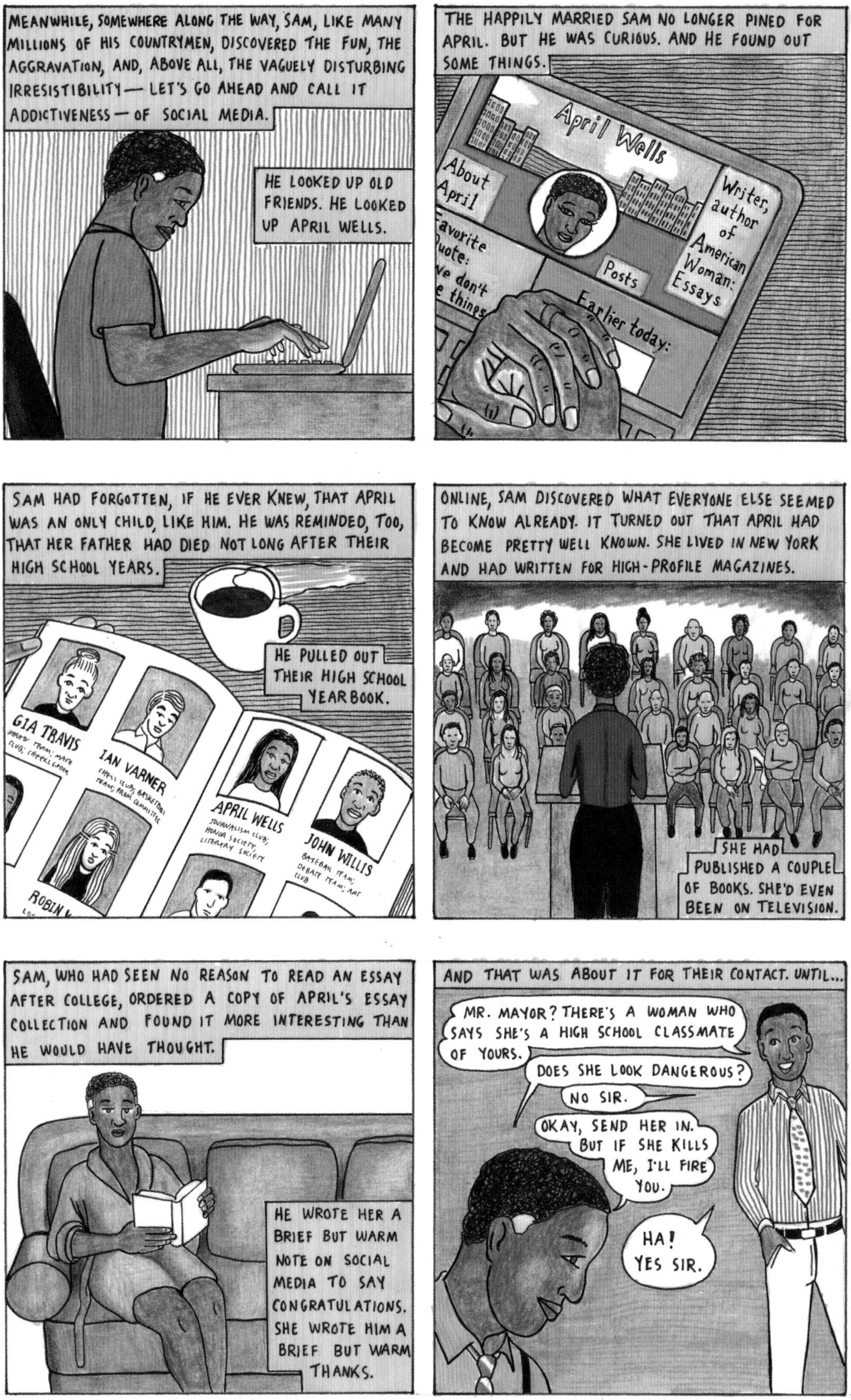
MEANWHILE, SOMEWHERE ALONG THE WAY, SAM, LIKE MANY MILLIONS OF HIS COUNTRYMEN, DISCOVERED THE FUN, THE AGGRAVATION, AND, ABOVE ALL, THE VAGUELY DISTURBING IRRESISTIBILITY— LET'S GO AHEAD AND CALL IT ADDICTIVENESS— OF SOCIAL MEDIA.
HE LOOKED UP OLD FRIENDS. HE LOOKED UP APRIL WELLS.
THE HAPPILY MARRIED SAM NO LONGER PINED FOR APRIL. BUT HE WAS CURIOUS. AND HE FOUND OUT SOME THINGS.
April Wells
About April
Writer, author of American Woman: Essays
Posts
Earlier today:
SAM HAD FORGOTTEN, IF HE EVER KNEW, THAT APRIL WAS AN ONLY CHILD, LIKE HIM. HE WAS REMINDED, TOO, THAT HER FATHER HAD DIED NOT LONG AFTER THEIR HIGH SCHOOL YEARS.
HE PULLED OUT THEIR HIGH SCHOOL YEARBOOK.
GIA TRAVIS
IAN VARNER
APRIL WELLS
JOURNALISM CLUB; HONOR SOCIETY; LITERARY SOCIETY
JOHN WILLIS
BASEBALL TEAM; DEBATE TEAM; ART CLUB
ONLINE, SAM DISCOVERED WHAT EVERYONE ELSE SEEMED TO KNOW ALREADY. IT TURNED OUT THAT APRIL HAD BECOME PRETTY WELL KNOWN. SHE LIVED IN NEW YORK AND HAD WRITTEN FOR HIGH-PROFILE MAGAZINES.
SHE HAD PUBLISHED A COUPLE OF BOOKS. SHE'D EVEN BEEN ON TELEVISION.
SAM, WHO HAD SEEN NO REASON TO READ AN ESSAY AFTER COLLEGE, ORDERED A COPY OF APRIL'S ESSAY COLLECTION AND FOUND IT MORE INTERESTING THAN HE WOULD HAVE THOUGHT.
HE WROTE HER A BRIEF BUT WARM NOTE ON SOCIAL MEDIA TO SAY CONGRATULATIONS. SHE WROTE HIM A BRIEF BUT WARM THANKS.
AND THAT WAS ABOUT IT FOR THEIR CONTACT. UNTIL...
MR. MAYOR? THERE'S A WOMAN WHO SAYS SHE'S A HIGH SCHOOL CLASSMATE OF YOURS.
DOES SHE LOOK DANGEROUS?
NO SIR.
OKAY, SEND HER IN. BUT IF SHE KILLS ME, I'LL FIRE YOU.
HA! YES SIR.

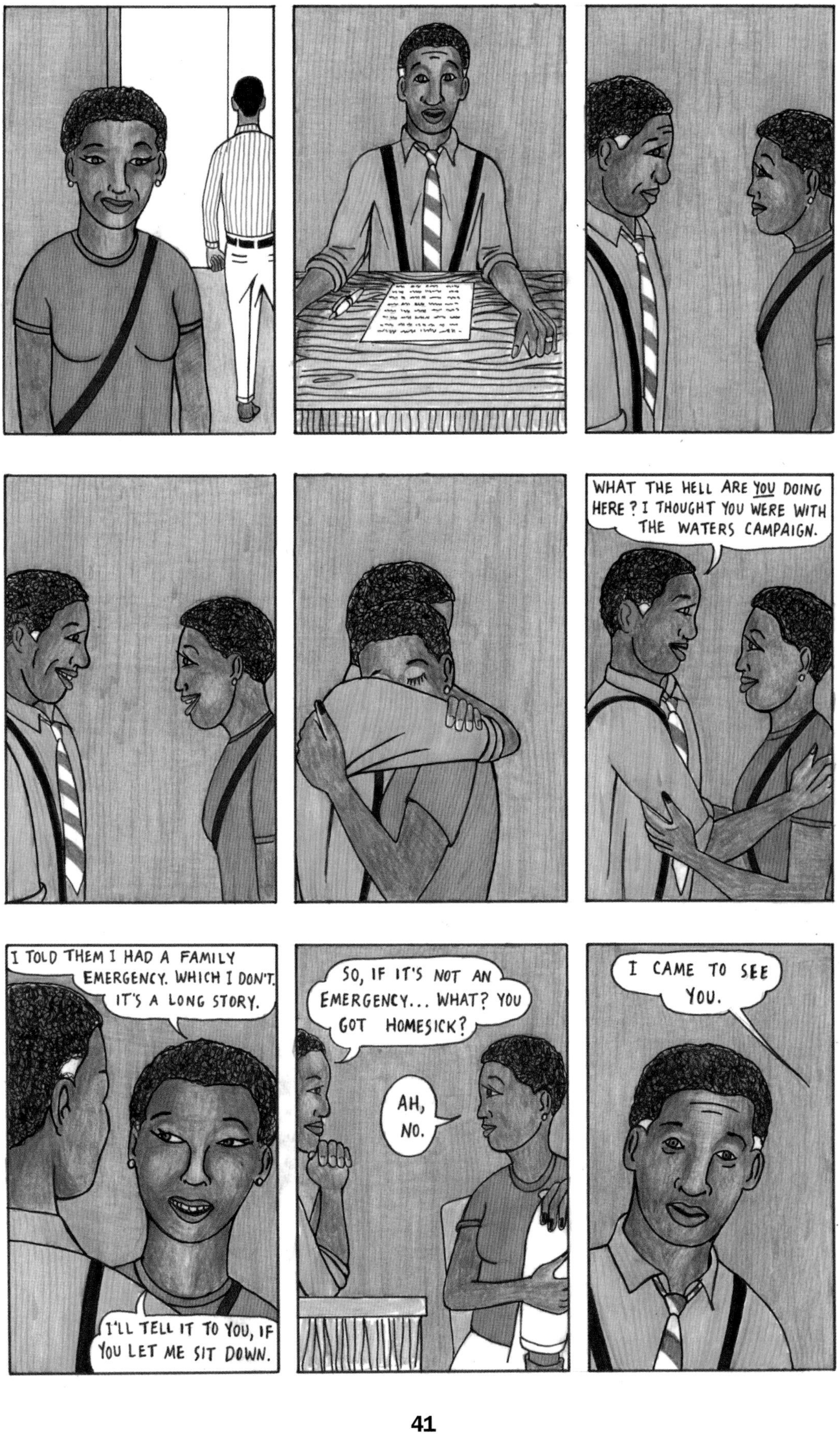

WHAT THE HELL ARE YOU DOING HERE? I THOUGHT YOU WERE WITH THE WATERS CAMPAIGN.
I TOLD THEM I HAD A FAMILY EMERGENCY. WHICH I DON'T. IT'S A LONG STORY.
I'LL TELL IT TO YOU, IF YOU LET ME SIT DOWN.
SO, IF IT'S NOT AN EMERGENCY... WHAT? YOU GOT HOMESICK?
AH, NO.
I CAME TO SEE YOU.

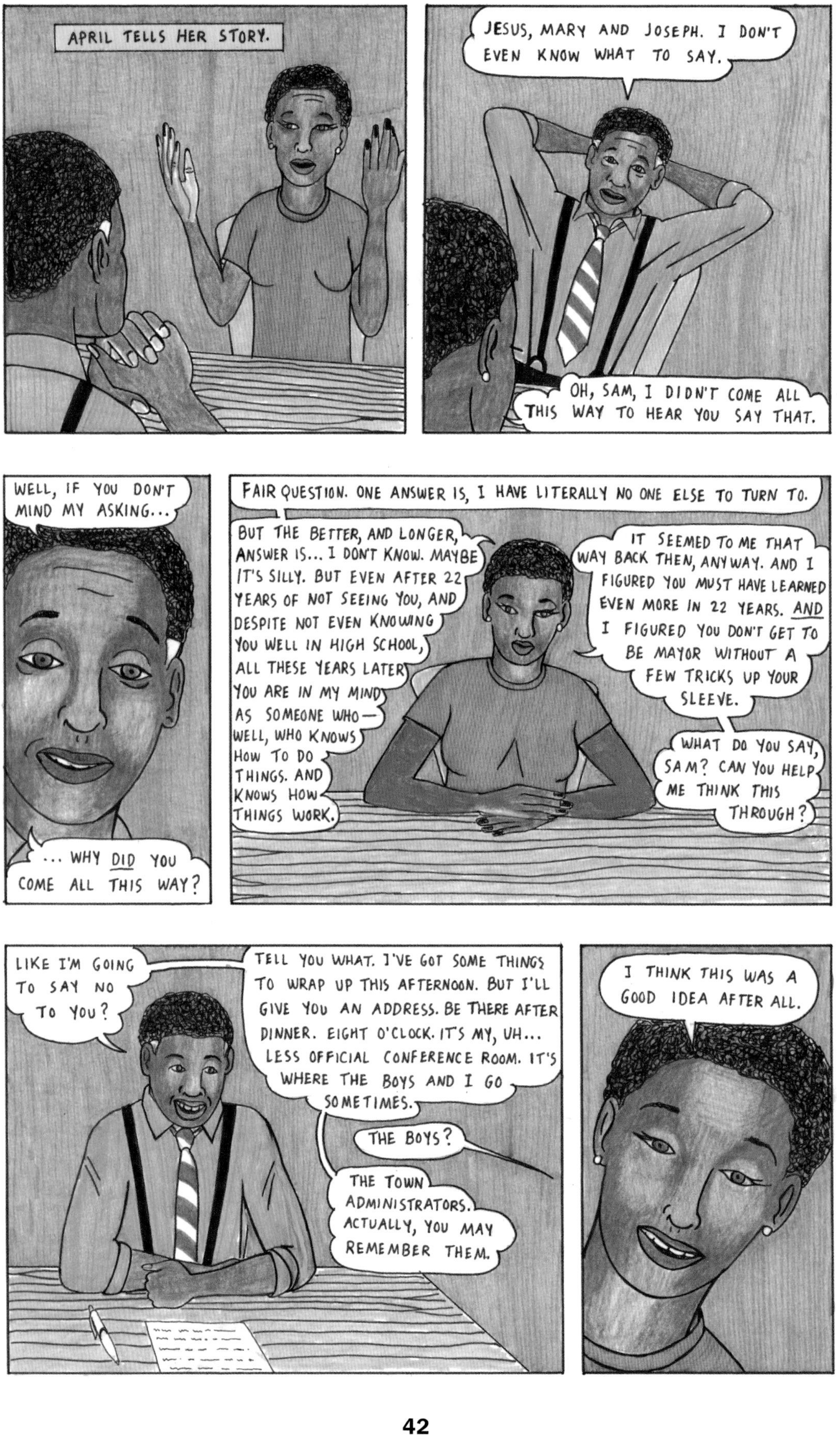
APRIL TELLS HER STORY.
JESUS, MARY AND JOSEPH. I DON'T EVEN KNOW WHAT TO SAY.
OH, SAM, I DIDN'T COME ALL THIS WAY TO HEAR YOU SAY THAT.
WELL, IF YOU DON'T MIND MY ASKING...
... WHY DID YOU COME ALL THIS WAY?
FAIR QUESTION. ONE ANSWER IS, I HAVE LITERALLY NO ONE ELSE TO TURN TO.
BUT THE BETTER, AND LONGER, ANSWER IS... I DON'T KNOW. MAYBE IT'S SILLY. BUT EVEN AFTER 22 YEARS OF NOT SEEING YOU, AND DESPITE NOT EVEN KNOWING YOU WELL IN HIGH SCHOOL, ALL THESE YEARS LATER YOU ARE IN MY MIND AS SOMEONE WHO— WELL, WHO KNOWS HOW TO DO THINGS. AND KNOWS HOW THINGS WORK.
IT SEEMED TO ME THAT WAY BACK THEN, ANYWAY. AND I FIGURED YOU MUST HAVE LEARNED EVEN MORE IN 22 YEARS. AND I FIGURED YOU DON'T GET TO BE MAYOR WITHOUT A FEW TRICKS UP YOUR SLEEVE.
WHAT DO YOU SAY, SAM? CAN YOU HELP ME THINK THIS THROUGH?
LIKE I'M GOING TO SAY NO TO YOU?
TELL YOU WHAT. I'VE GOT SOME THINGS TO WRAP UP THIS AFTERNOON. BUT I'LL GIVE YOU AN ADDRESS. BE THERE AFTER DINNER. EIGHT O'CLOCK. IT'S MY, UH... LESS OFFICIAL CONFERENCE ROOM. IT'S WHERE THE BOYS AND I GO SOMETIMES.
THE BOYS?
THE TOWN ADMINISTRATORS. ACTUALLY, YOU MAY REMEMBER THEM.
I THINK THIS WAS A GOOD IDEA AFTER ALL.

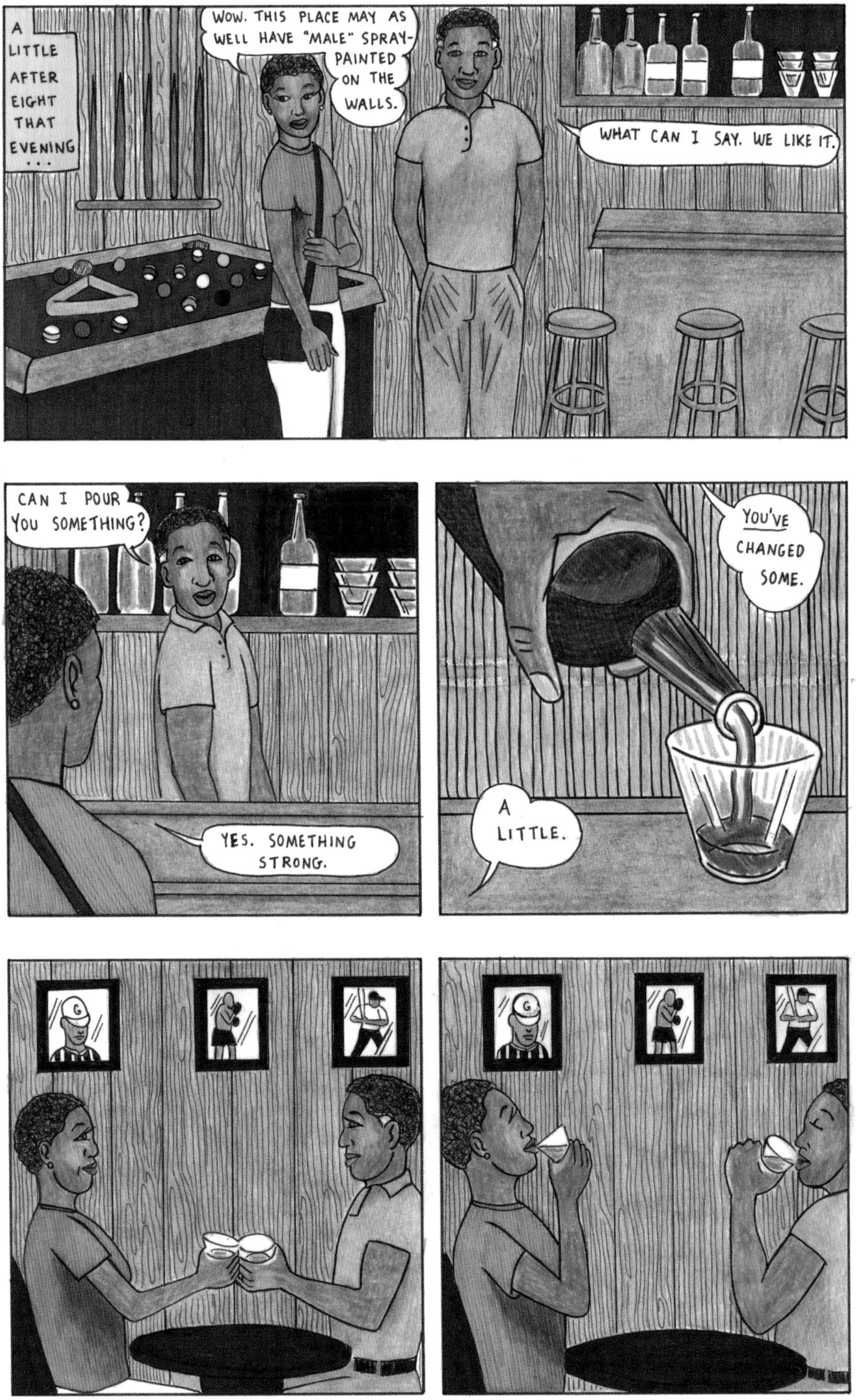
A LITTLE AFTER EIGHT THAT EVENING...
WOW. THIS PLACE MAY AS WELL HAVE "MALE" SPRAY-PAINTED ON THE WALLS.
WHAT CAN I SAY. WE LIKE IT.
CAN I POUR YOU SOMETHING?
YES. SOMETHING STRONG.
YOU'VE CHANGED SOME.
A LITTLE.
G
G

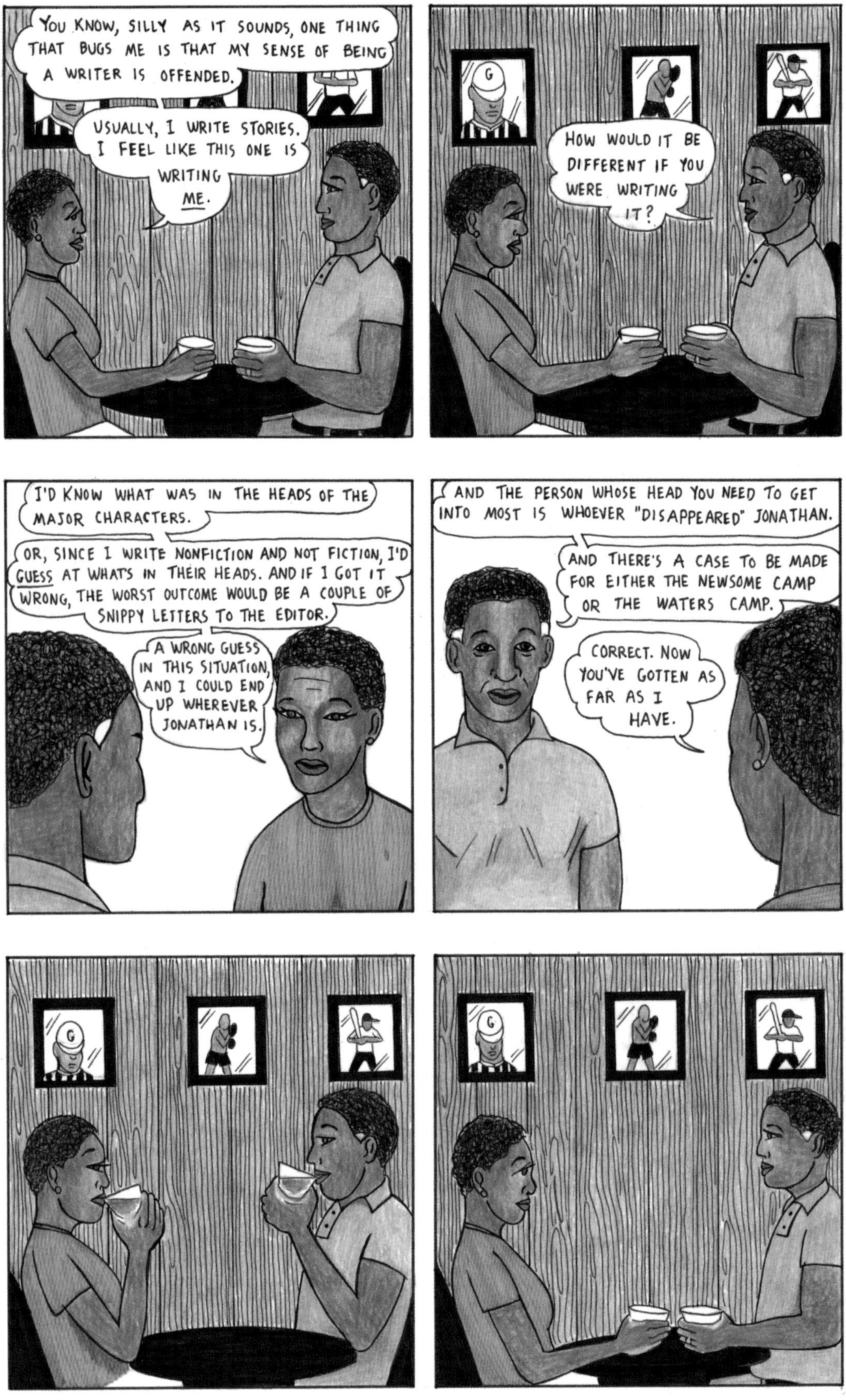
YOU KNOW, SILLY AS IT SOUNDS, ONE THING THAT BUGS ME IS THAT MY SENSE OF BEING A WRITER IS OFFENDED.
USUALLY, I WRITE STORIES. I FEEL LIKE THIS ONE IS WRITING ME.
HOW WOULD IT BE DIFFERENT IF YOU WERE WRITING IT?
I'D KNOW WHAT WAS IN THE HEADS OF THE MAJOR CHARACTERS.
OR, SINCE I WRITE NONFICTION AND NOT FICTION, I'D GUESS AT WHAT'S IN THEIR HEADS. AND IF I GOT IT WRONG, THE WORST OUTCOME WOULD BE A COUPLE OF SNIPPY LETTERS TO THE EDITOR.
A WRONG GUESS IN THIS SITUATION, AND I COULD END UP WHEREVER JONATHAN IS.
AND THE PERSON WHOSE HEAD YOU NEED TO GET INTO MOST IS WHOEVER "DISAPPEARED" JONATHAN.
AND THERE'S A CASE TO BE MADE FOR EITHER THE NEWSOME CAMP OR THE WATERS CAMP.
CORRECT. NOW YOU'VE GOTTEN AS FAR AS I HAVE.

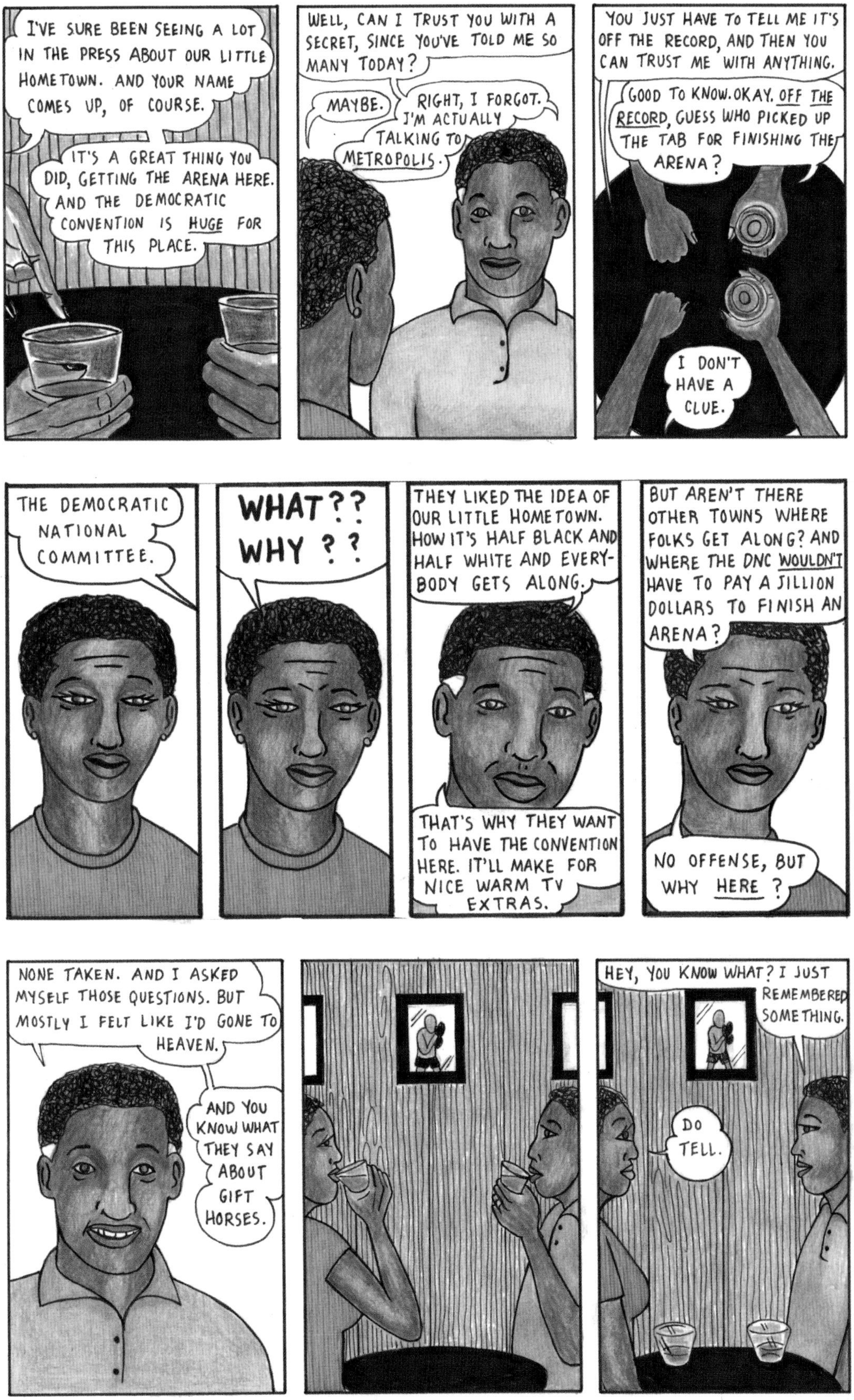
I'VE SURE BEEN SEEING A LOT IN THE PRESS ABOUT OUR LITTLE HOMETOWN. AND YOUR NAME COMES UP, OF COURSE.
IT'S A GREAT THING YOU DID, GETTING THE ARENA HERE. AND THE DEMOCRATIC CONVENTION IS HUGE FOR THIS PLACE.
WELL, CAN I TRUST YOU WITH A SECRET, SINCE YOU'VE TOLD ME SO MANY TODAY?
MAYBE.
RIGHT, I FORGOT. I'M ACTUALLY TALKING TO METROPOLIS.
YOU JUST HAVE TO TELL ME IT'S OFF THE RECORD, AND THEN YOU CAN TRUST ME WITH ANYTHING.
GOOD TO KNOW. OKAY. OFF THE RECORD, GUESS WHO PICKED UP THE TAB FOR FINISHING THE ARENA?
I DON'T HAVE A CLUE.
THE DEMOCRATIC NATIONAL COMMITTEE.
WHAT?? WHY??
THEY LIKED THE IDEA OF OUR LITTLE HOMETOWN. HOW IT'S HALF BLACK AND HALF WHITE AND EVERYBODY GETS ALONG.
THAT'S WHY THEY WANT TO HAVE THE CONVENTION HERE. IT'LL MAKE FOR NICE WARM TV EXTRAS.
BUT AREN'T THERE OTHER TOWNS WHERE FOLKS GET ALONG? AND WHERE THE DNC WOULDN'T HAVE TO PAY A JILLION DOLLARS TO FINISH AN ARENA?
NO OFFENSE, BUT WHY HERE?
NONE TAKEN. AND I ASKED MYSELF THOSE QUESTIONS. BUT MOSTLY I FELT LIKE I'D GONE TO HEAVEN.
AND YOU KNOW WHAT THEY SAY ABOUT GIFT HORSES.
HEY, YOU KNOW WHAT? I JUST REMEMBERED SOMETHING.
DO TELL.

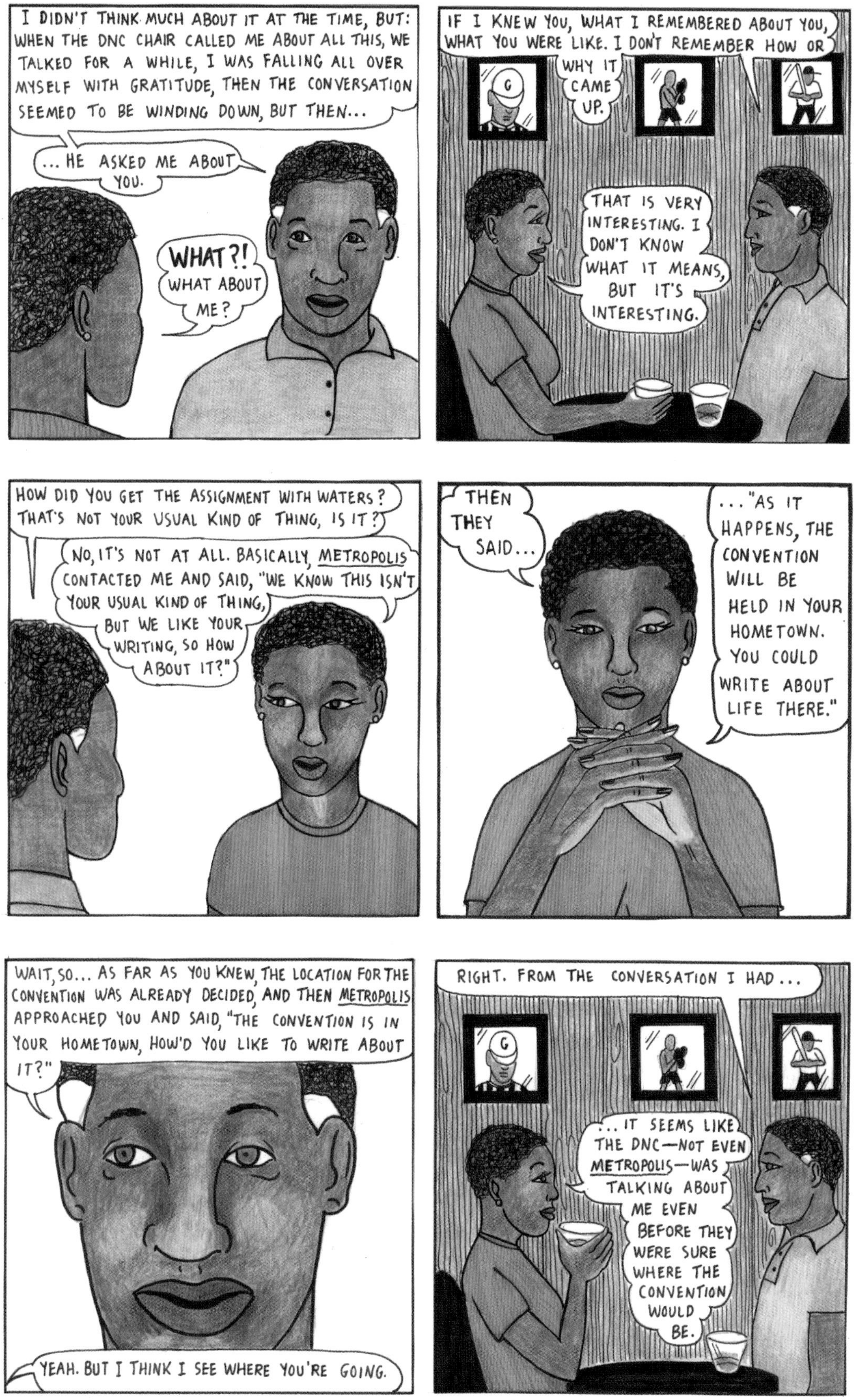
I DIDN'T THINK MUCH ABOUT IT AT THE TIME, BUT: WHEN THE DNC CHAIR CALLED ME ABOUT ALL THIS, WE TALKED FOR A WHILE, I WAS FALLING ALL OVER MYSELF WITH GRATITUDE, THEN THE CONVERSATION SEEMED TO BE WINDING DOWN, BUT THEN...
...HE ASKED ME ABOUT YOU.
WHAT?! WHAT ABOUT ME?
IF I KNEW YOU, WHAT I REMEMBERED ABOUT YOU, WHAT YOU WERE LIKE. I DON'T REMEMBER HOW OR
WHY IT CAME UP.
THAT IS VERY INTERESTING. I DON'T KNOW WHAT IT MEANS, BUT IT'S INTERESTING.
HOW DID YOU GET THE ASSIGNMENT WITH WATERS? THAT'S NOT YOUR USUAL KIND OF THING, IS IT?
NO, IT'S NOT AT ALL. BASICALLY, METROPOLIS CONTACTED ME AND SAID, "WE KNOW THIS ISN'T YOUR USUAL KIND OF THING,
BUT WE LIKE YOUR WRITING, SO HOW ABOUT IT?"
THEN THEY SAID...
..."AS IT HAPPENS, THE CONVENTION WILL BE HELD IN YOUR HOMETOWN. YOU COULD WRITE ABOUT LIFE THERE."
WAIT, SO... AS FAR AS YOU KNEW, THE LOCATION FOR THE CONVENTION WAS ALREADY DECIDED, AND THEN METROPOLIS APPROACHED YOU AND SAID, "THE CONVENTION IS IN YOUR HOMETOWN, HOW'D YOU LIKE TO WRITE ABOUT IT?"
YEAH. BUT I THINK I SEE WHERE YOU'RE GOING.
RIGHT. FROM THE CONVERSATION I HAD...
...IT SEEMS LIKE THE DNC—NOT EVEN METROPOLIS—WAS TALKING ABOUT ME EVEN BEFORE THEY WERE SURE WHERE THE CONVENTION WOULD BE.

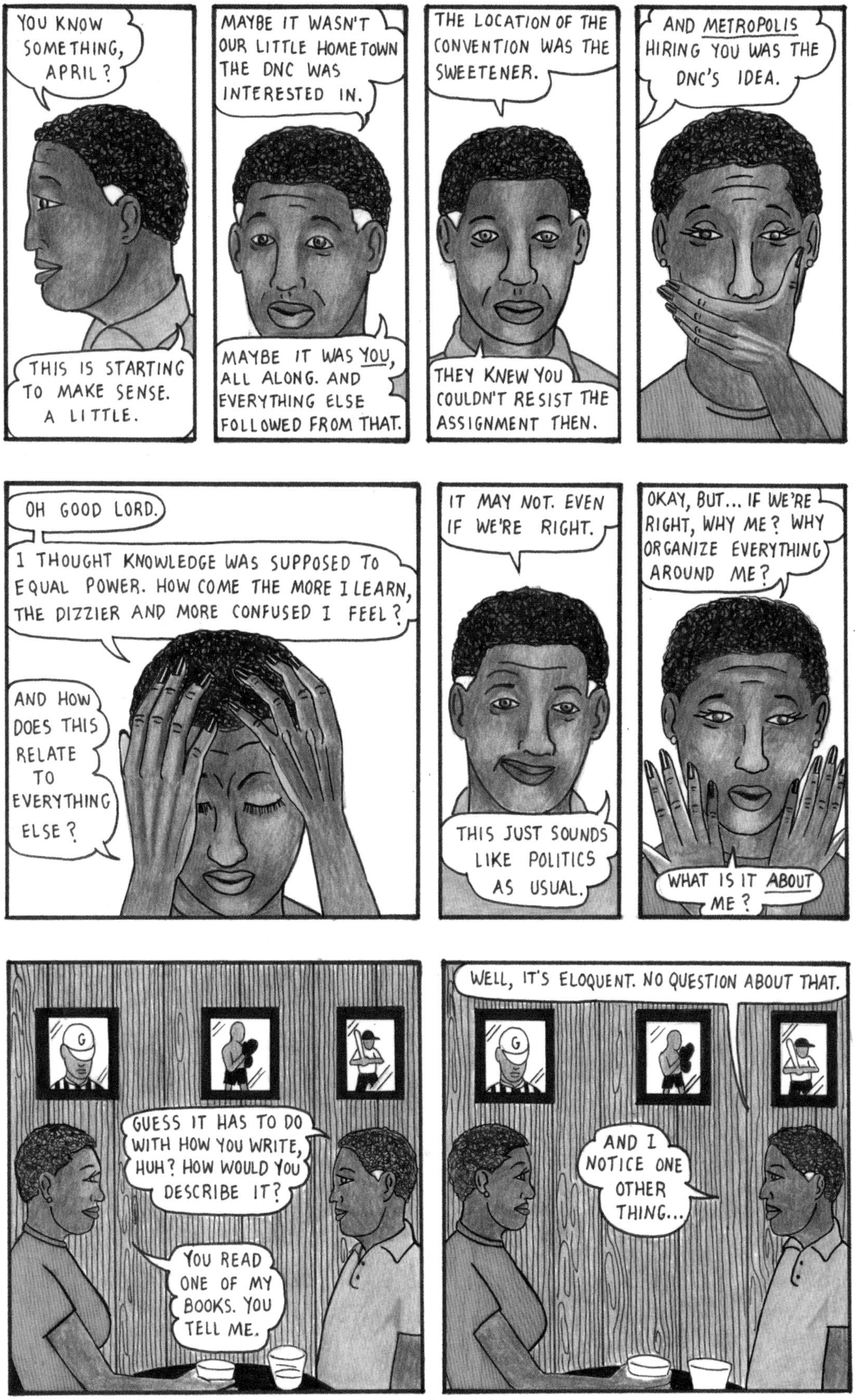
YOU KNOW SOMETHING, APRIL?
THIS IS STARTING TO MAKE SENSE. A LITTLE.
MAYBE IT WASN'T OUR LITTLE HOMETOWN THE DNC WAS INTERESTED IN.
MAYBE IT WAS YOU, ALL ALONG. AND EVERYTHING ELSE FOLLOWED FROM THAT.
THE LOCATION OF THE CONVENTION WAS THE SWEETENER.
THEY KNEW YOU COULDN'T RESIST THE ASSIGNMENT THEN.
AND METROPOLIS HIRING YOU WAS THE DNC'S IDEA.
OH GOOD LORD.
I THOUGHT KNOWLEDGE WAS SUPPOSED TO EQUAL POWER. HOW COME THE MORE I LEARN, THE DIZZIER AND MORE CONFUSED I FEEL?
AND HOW DOES THIS RELATE TO EVERYTHING ELSE?
IT MAY NOT. EVEN IF WE'RE RIGHT.
THIS JUST SOUNDS LIKE POLITICS AS USUAL.
OKAY, BUT... IF WE'RE RIGHT, WHY ME? WHY ORGANIZE EVERYTHING AROUND ME?
WHAT IS IT ABOUT ME?
GUESS IT HAS TO DO WITH HOW YOU WRITE, HUH? HOW WOULD YOU DESCRIBE IT?
YOU READ ONE OF MY BOOKS. YOU TELL ME.
WELL, IT'S ELOQUENT. NO QUESTION ABOUT THAT.
AND I NOTICE ONE OTHER THING...

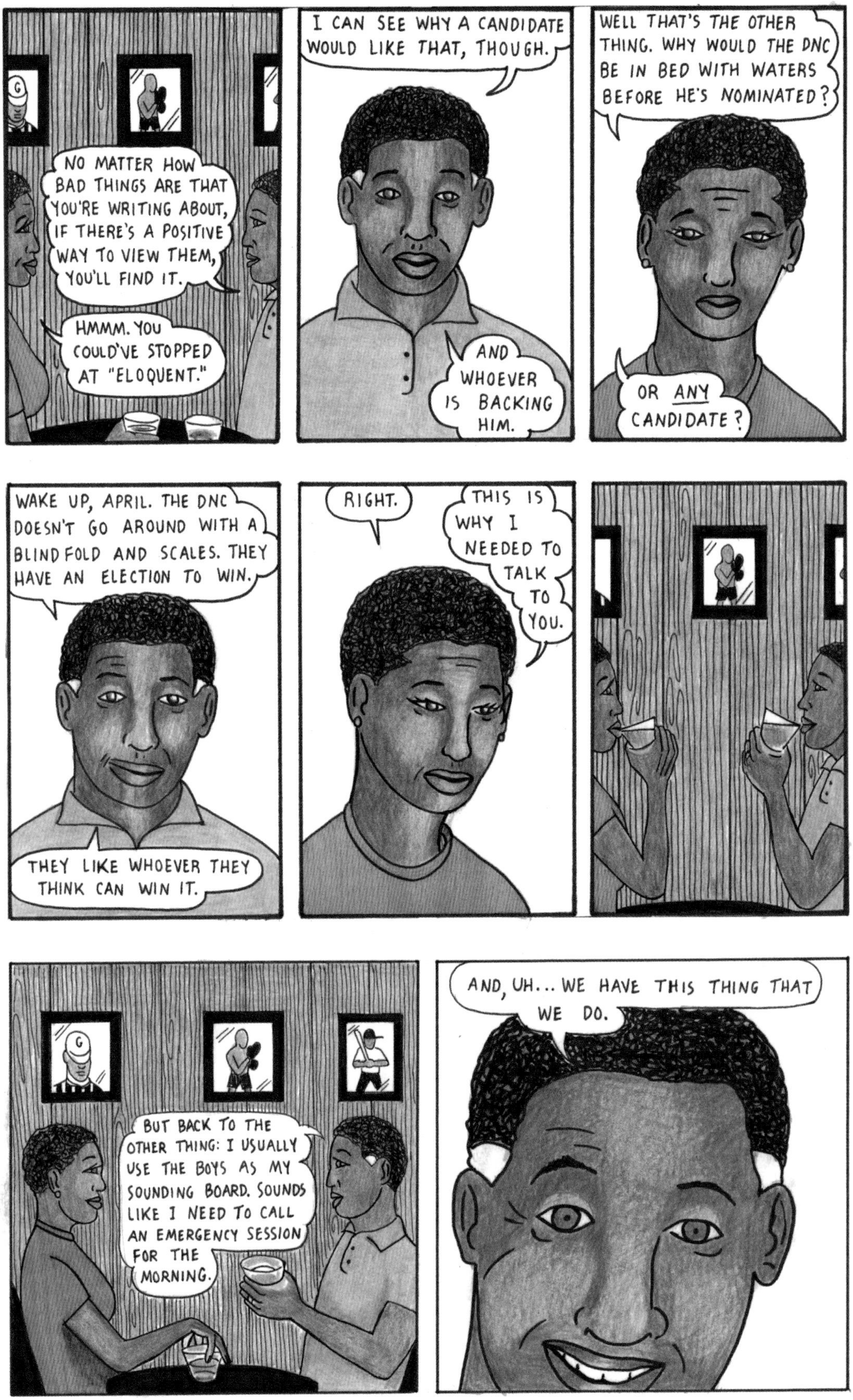
NO MATTER HOW BAD THINGS ARE THAT YOU'RE WRITING ABOUT, IF THERE'S A POSITIVE WAY TO VIEW THEM, YOU'LL FIND IT.
HMMM. YOU COULD'VE STOPPED AT "ELOQUENT."
I CAN SEE WHY A CANDIDATE WOULD LIKE THAT, THOUGH.
AND WHOEVER IS BACKING HIM.
WELL THAT'S THE OTHER THING. WHY WOULD THE DNC BE IN BED WITH WATERS BEFORE HE'S NOMINATED?
OR ANY CANDIDATE?
WAKE UP, APRIL. THE DNC DOESN'T GO AROUND WITH A BLINDFOLD AND SCALES. THEY HAVE AN ELECTION TO WIN.
THEY LIKE WHOEVER THEY THINK CAN WIN IT.
RIGHT.
THIS IS WHY I NEEDED TO TALK TO YOU.
BUT BACK TO THE OTHER THING: I USUALLY USE THE BOYS AS MY SOUNDING BOARD. SOUNDS LIKE I NEED TO CALL AN EMERGENCY SESSION FOR THE MORNING.
AND, UH... WE HAVE THIS THING THAT WE DO.

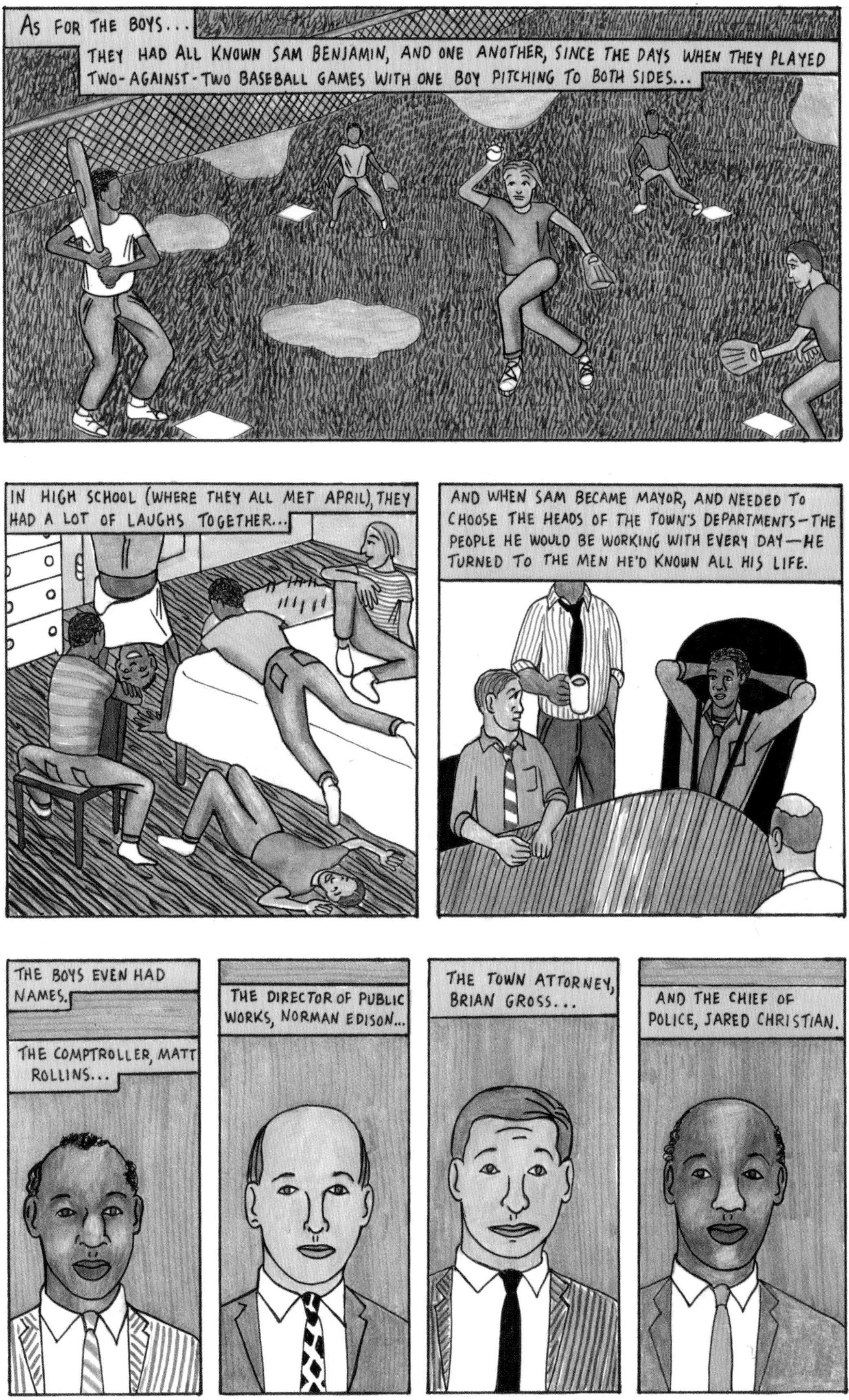
AS FOR THE BOYS...
THEY HAD ALL KNOWN SAM BENJAMIN, AND ONE ANOTHER, SINCE THE DAYS WHEN THEY PLAYED TWO-AGAINST-TWO BASEBALL GAMES WITH ONE BOY PITCHING TO BOTH SIDES...
IN HIGH SCHOOL (WHERE THEY ALL MET APRIL), THEY HAD A LOT OF LAUGHS TOGETHER...
AND WHEN SAM BECAME MAYOR, AND NEEDED TO CHOOSE THE HEADS OF THE TOWN'S DEPARTMENTS—THE PEOPLE HE WOULD BE WORKING WITH EVERY DAY—HE TURNED TO THE MEN HE'D KNOWN ALL HIS LIFE.
THE BOYS EVEN HAD NAMES.
THE COMPTROLLER, MATT ROLLINS...
THE DIRECTOR OF PUBLIC WORKS, NORMAN EDISON...
THE TOWN ATTORNEY, BRIAN GROSS...
AND THE CHIEF OF POLICE, JARED CHRISTIAN.

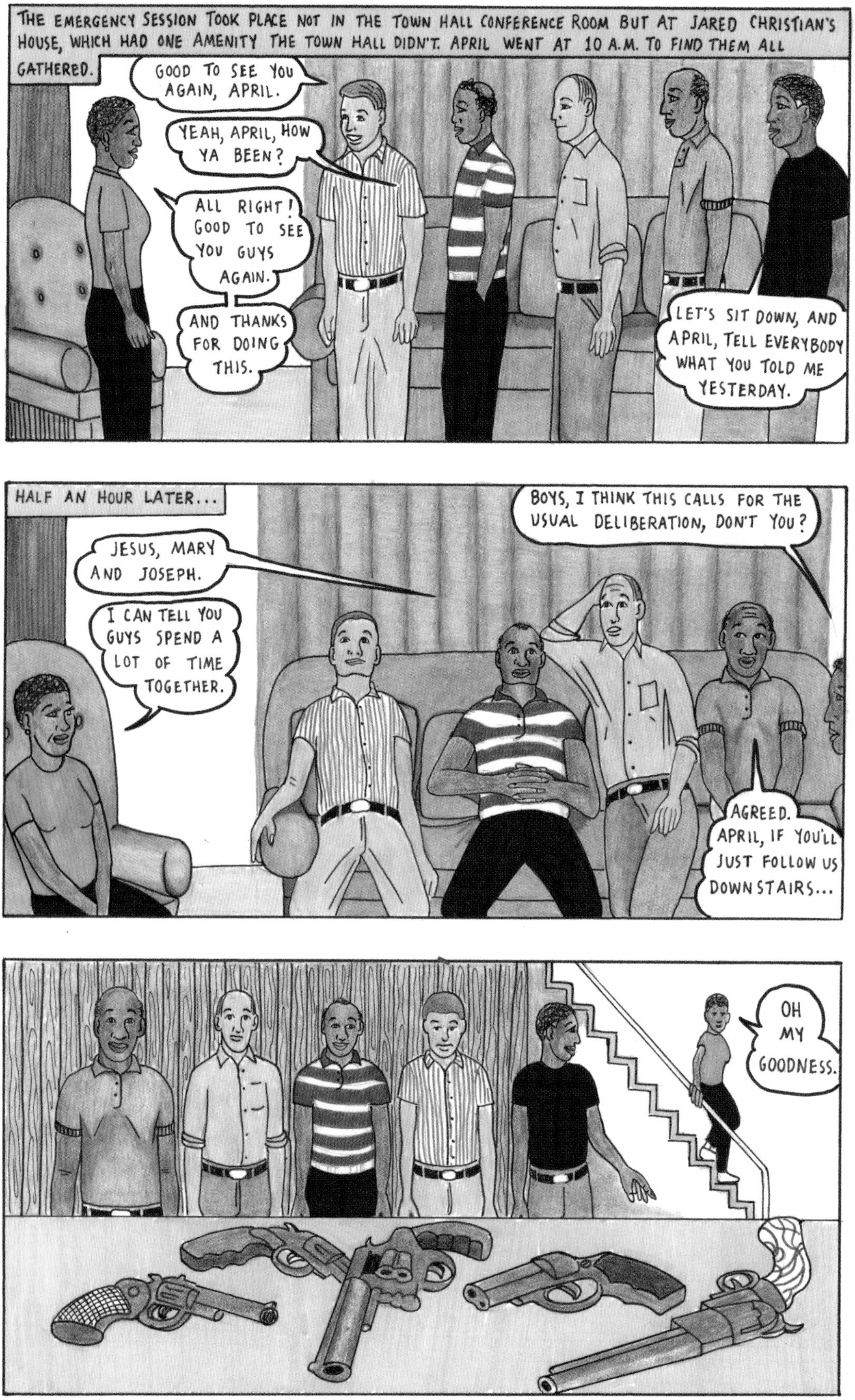
THE EMERGENCY SESSION TOOK PLACE NOT IN THE TOWN HALL CONFERENCE ROOM BUT AT JARED CHRISTIAN'S HOUSE, WHICH HAD ONE AMENITY THE TOWN HALL DIDN'T. APRIL WENT AT 10 A.M. TO FIND THEM ALL GATHERED.
GOOD TO SEE YOU AGAIN, APRIL.
YEAH, APRIL, HOW YA BEEN?
ALL RIGHT! GOOD TO SEE YOU GUYS AGAIN.
AND THANKS FOR DOING THIS.
LET'S SIT DOWN, AND APRIL, TELL EVERYBODY WHAT YOU TOLD ME YESTERDAY.
HALF AN HOUR LATER...
JESUS, MARY AND JOSEPH.
I CAN TELL YOU GUYS SPEND A LOT OF TIME TOGETHER.
BOYS, I THINK THIS CALLS FOR THE USUAL DELIBERATION, DON'T YOU?
AGREED. APRIL, IF YOU'LL JUST FOLLOW US DOWNSTAIRS...
OH MY GOODNESS.

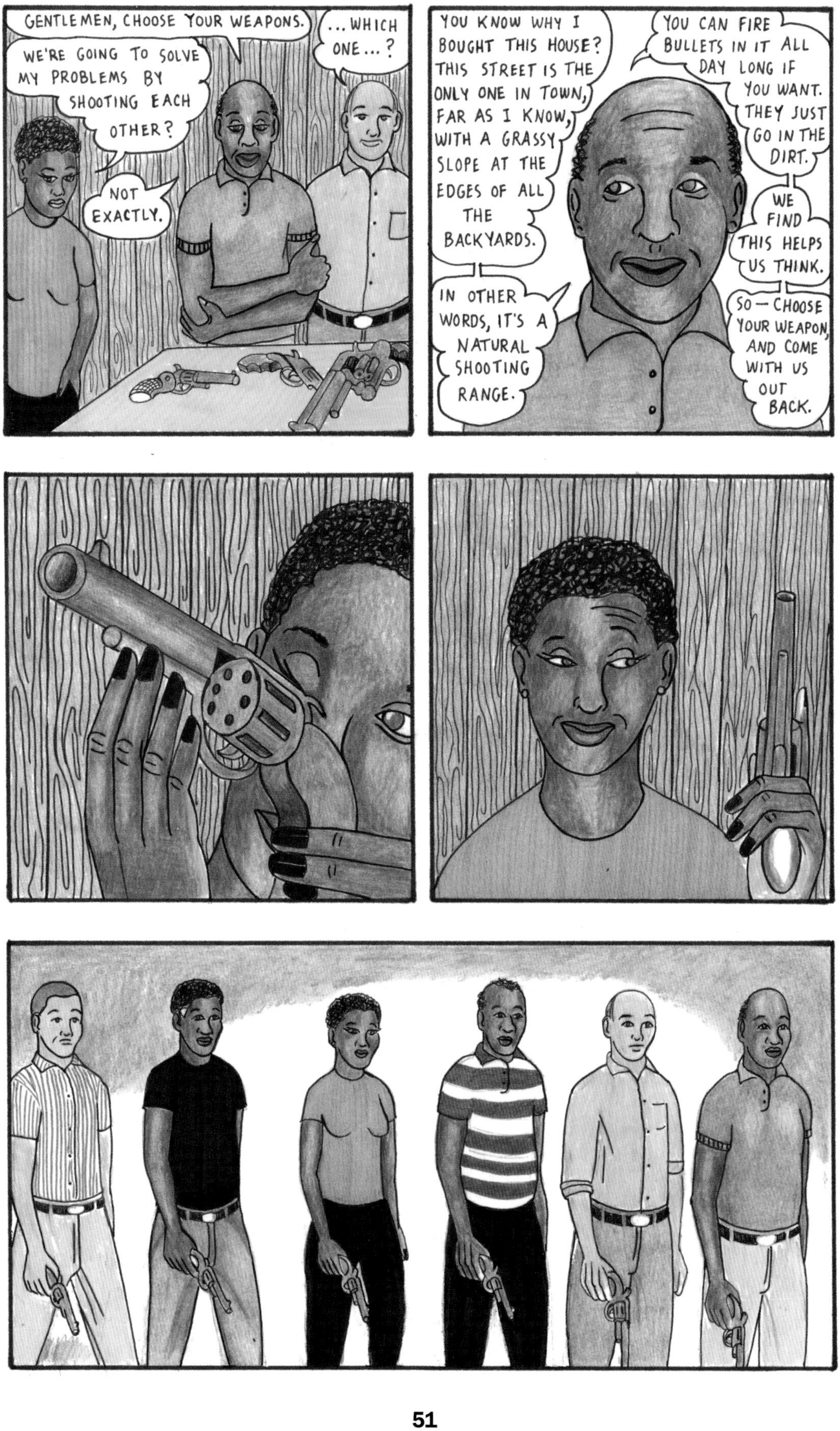
GENTLEMEN, CHOOSE YOUR WEAPONS.
WE'RE GOING TO SOLVE MY PROBLEMS BY SHOOTING EACH OTHER?
NOT EXACTLY.
...WHICH ONE...?
YOU KNOW WHY I BOUGHT THIS HOUSE? THIS STREET IS THE ONLY ONE IN TOWN, FAR AS I KNOW, WITH A GRASSY SLOPE AT THE EDGES OF ALL THE BACKYARDS.
IN OTHER WORDS, IT'S A NATURAL SHOOTING RANGE.
YOU CAN FIRE BULLETS IN IT ALL DAY LONG IF YOU WANT. THEY JUST GO IN THE DIRT.
WE FIND THIS HELPS US THINK.
SO—CHOOSE YOUR WEAPON, AND COME WITH US OUT BACK.

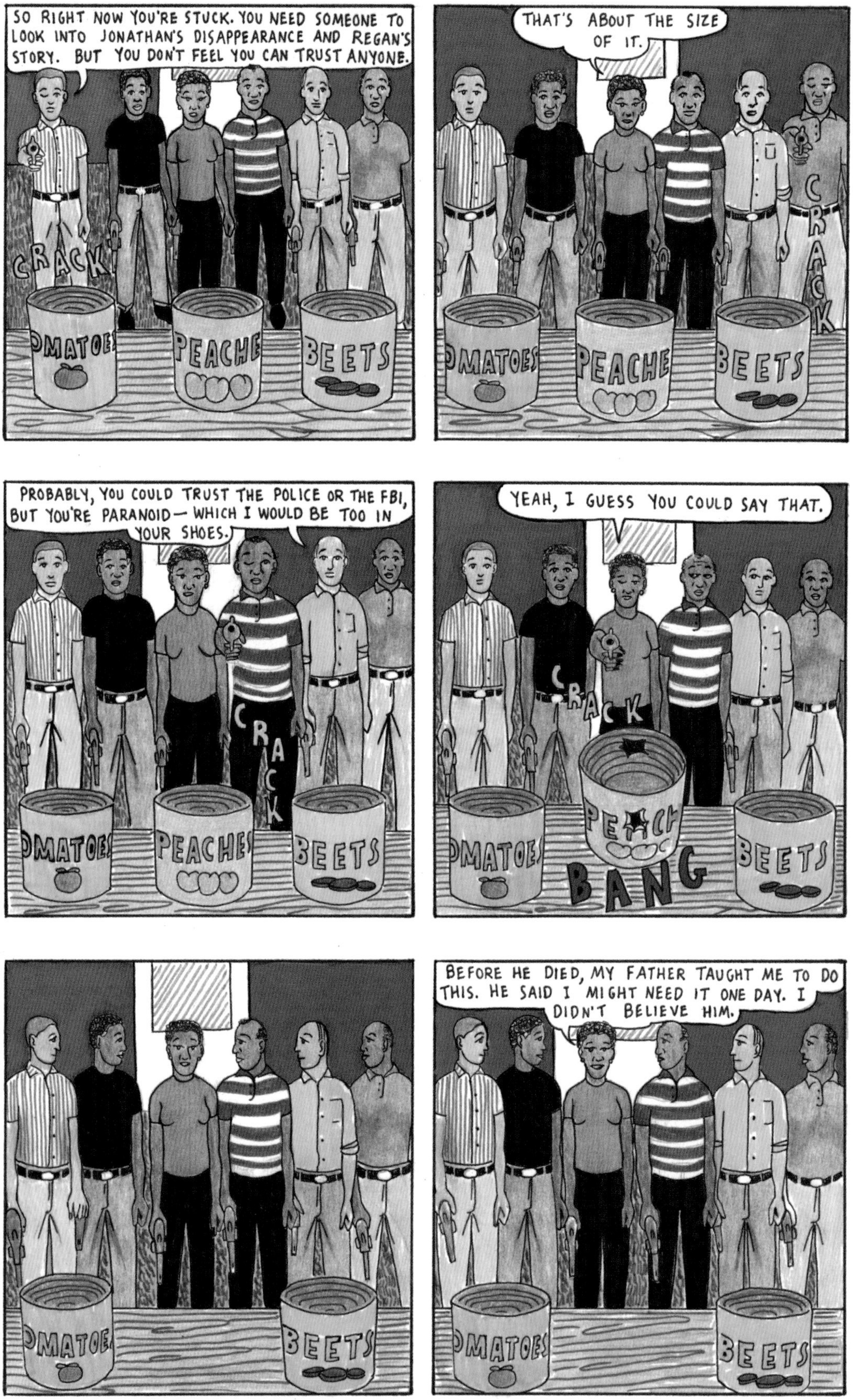
SO RIGHT NOW YOU'RE STUCK. YOU NEED SOMEONE TO LOOK INTO JONATHAN'S DISAPPEARANCE AND REGAN'S STORY. BUT YOU DON'T FEEL YOU CAN TRUST ANYONE.
CRACK
OMATOES
PEACHE
BEETS
THAT'S ABOUT THE SIZE OF IT.
CRACK
OMATOES
PEACHE
BEETS
PROBABLY, YOU COULD TRUST THE POLICE OR THE FBI, BUT YOU'RE PARANOID— WHICH I WOULD BE TOO IN YOUR SHOES.
CRACK
OMATOES
PEACHES
BEETS
YEAH, I GUESS YOU COULD SAY THAT.
CRACK
OMATOES
BANG
BEETS
OMATOE
BEETS
BEFORE HE DIED, MY FATHER TAUGHT ME TO DO THIS. HE SAID I MIGHT NEED IT ONE DAY. I DIDN'T BELIEVE HIM.
OMATOES
BEETS

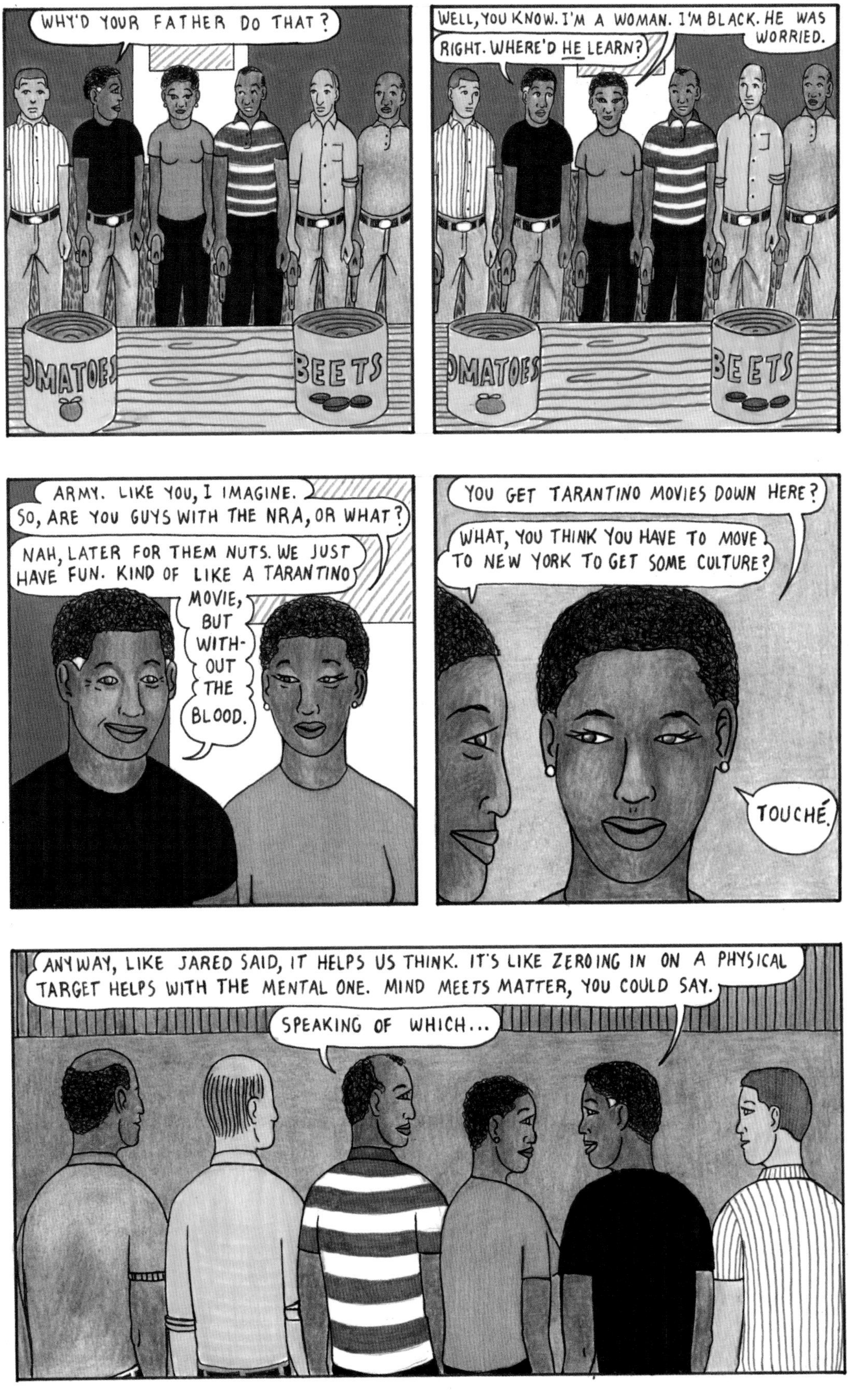
WHY'D YOUR FATHER DO THAT?
WELL, YOU KNOW. I'M A WOMAN. I'M BLACK. HE WAS WORRIED.
RIGHT. WHERE'D HE LEARN?
ARMY. LIKE YOU, I IMAGINE.
SO, ARE YOU GUYS WITH THE NRA, OR WHAT?
NAH, LATER FOR THEM NUTS. WE JUST HAVE FUN. KIND OF LIKE A TARANTINO MOVIE, BUT WITHOUT THE BLOOD.
YOU GET TARANTINO MOVIES DOWN HERE?
WHAT, YOU THINK YOU HAVE TO MOVE TO NEW YORK TO GET SOME CULTURE?
TOUCHÉ.
ANYWAY, LIKE JARED SAID, IT HELPS US THINK. IT'S LIKE ZEROING IN ON A PHYSICAL TARGET HELPS WITH THE MENTAL ONE. MIND MEETS MATTER, YOU COULD SAY.
SPEAKING OF WHICH...

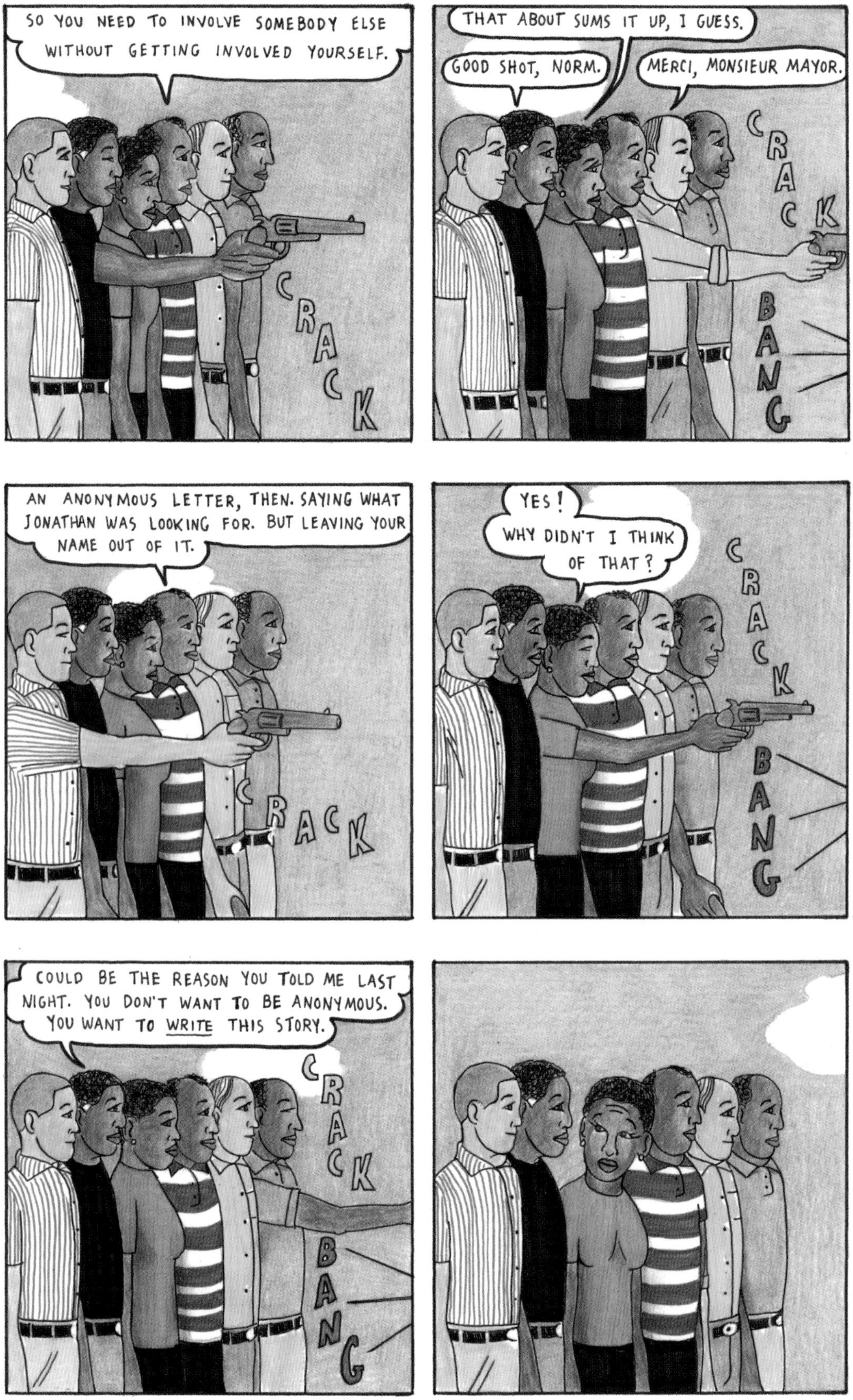
SO YOU NEED TO INVOLVE SOMEBODY ELSE WITHOUT GETTING INVOLVED YOURSELF.
CRACK
THAT ABOUT SUMS IT UP, I GUESS.
GOOD SHOT, NORM.
MERCI, MONSIEUR MAYOR.
CRACK
BANG
AN ANONYMOUS LETTER, THEN. SAYING WHAT JONATHAN WAS LOOKING FOR. BUT LEAVING YOUR NAME OUT OF IT.
CRACK
YES!
WHY DIDN'T I THINK OF THAT?
CRACK
BANG
COULD BE THE REASON YOU TOLD ME LAST NIGHT. YOU DON'T WANT TO BE ANONYMOUS. YOU WANT TO WRITE THIS STORY.
CRACK
BANG

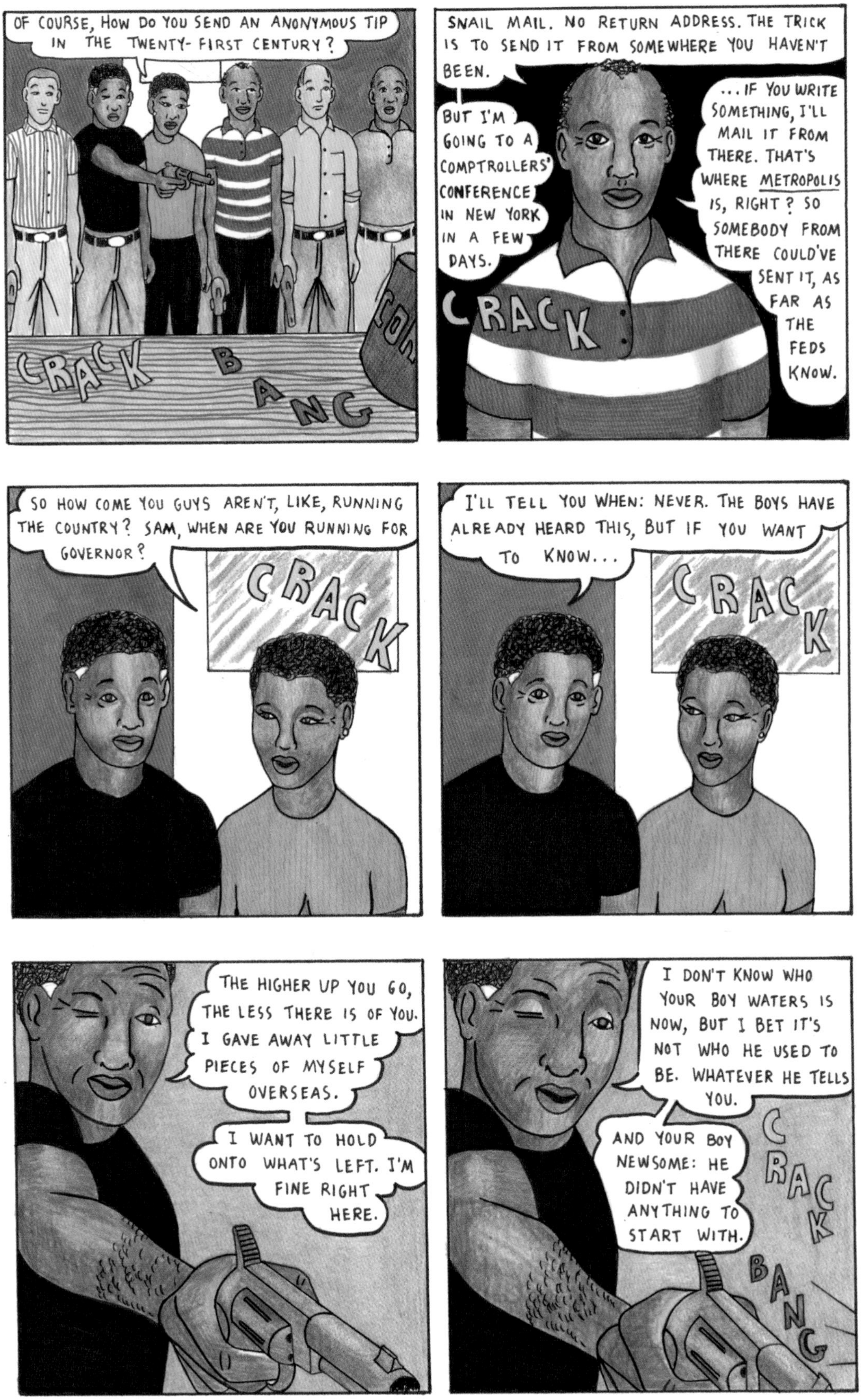
OF COURSE, HOW DO YOU SEND AN ANONYMOUS TIP IN THE TWENTY-FIRST CENTURY?
CRACK
BANG
SNAIL MAIL. NO RETURN ADDRESS. THE TRICK IS TO SEND IT FROM SOMEWHERE YOU HAVEN'T BEEN.
BUT I'M GOING TO A COMPTROLLERS' CONFERENCE IN NEW YORK IN A FEW DAYS.
...IF YOU WRITE SOMETHING, I'LL MAIL IT FROM THERE. THAT'S WHERE METROPOLIS IS, RIGHT? SO SOMEBODY FROM THERE COULD'VE SENT IT, AS FAR AS THE FEDS KNOW.
CRACK
SO HOW COME YOU GUYS AREN'T, LIKE, RUNNING THE COUNTRY? SAM, WHEN ARE YOU RUNNING FOR GOVERNOR?
CRACK
I'LL TELL YOU WHEN: NEVER. THE BOYS HAVE ALREADY HEARD THIS, BUT IF YOU WANT TO KNOW...
CRACK
THE HIGHER UP YOU GO, THE LESS THERE IS OF YOU. I GAVE AWAY LITTLE PIECES OF MYSELF OVERSEAS.
I WANT TO HOLD ONTO WHAT'S LEFT. I'M FINE RIGHT HERE.
I DON'T KNOW WHO YOUR BOY WATERS IS NOW, BUT I BET IT'S NOT WHO HE USED TO BE. WHATEVER HE TELLS YOU.
AND YOUR BOY NEWSOME: HE DIDN'T HAVE ANYTHING TO START WITH.
CRACK
BANG

WELL, WHAT DO YOU THINK, APRIL WELLS?

I THINK I CAME HERE TO LEARN SOME THINGS I ALREADY KNEW. IF I COULD HAVE GOTTEN OUT OF MY OWN WAY LONG ENOUGH TO SEE THEM.

THAT'S HOW IT IS SOMETIMES.

SO WRITE YOUR LETTER, GIVE IT TO MATT, AND GET BACK ON THAT CAMPAIGN BUS AND KICK SOME PRESIDENTIAL ASS.

HA. I'LL TRY.

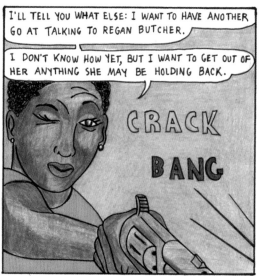

I'LL TELL YOU WHAT ELSE: I WANT TO HAVE ANOTHER GO AT TALKING TO REGAN BUTCHER.

I DON'T KNOW HOW YET, BUT I WANT TO GET OUT OF HER ANYTHING SHE MAY BE HOLDING BACK.

CRACK

BANG

56

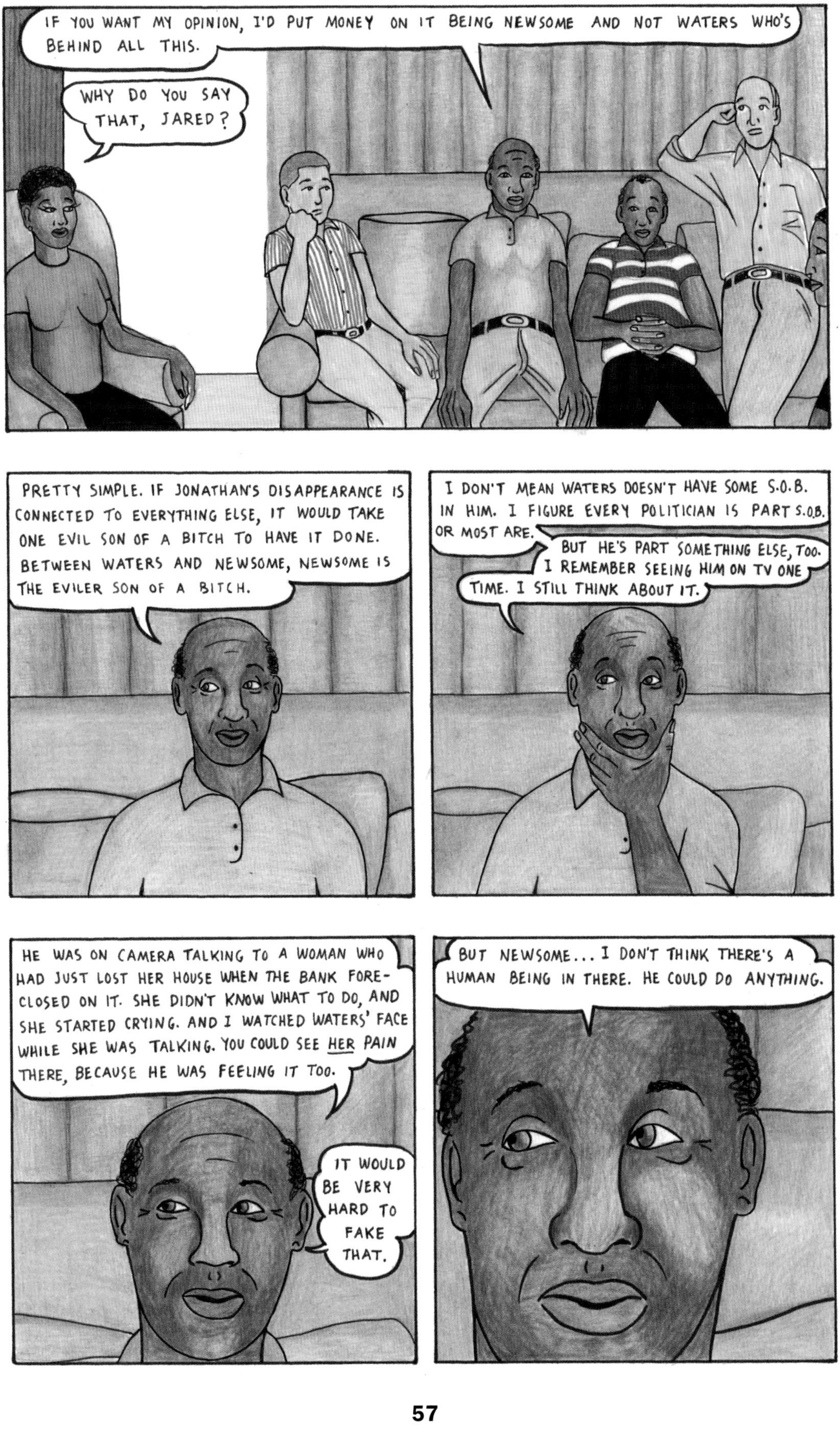
IF YOU WANT MY OPINION, I'D PUT MONEY ON IT BEING NEWSOME AND NOT WATERS WHO'S BEHIND ALL THIS.
WHY DO YOU SAY THAT, JARED?
PRETTY SIMPLE. IF JONATHAN'S DISAPPEARANCE IS CONNECTED TO EVERYTHING ELSE, IT WOULD TAKE ONE EVIL SON OF A BITCH TO HAVE IT DONE. BETWEEN WATERS AND NEWSOME, NEWSOME IS THE EVILER SON OF A BITCH.
I DON'T MEAN WATERS DOESN'T HAVE SOME S.O.B. IN HIM. I FIGURE EVERY POLITICIAN IS PART S.O.B. OR MOST ARE.
BUT HE'S PART SOMETHING ELSE, TOO. I REMEMBER SEEING HIM ON TV ONE TIME. I STILL THINK ABOUT IT.
HE WAS ON CAMERA TALKING TO A WOMAN WHO HAD JUST LOST HER HOUSE WHEN THE BANK FORECLOSED ON IT. SHE DIDN'T KNOW WHAT TO DO, AND SHE STARTED CRYING. AND I WATCHED WATERS' FACE WHILE SHE WAS TALKING. YOU COULD SEE HER PAIN THERE, BECAUSE HE WAS FEELING IT TOO.
IT WOULD BE VERY HARD TO FAKE THAT.
BUT NEWSOME... I DON'T THINK THERE'S A HUMAN BEING IN THERE. HE COULD DO ANYTHING.

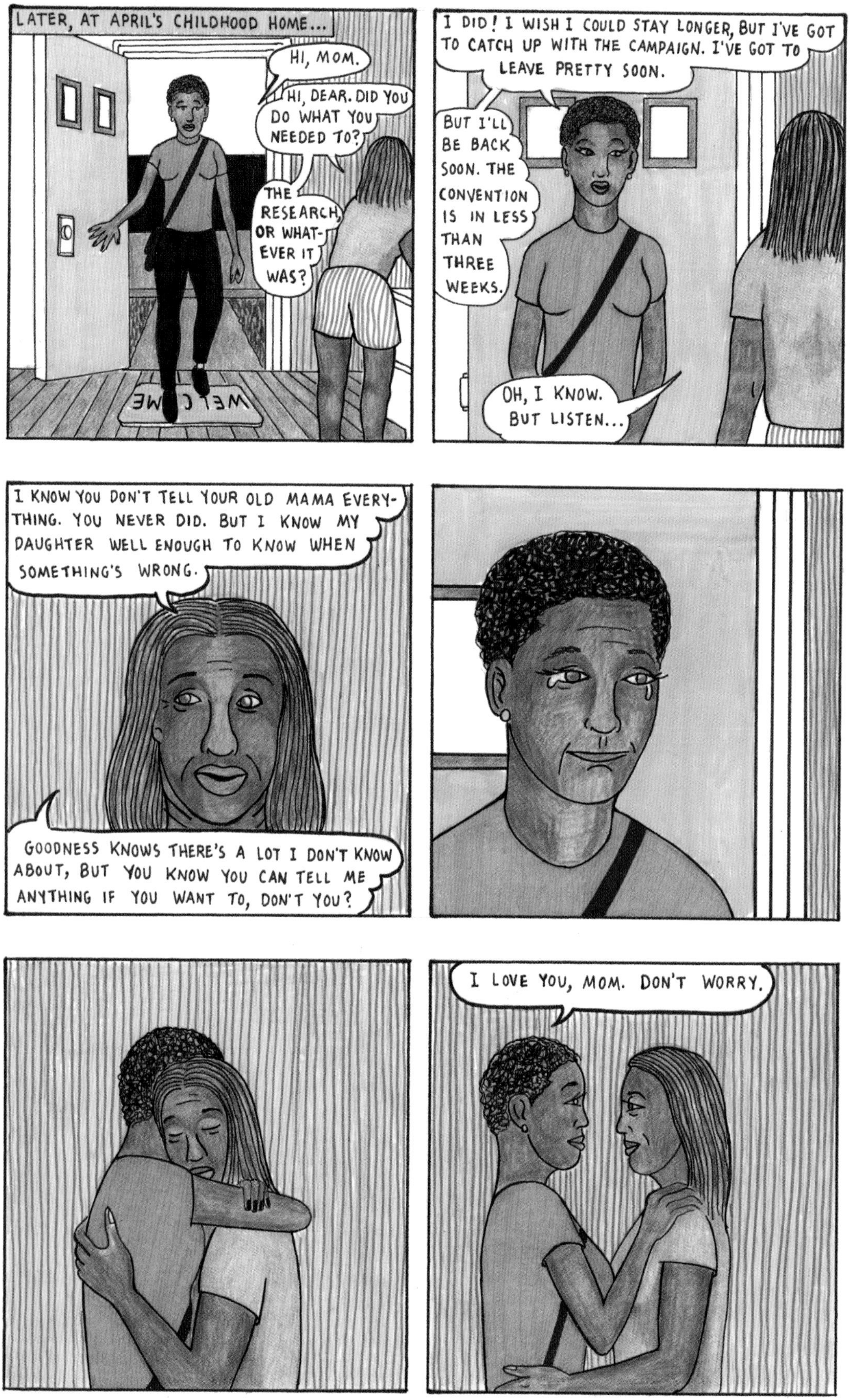
LATER, AT APRIL'S CHILDHOOD HOME...
HI, MOM.
HI, DEAR. DID YOU DO WHAT YOU NEEDED TO?
THE RESEARCH, OR WHAT-EVER IT WAS?
WELCOME
I DID! I WISH I COULD STAY LONGER, BUT I'VE GOT TO CATCH UP WITH THE CAMPAIGN. I'VE GOT TO LEAVE PRETTY SOON.
BUT I'LL BE BACK SOON. THE CONVENTION IS IN LESS THAN THREE WEEKS.
OH, I KNOW. BUT LISTEN...
I KNOW YOU DON'T TELL YOUR OLD MAMA EVERY-THING. YOU NEVER DID. BUT I KNOW MY DAUGHTER WELL ENOUGH TO KNOW WHEN SOMETHING'S WRONG.
GOODNESS KNOWS THERE'S A LOT I DON'T KNOW ABOUT, BUT YOU KNOW YOU CAN TELL ME ANYTHING IF YOU WANT TO, DON'T YOU?
I LOVE YOU, MOM. DON'T WORRY.

PART THREE

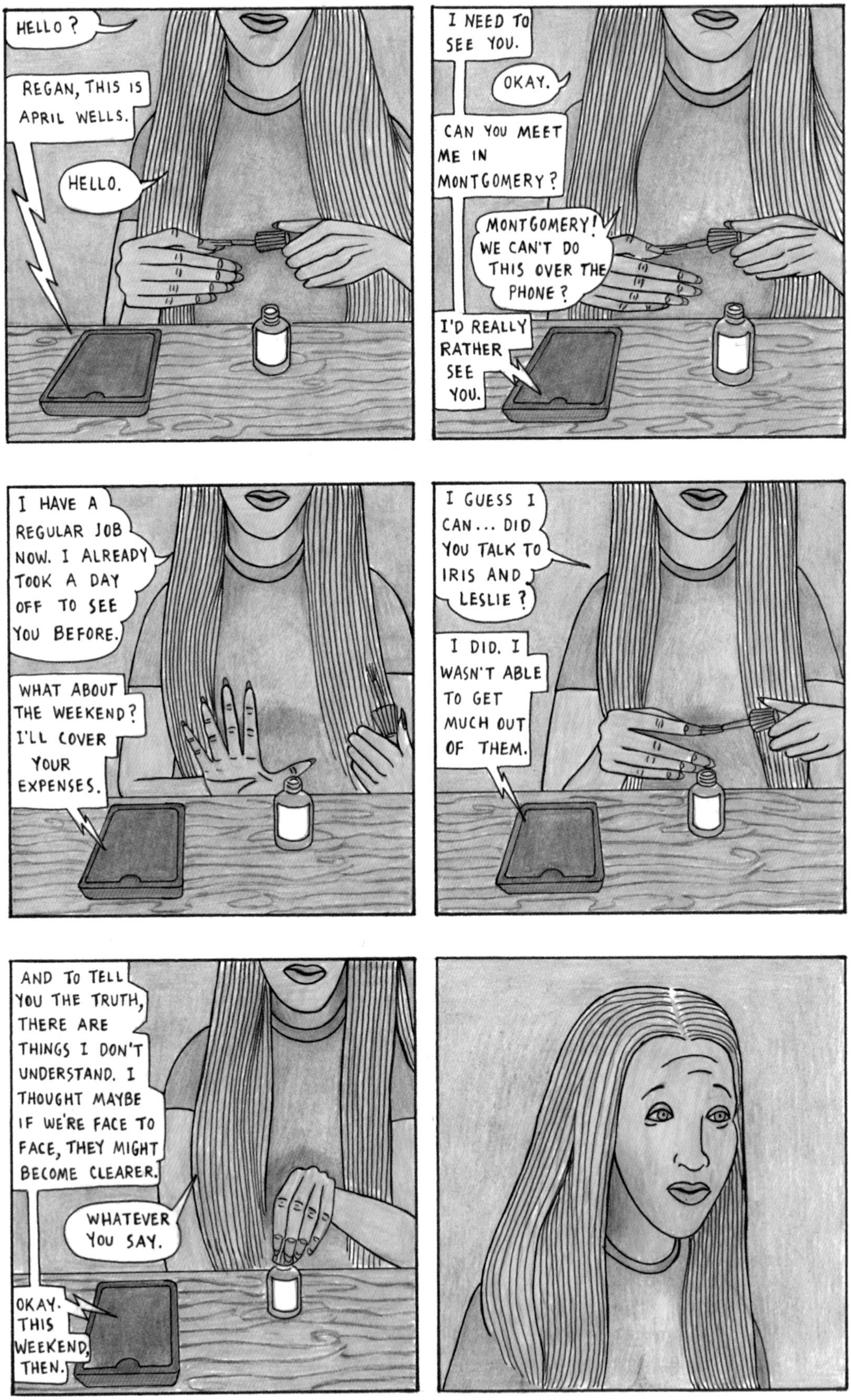
HELLO?
REGAN, THIS IS APRIL WELLS.
HELLO.
I NEED TO SEE YOU.
OKAY.
CAN YOU MEET ME IN MONTGOMERY?
MONTGOMERY! WE CAN'T DO THIS OVER THE PHONE?
I'D REALLY RATHER SEE YOU.
I HAVE A REGULAR JOB NOW. I ALREADY TOOK A DAY OFF TO SEE YOU BEFORE.
WHAT ABOUT THE WEEKEND? I'LL COVER YOUR EXPENSES.
I GUESS I CAN... DID YOU TALK TO IRIS AND LESLIE?
I DID. I WASN'T ABLE TO GET MUCH OUT OF THEM.
AND TO TELL YOU THE TRUTH, THERE ARE THINGS I DON'T UNDERSTAND. I THOUGHT MAYBE IF WE'RE FACE TO FACE, THEY MIGHT BECOME CLEARER.
WHATEVER YOU SAY.
OKAY. THIS WEEKEND, THEN.

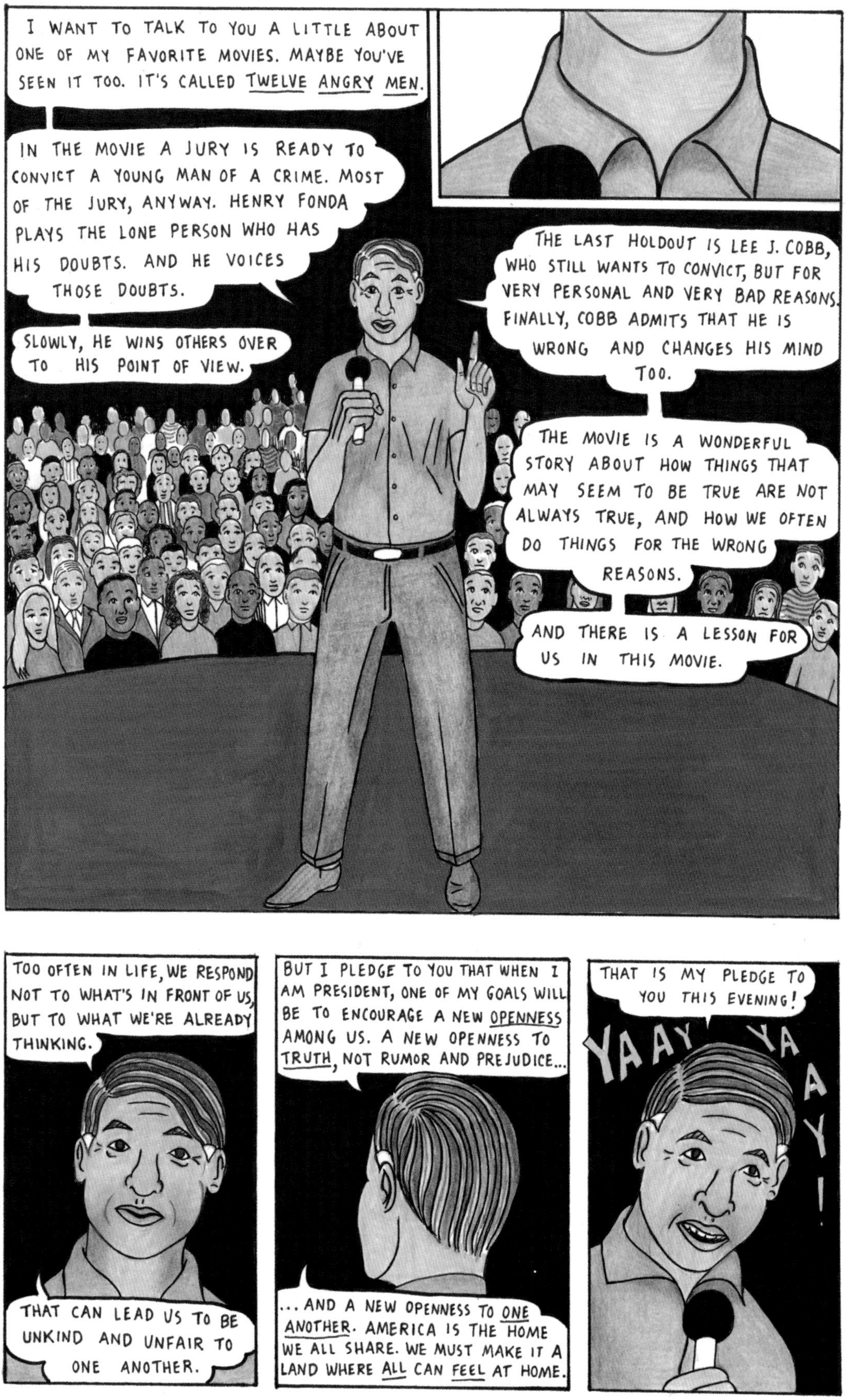
I WANT TO TALK TO YOU A LITTLE ABOUT ONE OF MY FAVORITE MOVIES. MAYBE YOU'VE SEEN IT TOO. IT'S CALLED TWELVE ANGRY MEN.
IN THE MOVIE A JURY IS READY TO CONVICT A YOUNG MAN OF A CRIME. MOST OF THE JURY, ANYWAY. HENRY FONDA PLAYS THE LONE PERSON WHO HAS HIS DOUBTS. AND HE VOICES THOSE DOUBTS.
SLOWLY, HE WINS OTHERS OVER TO HIS POINT OF VIEW.
THE LAST HOLDOUT IS LEE J. COBB, WHO STILL WANTS TO CONVICT, BUT FOR VERY PERSONAL AND VERY BAD REASONS. FINALLY, COBB ADMITS THAT HE IS WRONG AND CHANGES HIS MIND TOO.
THE MOVIE IS A WONDERFUL STORY ABOUT HOW THINGS THAT MAY SEEM TO BE TRUE ARE NOT ALWAYS TRUE, AND HOW WE OFTEN DO THINGS FOR THE WRONG REASONS.
AND THERE IS A LESSON FOR US IN THIS MOVIE.
TOO OFTEN IN LIFE, WE RESPOND NOT TO WHAT'S IN FRONT OF US, BUT TO WHAT WE'RE ALREADY THINKING.
THAT CAN LEAD US TO BE UNKIND AND UNFAIR TO ONE ANOTHER.
BUT I PLEDGE TO YOU THAT WHEN I AM PRESIDENT, ONE OF MY GOALS WILL BE TO ENCOURAGE A NEW OPENNESS AMONG US. A NEW OPENNESS TO TRUTH, NOT RUMOR AND PREJUDICE...
...AND A NEW OPENNESS TO ONE ANOTHER. AMERICA IS THE HOME WE ALL SHARE. WE MUST MAKE IT A LAND WHERE ALL CAN FEEL AT HOME.
THAT IS MY PLEDGE TO YOU THIS EVENING!
YAAY YAAAY!

LATER, IN APRIL'S HOTEL ROOM...

TODAY NEWSOME RESPONDED TO ALLEGATIONS OF SEXUAL MISCONDUCT:

LISTEN. I SAID SOME THINGS OUT OF CONTEXT. NOW PEOPLE ARE TRYING TO MAKE ME OUT TO BE A RAPIST. ASSAULTER. WHATEVER.

HERE'S THE THING ABOUT THOSE ALLEGATIONS: THEY ARE FALSE. THEY ARE FALSE BECAUSE THE PEOPLE MAKING THEM ARE LOSERS. AND JEALOUS.

THE PEOPLE MAKING THEM PROBABLY WISH THEY WERE THE KIND OF LADIES I'D WANT TO MOLEST. HA. SADLY, THEY ARE NOT.

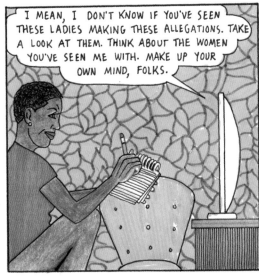

I MEAN, I DON'T KNOW IF YOU'VE SEEN THESE LADIES MAKING THESE ALLEGATIONS. TAKE A LOOK AT THEM. THINK ABOUT THE WOMEN YOU'VE SEEN ME WITH. MAKE UP YOUR OWN MIND, FOLKS.

SO LET'S NOT GET DISTRACTED BY THESE LIES. LET'S GET BACK TO TALKING ABOUT WHAT'S IMPORTANT: MAKING AMERICA WHAT IT SHOULD BE...

...A PLACE WHERE THE RIGHT KIND OF PEOPLE CAN LIVE IN PEACE AND SAFETY!

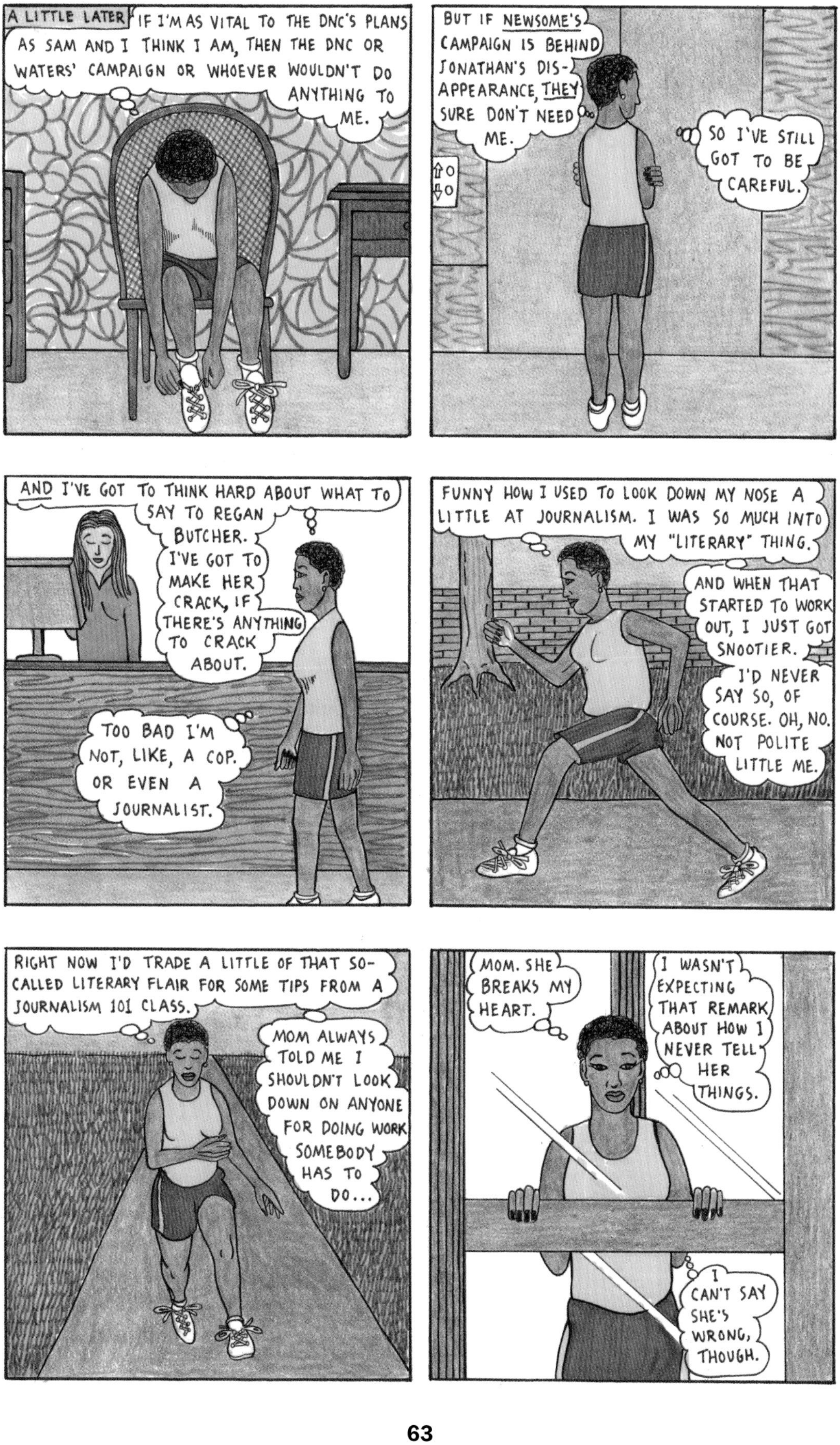
A LITTLE LATER
IF I'M AS VITAL TO THE DNC'S PLANS AS SAM AND I THINK I AM, THEN THE DNC OR WATERS' CAMPAIGN OR WHOEVER WOULDN'T DO ANYTHING TO ME.
BUT IF NEWSOME'S CAMPAIGN IS BEHIND JONATHAN'S DISAPPEARANCE, THEY SURE DON'T NEED ME.
SO I'VE STILL GOT TO BE CAREFUL.
AND I'VE GOT TO THINK HARD ABOUT WHAT TO SAY TO REGAN BUTCHER. I'VE GOT TO MAKE HER CRACK, IF THERE'S ANYTHING TO CRACK ABOUT.
TOO BAD I'M NOT, LIKE, A COP. OR EVEN A JOURNALIST.
FUNNY HOW I USED TO LOOK DOWN MY NOSE A LITTLE AT JOURNALISM. I WAS SO MUCH INTO MY "LITERARY" THING.
AND WHEN THAT STARTED TO WORK OUT, I JUST GOT SNOOTIER.
I'D NEVER SAY SO, OF COURSE. OH, NO. NOT POLITE LITTLE ME.
RIGHT NOW I'D TRADE A LITTLE OF THAT SO-CALLED LITERARY FLAIR FOR SOME TIPS FROM A JOURNALISM 101 CLASS.
MOM ALWAYS TOLD ME I SHOULDN'T LOOK DOWN ON ANYONE FOR DOING WORK SOMEBODY HAS TO DO...
MOM. SHE BREAKS MY HEART.
I WASN'T EXPECTING THAT REMARK ABOUT HOW I NEVER TELL HER THINGS.
I CAN'T SAY SHE'S WRONG, THOUGH.

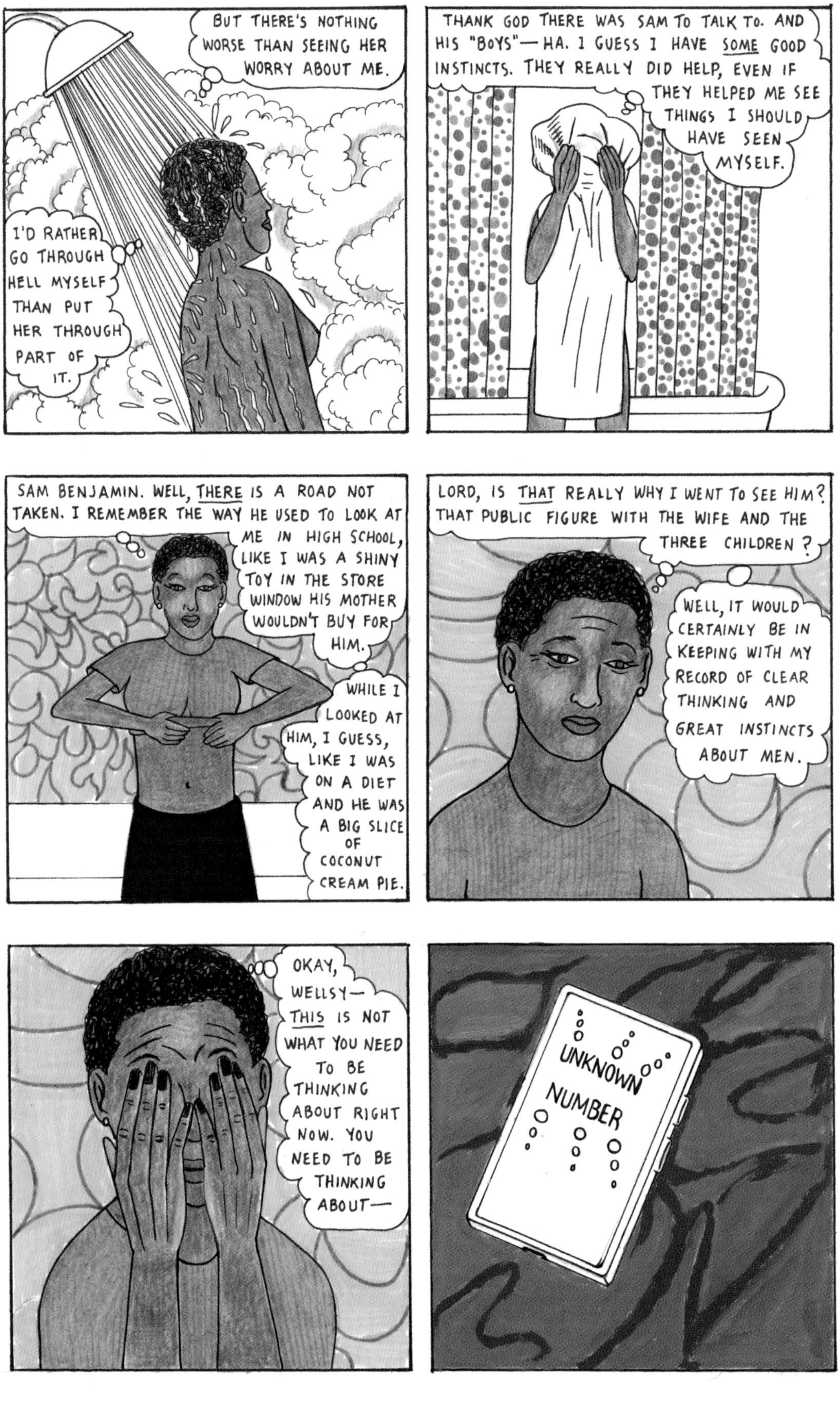
BUT THERE'S NOTHING WORSE THAN SEEING HER WORRY ABOUT ME.
I'D RATHER GO THROUGH HELL MYSELF THAN PUT HER THROUGH PART OF IT.
THANK GOD THERE WAS SAM TO TALK TO. AND HIS "BOYS"—HA. I GUESS I HAVE SOME GOOD INSTINCTS. THEY REALLY DID HELP, EVEN IF THEY HELPED ME SEE THINGS I SHOULD HAVE SEEN MYSELF.
SAM BENJAMIN. WELL, THERE IS A ROAD NOT TAKEN. I REMEMBER THE WAY HE USED TO LOOK AT ME IN HIGH SCHOOL, LIKE I WAS A SHINY TOY IN THE STORE WINDOW HIS MOTHER WOULDN'T BUY FOR HIM.
WHILE I LOOKED AT HIM, I GUESS, LIKE I WAS ON A DIET AND HE WAS A BIG SLICE OF COCONUT CREAM PIE.
LORD, IS THAT REALLY WHY I WENT TO SEE HIM? THAT PUBLIC FIGURE WITH THE WIFE AND THE THREE CHILDREN?
WELL, IT WOULD CERTAINLY BE IN KEEPING WITH MY RECORD OF CLEAR THINKING AND GREAT INSTINCTS ABOUT MEN.
OKAY, WELLSY—THIS IS NOT WHAT YOU NEED TO BE THINKING ABOUT RIGHT NOW. YOU NEED TO BE THINKING ABOUT—
UNKNOWN NUMBER

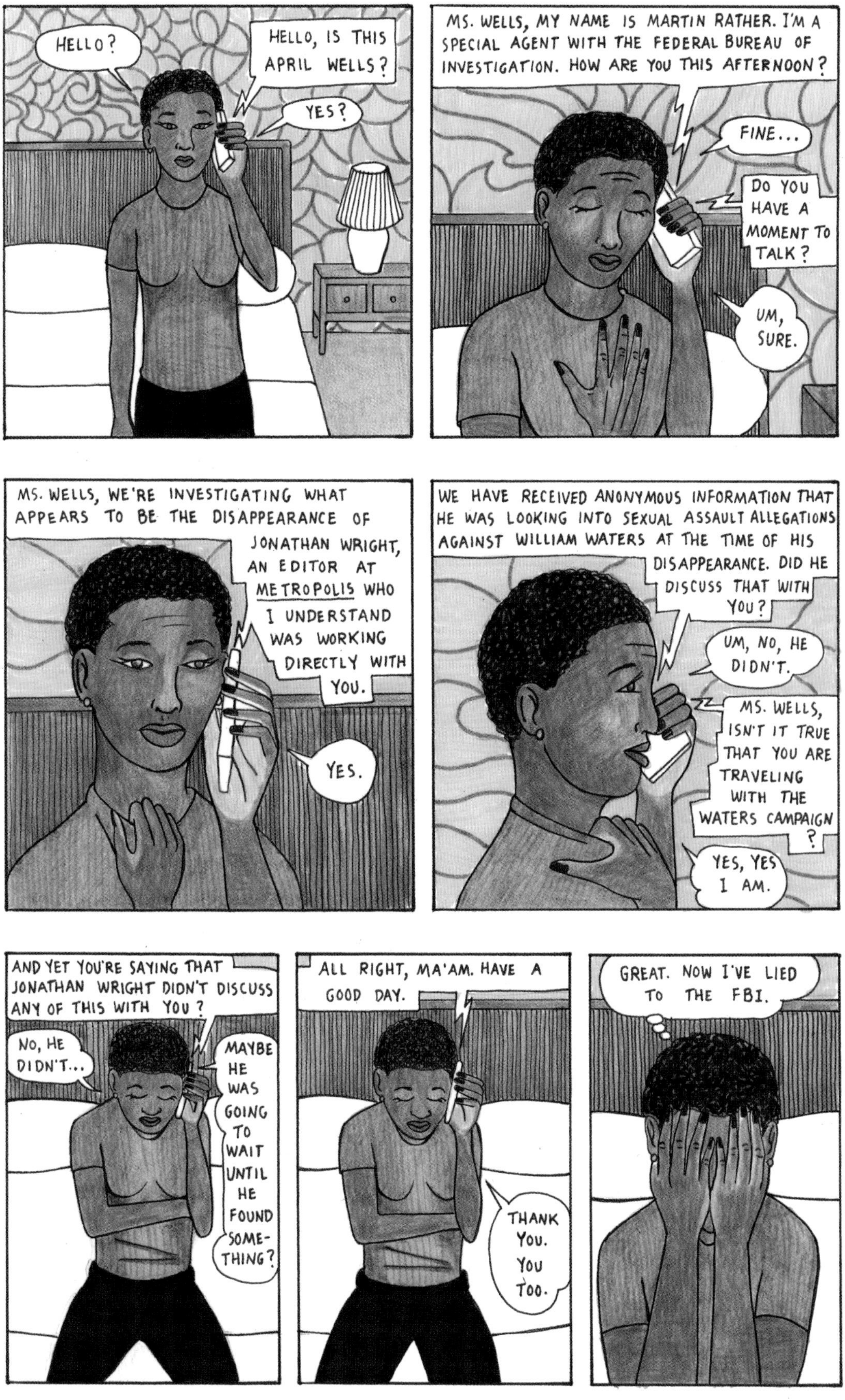
HELLO?
HELLO, IS THIS APRIL WELLS?
YES?
MS. WELLS, MY NAME IS MARTIN RATHER. I'M A SPECIAL AGENT WITH THE FEDERAL BUREAU OF INVESTIGATION. HOW ARE YOU THIS AFTERNOON?
FINE...
DO YOU HAVE A MOMENT TO TALK?
UM, SURE.
MS. WELLS, WE'RE INVESTIGATING WHAT APPEARS TO BE THE DISAPPEARANCE OF JONATHAN WRIGHT, AN EDITOR AT METROPOLIS WHO I UNDERSTAND WAS WORKING DIRECTLY WITH YOU.
YES.
WE HAVE RECEIVED ANONYMOUS INFORMATION THAT HE WAS LOOKING INTO SEXUAL ASSAULT ALLEGATIONS AGAINST WILLIAM WATERS AT THE TIME OF HIS DISAPPEARANCE. DID HE DISCUSS THAT WITH YOU?
UM, NO, HE DIDN'T.
MS. WELLS, ISN'T IT TRUE THAT YOU ARE TRAVELING WITH THE WATERS CAMPAIGN?
YES, YES I AM.
AND YET YOU'RE SAYING THAT JONATHAN WRIGHT DIDN'T DISCUSS ANY OF THIS WITH YOU?
NO, HE DIDN'T...
MAYBE HE WAS GOING TO WAIT UNTIL HE FOUND SOME-THING?
ALL RIGHT, MA'AM. HAVE A GOOD DAY.
THANK YOU. YOU TOO.
GREAT. NOW I'VE LIED TO THE FBI.

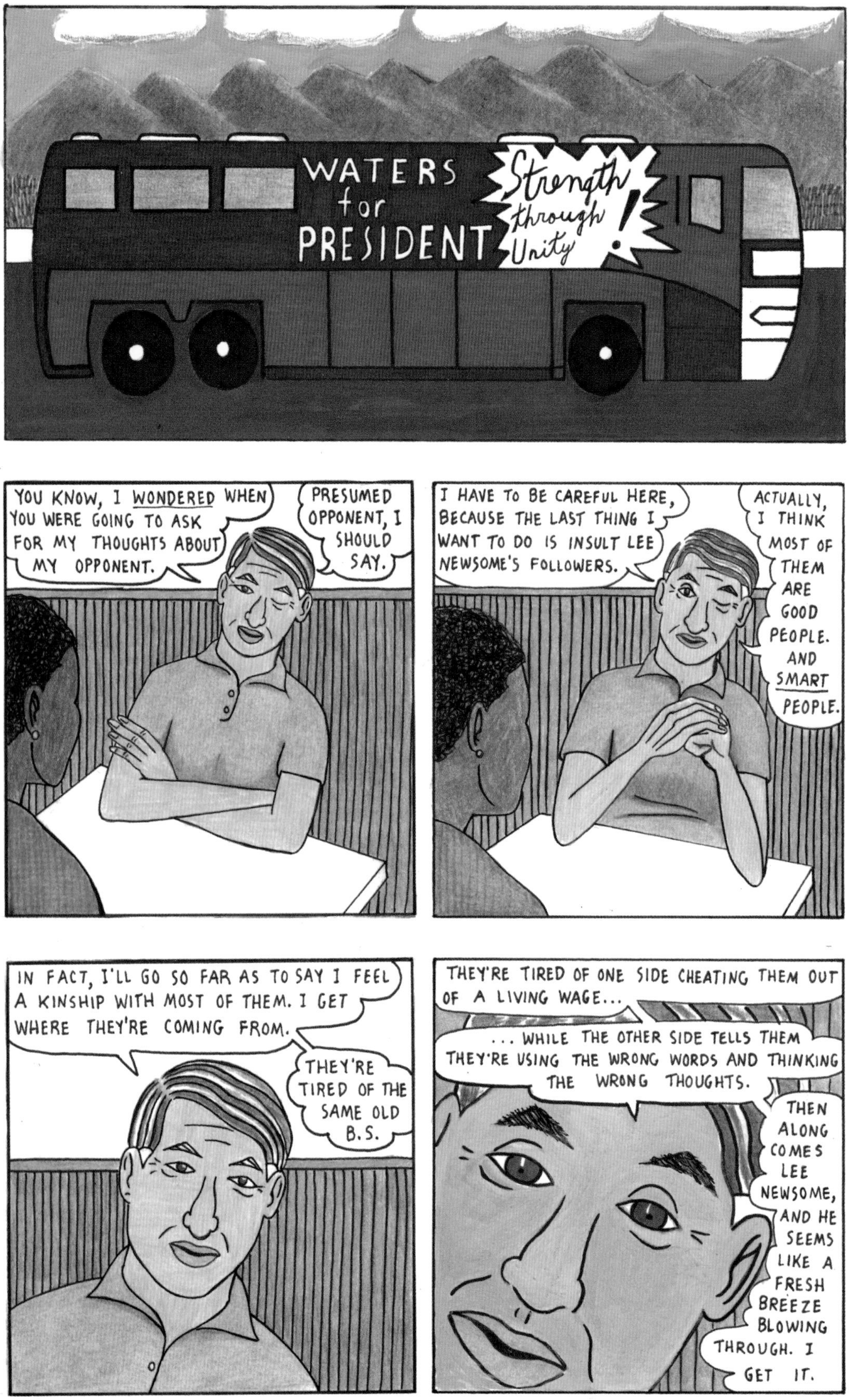
WATERS for PRESIDENT
Strength through Unity!
YOU KNOW, I WONDERED WHEN YOU WERE GOING TO ASK FOR MY THOUGHTS ABOUT MY OPPONENT.
PRESUMED OPPONENT, I SHOULD SAY.
I HAVE TO BE CAREFUL HERE, BECAUSE THE LAST THING I WANT TO DO IS INSULT LEE NEWSOME'S FOLLOWERS.
ACTUALLY, I THINK MOST OF THEM ARE GOOD PEOPLE. AND SMART PEOPLE.
IN FACT, I'LL GO SO FAR AS TO SAY I FEEL A KINSHIP WITH MOST OF THEM. I GET WHERE THEY'RE COMING FROM.
THEY'RE TIRED OF THE SAME OLD B.S.
THEY'RE TIRED OF ONE SIDE CHEATING THEM OUT OF A LIVING WAGE...
...WHILE THE OTHER SIDE TELLS THEM THEY'RE USING THE WRONG WORDS AND THINKING THE WRONG THOUGHTS.
THEN ALONG COMES LEE NEWSOME, AND HE SEEMS LIKE A FRESH BREEZE BLOWING THROUGH. I GET IT.

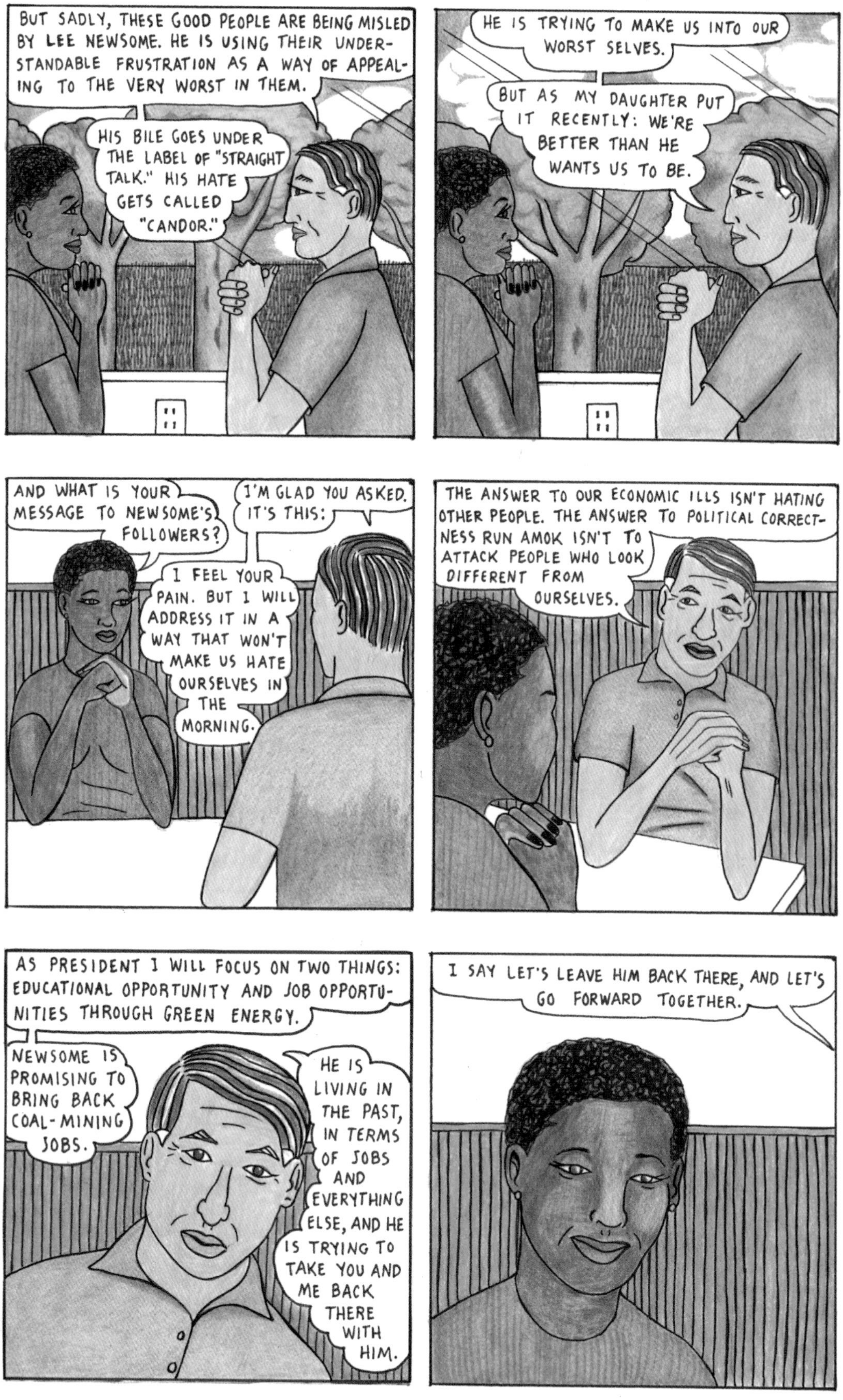
BUT SADLY, THESE GOOD PEOPLE ARE BEING MISLED BY LEE NEWSOME. HE IS USING THEIR UNDERSTANDABLE FRUSTRATION AS A WAY OF APPEALING TO THE VERY WORST IN THEM.
HIS BILE GOES UNDER THE LABEL OF "STRAIGHT TALK." HIS HATE GETS CALLED "CANDOR."
HE IS TRYING TO MAKE US INTO OUR WORST SELVES.
BUT AS MY DAUGHTER PUT IT RECENTLY: WE'RE BETTER THAN HE WANTS US TO BE.
AND WHAT IS YOUR MESSAGE TO NEWSOME'S FOLLOWERS?
I'M GLAD YOU ASKED. IT'S THIS:
I FEEL YOUR PAIN. BUT I WILL ADDRESS IT IN A WAY THAT WON'T MAKE US HATE OURSELVES IN THE MORNING.
THE ANSWER TO OUR ECONOMIC ILLS ISN'T HATING OTHER PEOPLE. THE ANSWER TO POLITICAL CORRECTNESS RUN AMOK ISN'T TO ATTACK PEOPLE WHO LOOK DIFFERENT FROM OURSELVES.
AS PRESIDENT I WILL FOCUS ON TWO THINGS: EDUCATIONAL OPPORTUNITY AND JOB OPPORTUNITIES THROUGH GREEN ENERGY.
NEWSOME IS PROMISING TO BRING BACK COAL-MINING JOBS.
HE IS LIVING IN THE PAST, IN TERMS OF JOBS AND EVERYTHING ELSE, AND HE IS TRYING TO TAKE YOU AND ME BACK THERE WITH HIM.
I SAY LET'S LEAVE HIM BACK THERE, AND LET'S GO FORWARD TOGETHER.

THAT WEEKEND...
MONT-GOMERY

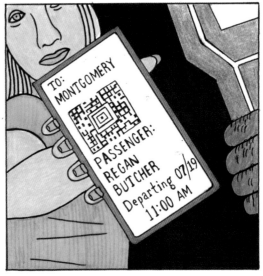
TO: MONTGOMERY

PASSENGER: REGAN BUTCHER

Departing 07/19 11:00 AM

IN PINE-LIGHT
THOMAS RAYFIEL

RAYFIEL IN PINELIGHT

MONTGOMERY
NEXT EXIT
1 MILE

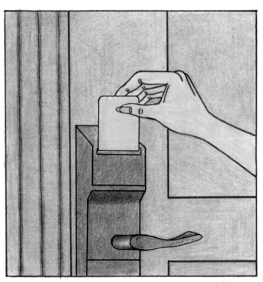

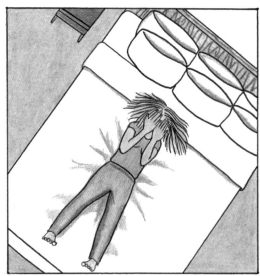

KNOCK KNOCK

WELL, THAT DIDN'T TAKE LONG.

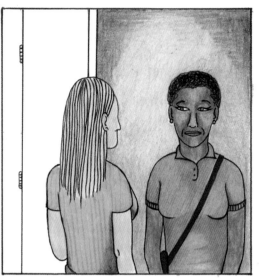

I KNOW ABOUT THAT EDITOR'S DISAPPEARANCE. I GOT A CALL FROM THE FBI. DON'T WORRY, I DIDN'T MENTION YOUR NAME OR MENTION THAT I TALKED TO YOU. I'D NEVER HAVE HAD ANY PEACE.

HOW DID YOU MANAGE TO AVOID MENTIONING MY NAME?

I SAID I HAD MENTIONED THE ASSAULT TO SOME FRIENDS. I SAID SOME OF THEM—I COULDN'T REMEMBER WHICH ONES, I SAID—HAD TALKED ABOUT TELLING SOMEONE... MAYBE ONE OF THEM HAD.

THE FBI CALLED ME, TOO.

REGAN... WHAT HAPPENED TO JONATHAN? WHO'S BEHIND IT?

I DON'T KNOW.

I FEEL LIKE YOU DO.

WELL, LOOK, WHO WOULD IT LOGICALLY BE? WHO STOOD TO GET HURT IF JONATHAN UNCOVERED SOMETHING? WATERS, RIGHT? SO WOULDN'T IT MAKE SENSE FOR IT TO BE SOMEBODY WORKING FOR HIS CAMPAIGN?

YES. EXCEPT FOR ONE THING.

THESE KINDS OF ALLEGATIONS HAPPEN ALL THE TIME. THE CANDIDATES DENY THEM. OR THEY SETTLE OUT OF COURT. OR BOTH. PEOPLE DON'T USUALLY DISAPPEAR, THOUGH.

WHAT'S GOING ON, REGAN?

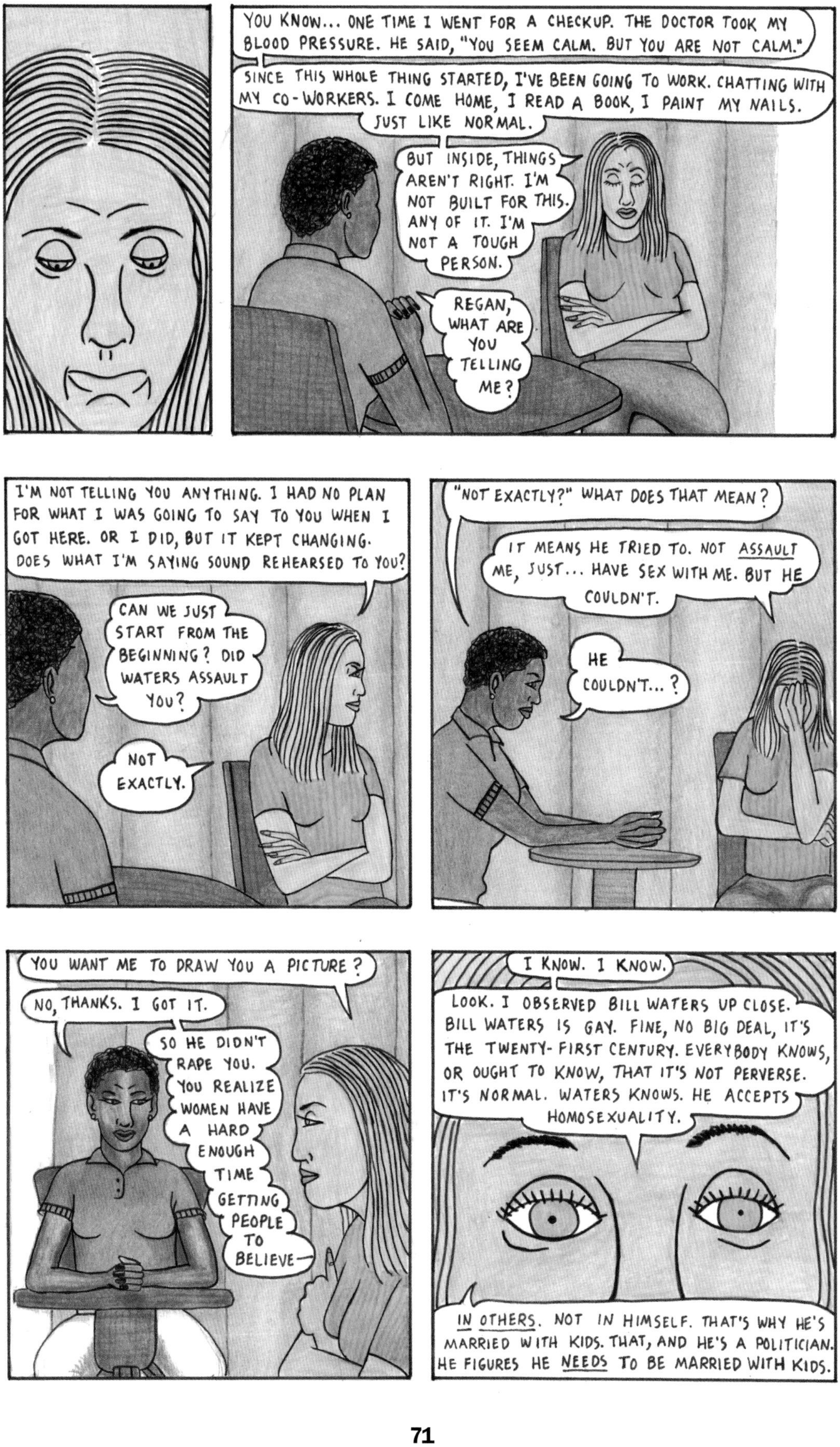
YOU KNOW... ONE TIME I WENT FOR A CHECKUP. THE DOCTOR TOOK MY BLOOD PRESSURE. HE SAID, "YOU SEEM CALM. BUT YOU ARE NOT CALM."
SINCE THIS WHOLE THING STARTED, I'VE BEEN GOING TO WORK. CHATTING WITH MY CO-WORKERS. I COME HOME, I READ A BOOK, I PAINT MY NAILS. JUST LIKE NORMAL.
BUT INSIDE, THINGS AREN'T RIGHT. I'M NOT BUILT FOR THIS. ANY OF IT. I'M NOT A TOUGH PERSON.
REGAN, WHAT ARE YOU TELLING ME?
I'M NOT TELLING YOU ANYTHING. I HAD NO PLAN FOR WHAT I WAS GOING TO SAY TO YOU WHEN I GOT HERE. OR I DID, BUT IT KEPT CHANGING. DOES WHAT I'M SAYING SOUND REHEARSED TO YOU?
CAN WE JUST START FROM THE BEGINNING? DID WATERS ASSAULT YOU?
NOT EXACTLY.
"NOT EXACTLY?" WHAT DOES THAT MEAN?
IT MEANS HE TRIED TO. NOT ASSAULT ME, JUST... HAVE SEX WITH ME. BUT HE COULDN'T.
HE COULDN'T...?
YOU WANT ME TO DRAW YOU A PICTURE?
NO, THANKS. I GOT IT.
SO HE DIDN'T RAPE YOU. YOU REALIZE WOMEN HAVE A HARD ENOUGH TIME GETTING PEOPLE TO BELIEVE—
I KNOW. I KNOW.
LOOK. I OBSERVED BILL WATERS UP CLOSE. BILL WATERS IS GAY. FINE, NO BIG DEAL, IT'S THE TWENTY-FIRST CENTURY. EVERYBODY KNOWS, OR OUGHT TO KNOW, THAT IT'S NOT PERVERSE. IT'S NORMAL. WATERS KNOWS. HE ACCEPTS HOMOSEXUALITY.
IN OTHERS. NOT IN HIMSELF. THAT'S WHY HE'S MARRIED WITH KIDS. THAT, AND HE'S A POLITICIAN. HE FIGURES HE NEEDS TO BE MARRIED WITH KIDS.

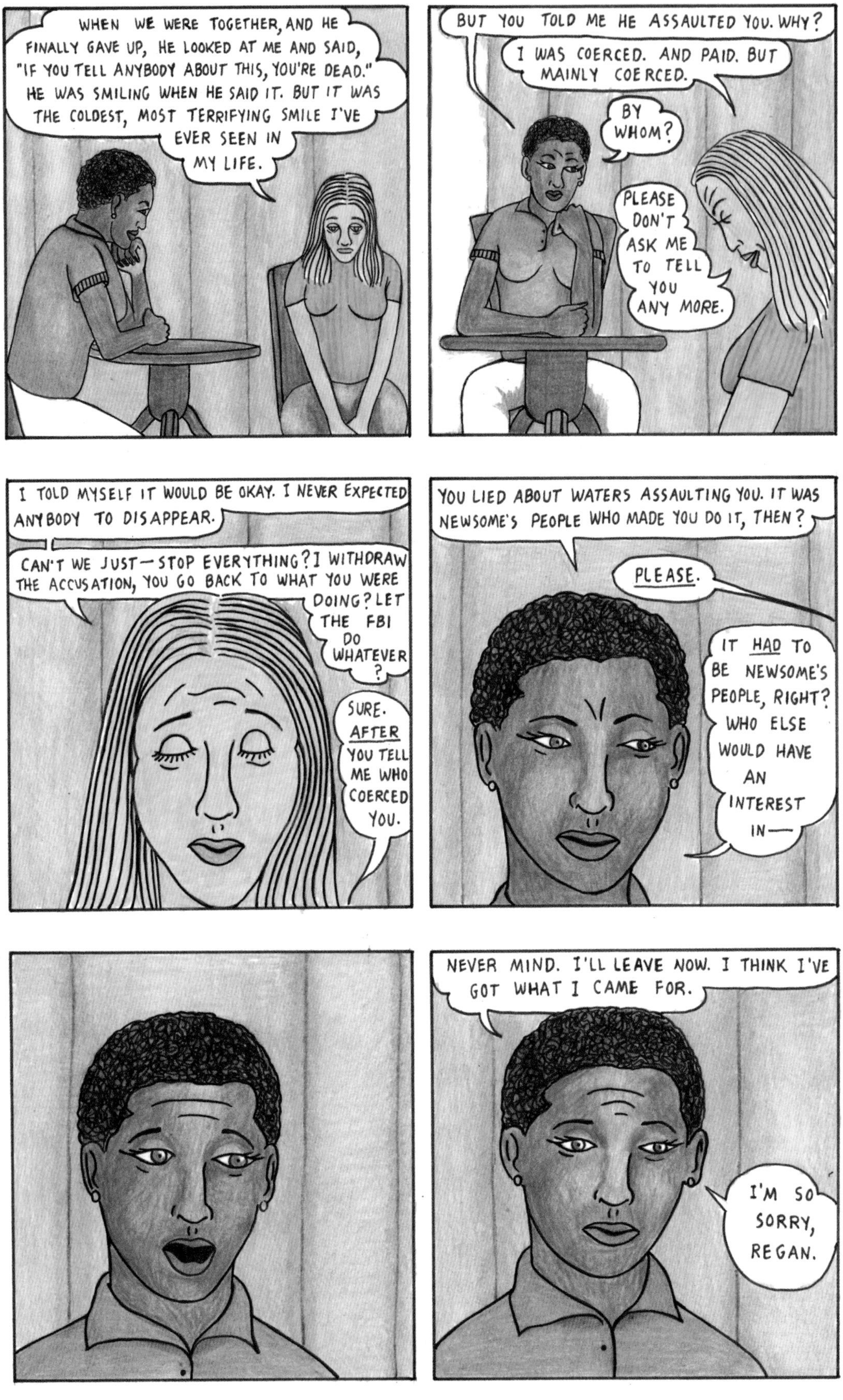
WHEN WE WERE TOGETHER, AND HE FINALLY GAVE UP, HE LOOKED AT ME AND SAID, "IF YOU TELL ANYBODY ABOUT THIS, YOU'RE DEAD." HE WAS SMILING WHEN HE SAID IT. BUT IT WAS THE COLDEST, MOST TERRIFYING SMILE I'VE EVER SEEN IN MY LIFE.
BUT YOU TOLD ME HE ASSAULTED YOU. WHY?
I WAS COERCED. AND PAID. BUT MAINLY COERCED.
BY WHOM?
PLEASE DON'T ASK ME TO TELL YOU ANY MORE.
I TOLD MYSELF IT WOULD BE OKAY. I NEVER EXPECTED ANYBODY TO DISAPPEAR.
CAN'T WE JUST—STOP EVERYTHING? I WITHDRAW THE ACCUSATION, YOU GO BACK TO WHAT YOU WERE DOING? LET THE FBI DO WHATEVER?
SURE. AFTER YOU TELL ME WHO COERCED YOU.
YOU LIED ABOUT WATERS ASSAULTING YOU. IT WAS NEWSOME'S PEOPLE WHO MADE YOU DO IT, THEN?
PLEASE.
IT HAD TO BE NEWSOME'S PEOPLE, RIGHT? WHO ELSE WOULD HAVE AN INTEREST IN—
NEVER MIND. I'LL LEAVE NOW. I THINK I'VE GOT WHAT I CAME FOR.
I'M SO SORRY, REGAN.

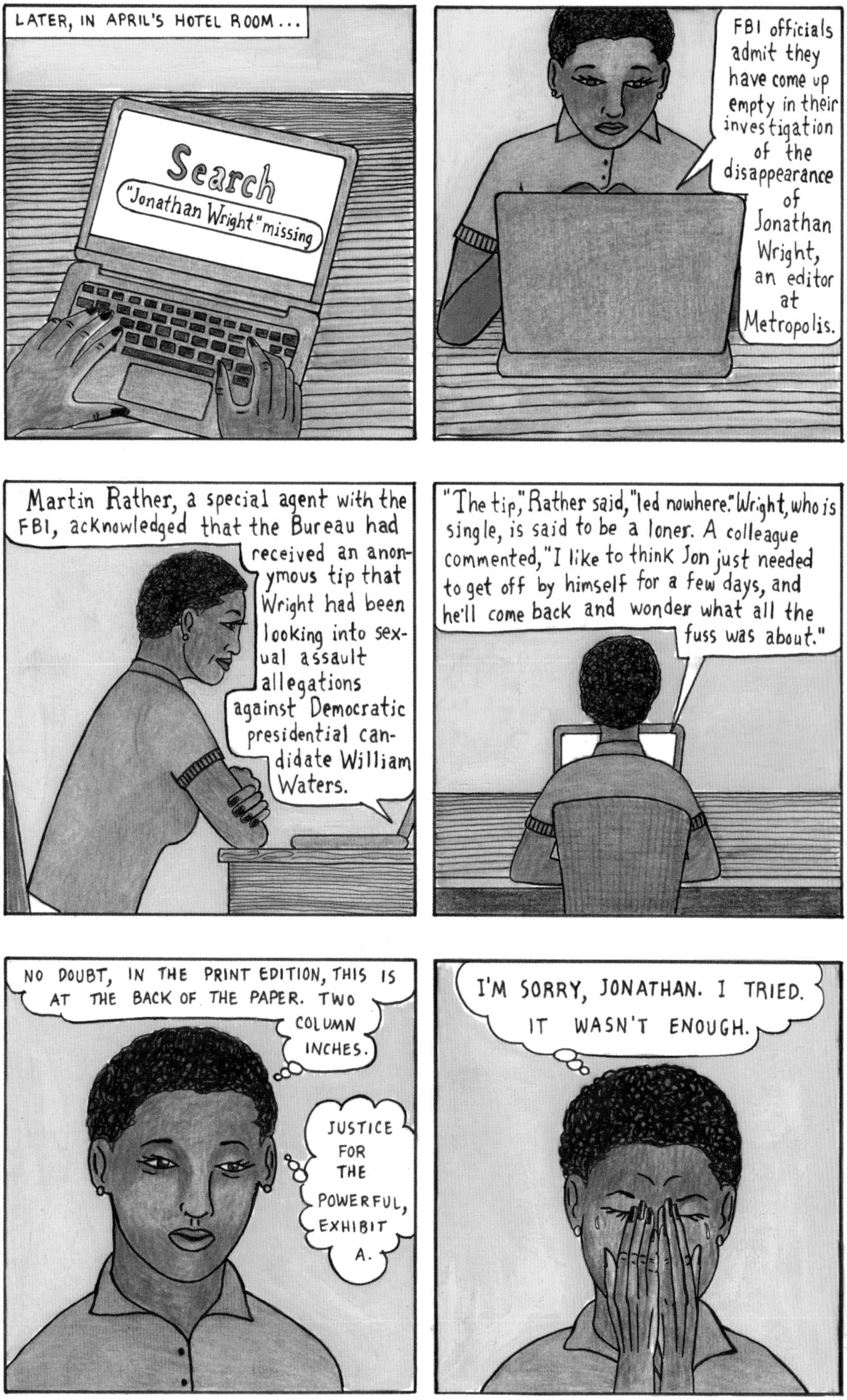
LATER, IN APRIL'S HOTEL ROOM...
Search
"Jonathan Wright" missing
FBI officials admit they have come up empty in their investigation of the disappearance of Jonathan Wright, an editor at Metropolis.
Martin Rather, a special agent with the FBI, acknowledged that the Bureau had received an anonymous tip that Wright had been looking into sexual assault allegations against Democratic presidential candidate William Waters.
"The tip," Rather said, "led nowhere." Wright, who is single, is said to be a loner. A colleague commented, "I like to think Jon just needed to get off by himself for a few days, and he'll come back and wonder what all the fuss was about."
NO DOUBT, IN THE PRINT EDITION, THIS IS AT THE BACK OF THE PAPER. TWO COLUMN INCHES.
JUSTICE FOR THE POWERFUL, EXHIBIT A.
I'M SORRY, JONATHAN. I TRIED. IT WASN'T ENOUGH.

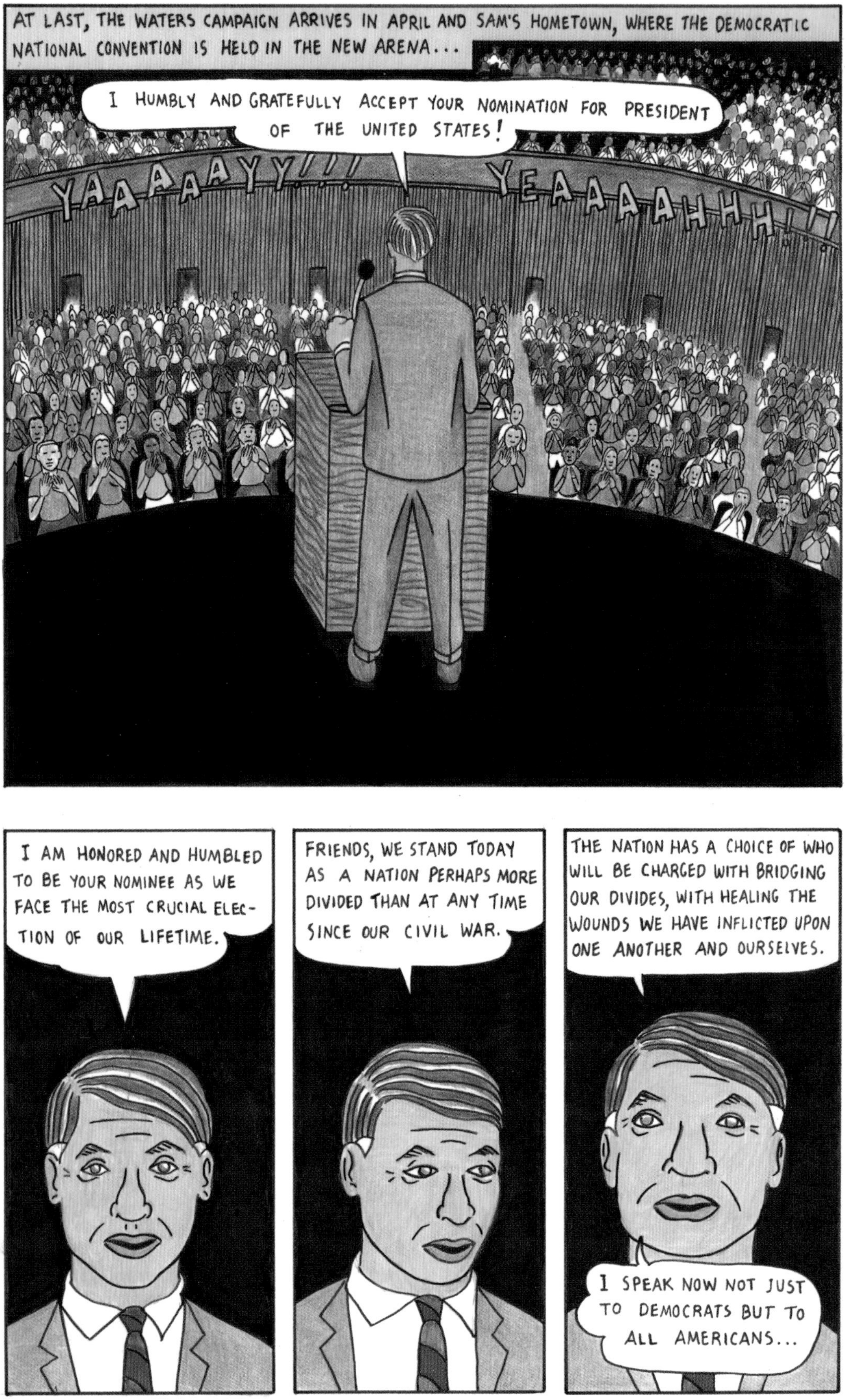
AT LAST, THE WATERS CAMPAIGN ARRIVES IN APRIL AND SAM'S HOMETOWN, WHERE THE DEMOCRATIC NATIONAL CONVENTION IS HELD IN THE NEW ARENA...
I HUMBLY AND GRATEFULLY ACCEPT YOUR NOMINATION FOR PRESIDENT OF THE UNITED STATES!
YAAAAAYY!!!
YEAAAAAHHH!!!
I AM HONORED AND HUMBLED TO BE YOUR NOMINEE AS WE FACE THE MOST CRUCIAL ELECTION OF OUR LIFETIME.
FRIENDS, WE STAND TODAY AS A NATION PERHAPS MORE DIVIDED THAN AT ANY TIME SINCE OUR CIVIL WAR.
THE NATION HAS A CHOICE OF WHO WILL BE CHARGED WITH BRIDGING OUR DIVIDES, WITH HEALING THE WOUNDS WE HAVE INFLICTED UPON ONE ANOTHER AND OURSELVES.
I SPEAK NOW NOT JUST TO DEMOCRATS BUT TO ALL AMERICANS...

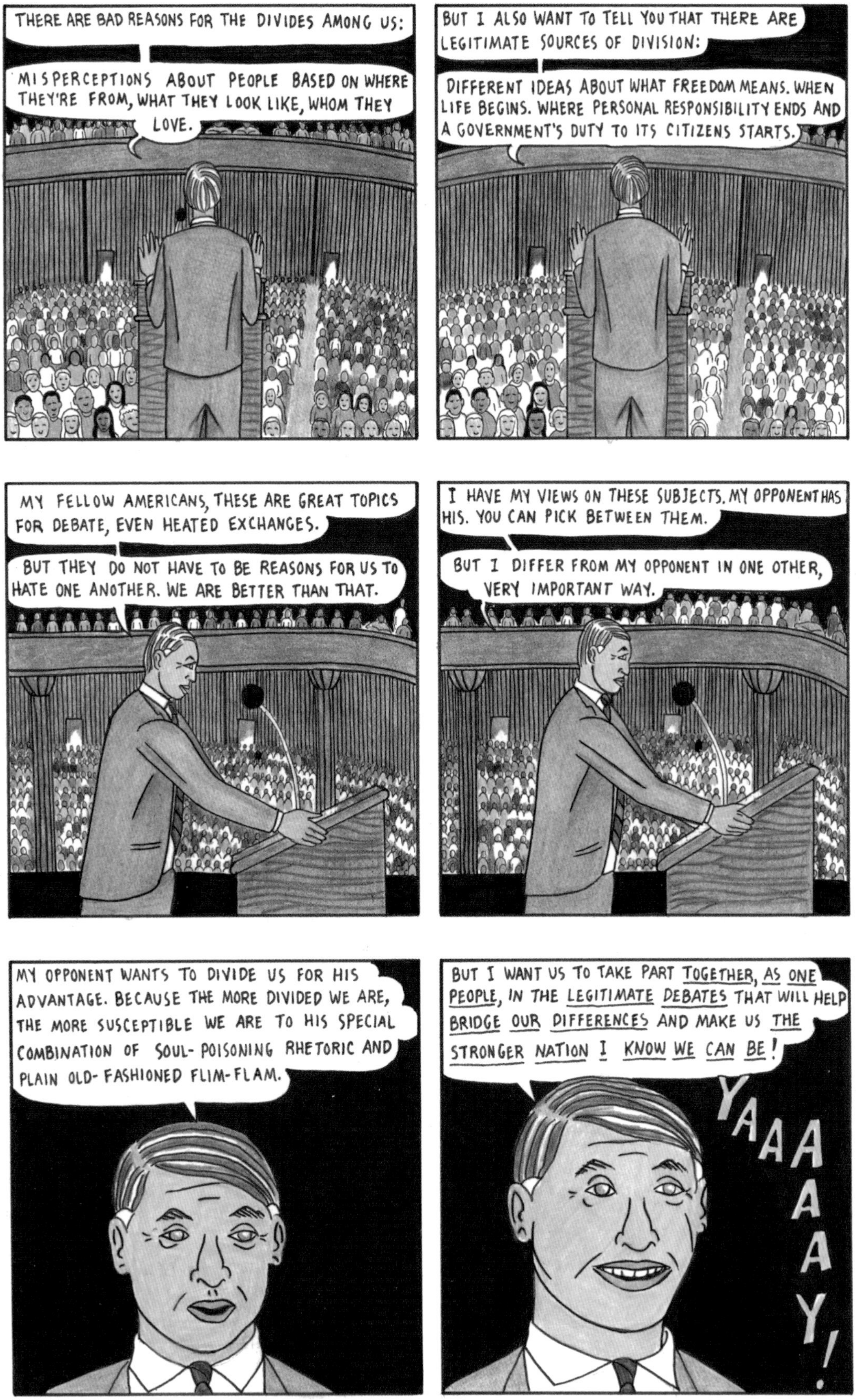
THERE ARE BAD REASONS FOR THE DIVIDES AMONG US:
MISPERCEPTIONS ABOUT PEOPLE BASED ON WHERE THEY'RE FROM, WHAT THEY LOOK LIKE, WHOM THEY LOVE.
BUT I ALSO WANT TO TELL YOU THAT THERE ARE LEGITIMATE SOURCES OF DIVISION:
DIFFERENT IDEAS ABOUT WHAT FREEDOM MEANS. WHEN LIFE BEGINS. WHERE PERSONAL RESPONSIBILITY ENDS AND A GOVERNMENT'S DUTY TO ITS CITIZENS STARTS.
MY FELLOW AMERICANS, THESE ARE GREAT TOPICS FOR DEBATE, EVEN HEATED EXCHANGES.
BUT THEY DO NOT HAVE TO BE REASONS FOR US TO HATE ONE ANOTHER. WE ARE BETTER THAN THAT.
I HAVE MY VIEWS ON THESE SUBJECTS. MY OPPONENT HAS HIS. YOU CAN PICK BETWEEN THEM.
BUT I DIFFER FROM MY OPPONENT IN ONE OTHER, VERY IMPORTANT WAY.
MY OPPONENT WANTS TO DIVIDE US FOR HIS ADVANTAGE. BECAUSE THE MORE DIVIDED WE ARE, THE MORE SUSCEPTIBLE WE ARE TO HIS SPECIAL COMBINATION OF SOUL-POISONING RHETORIC AND PLAIN OLD-FASHIONED FLIM-FLAM.
BUT I WANT US TO TAKE PART TOGETHER, AS ONE PEOPLE, IN THE LEGITIMATE DEBATES THAT WILL HELP BRIDGE OUR DIFFERENCES AND MAKE US THE STRONGER NATION I KNOW WE CAN BE!
YAAAAAAY!

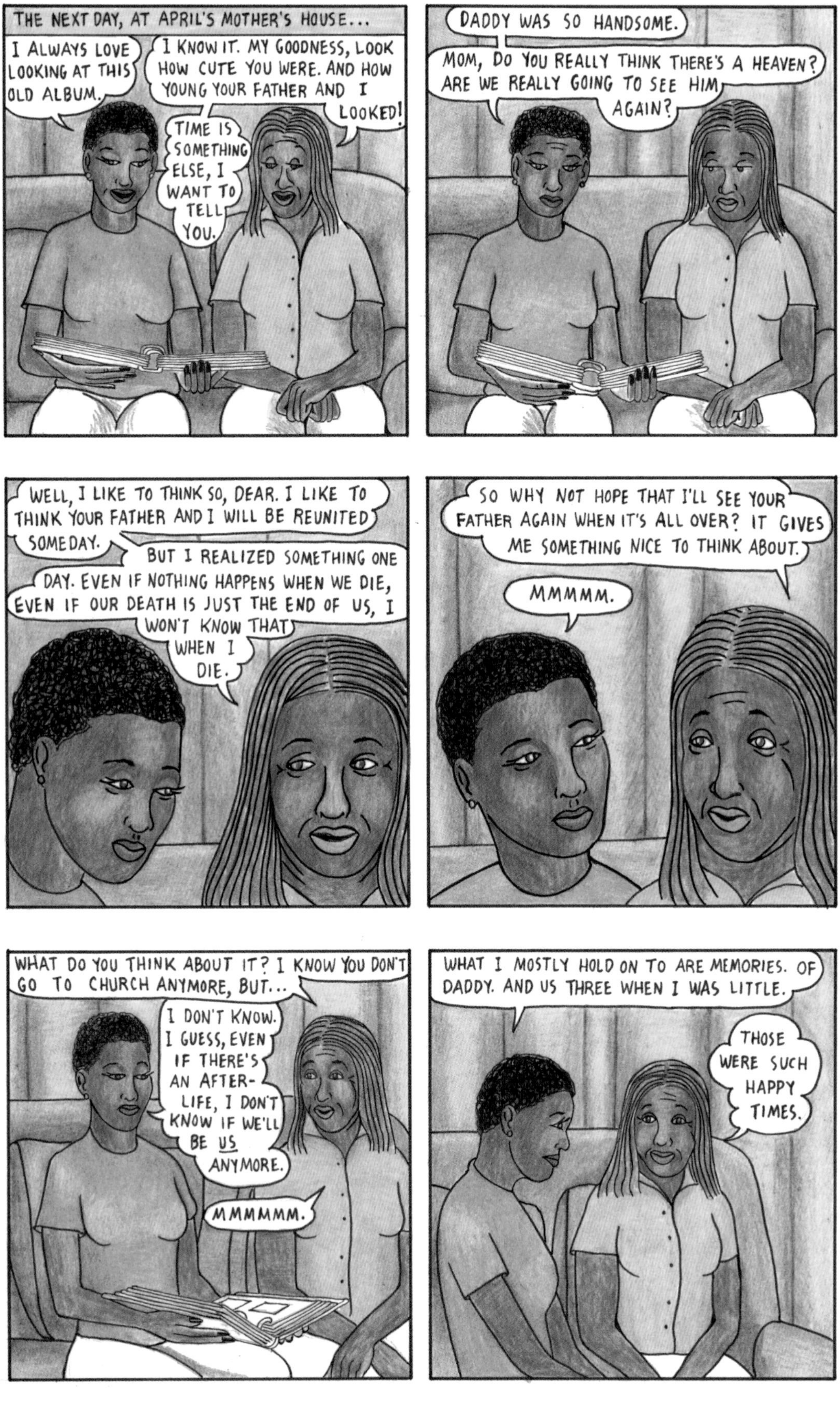
THE NEXT DAY, AT APRIL'S MOTHER'S HOUSE...
I ALWAYS LOVE LOOKING AT THIS OLD ALBUM.
I KNOW IT. MY GOODNESS, LOOK HOW CUTE YOU WERE. AND HOW YOUNG YOUR FATHER AND I LOOKED!
TIME IS SOMETHING ELSE, I WANT TO TELL YOU.
DADDY WAS SO HANDSOME.
MOM, DO YOU REALLY THINK THERE'S A HEAVEN? ARE WE REALLY GOING TO SEE HIM AGAIN?
WELL, I LIKE TO THINK SO, DEAR. I LIKE TO THINK YOUR FATHER AND I WILL BE REUNITED SOMEDAY.
BUT I REALIZED SOMETHING ONE DAY. EVEN IF NOTHING HAPPENS WHEN WE DIE, EVEN IF OUR DEATH IS JUST THE END OF US, I WON'T KNOW THAT WHEN I DIE.
SO WHY NOT HOPE THAT I'LL SEE YOUR FATHER AGAIN WHEN IT'S ALL OVER? IT GIVES ME SOMETHING NICE TO THINK ABOUT.
MMMMM.
WHAT DO YOU THINK ABOUT IT? I KNOW YOU DON'T GO TO CHURCH ANYMORE, BUT...
I DON'T KNOW. I GUESS, EVEN IF THERE'S AN AFTER-LIFE, I DON'T KNOW IF WE'LL BE US ANYMORE.
MMMMMM.
WHAT I MOSTLY HOLD ON TO ARE MEMORIES. OF DADDY. AND US THREE WHEN I WAS LITTLE.
THOSE WERE SUCH HAPPY TIMES.

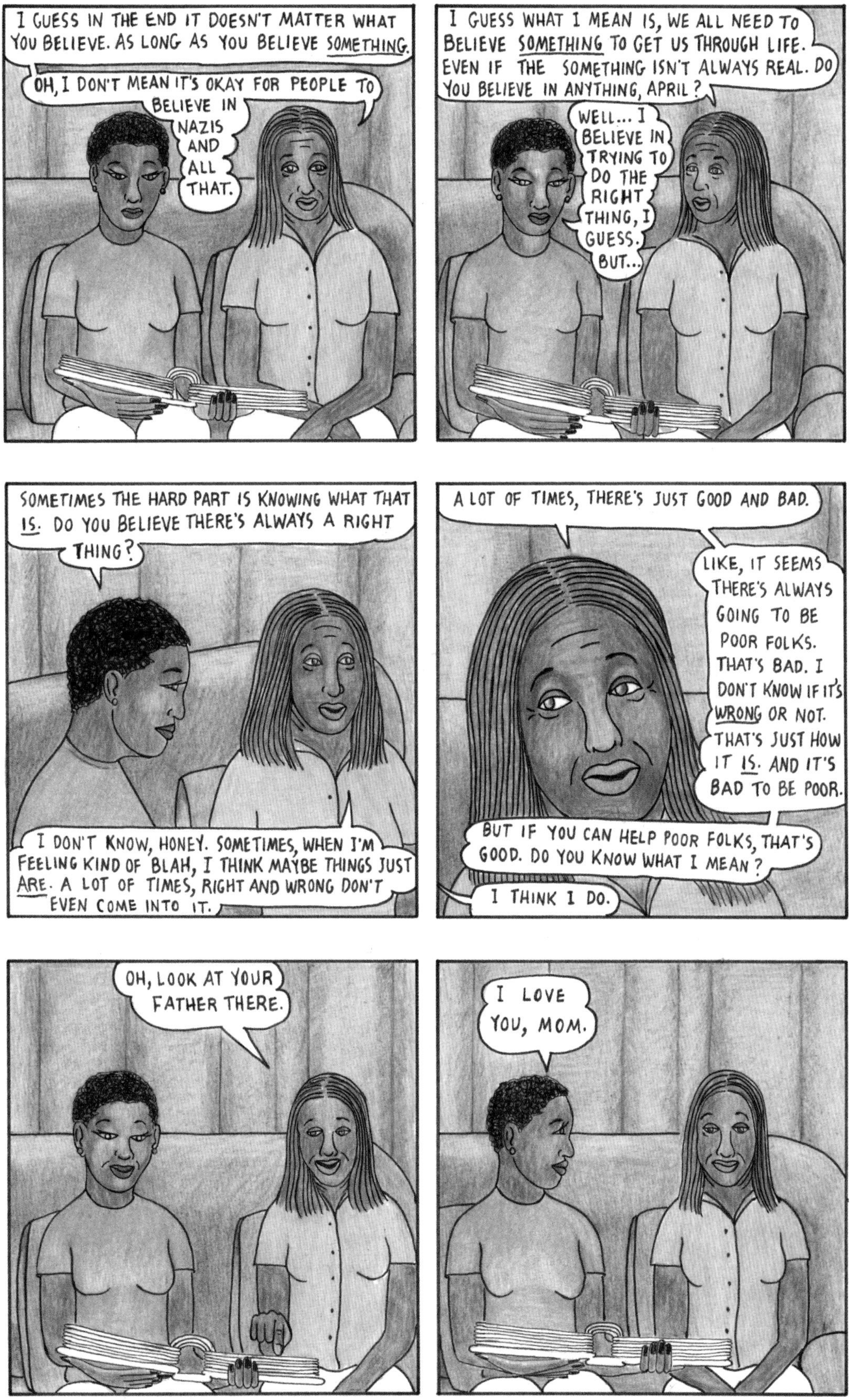
I GUESS IN THE END IT DOESN'T MATTER WHAT YOU BELIEVE. AS LONG AS YOU BELIEVE SOMETHING.
OH, I DON'T MEAN IT'S OKAY FOR PEOPLE TO BELIEVE IN NAZIS AND ALL THAT.
I GUESS WHAT I MEAN IS, WE ALL NEED TO BELIEVE SOMETHING TO GET US THROUGH LIFE. EVEN IF THE SOMETHING ISN'T ALWAYS REAL. DO YOU BELIEVE IN ANYTHING, APRIL?
WELL... I BELIEVE IN TRYING TO DO THE RIGHT THING, I GUESS. BUT...
SOMETIMES THE HARD PART IS KNOWING WHAT THAT IS. DO YOU BELIEVE THERE'S ALWAYS A RIGHT THING?
I DON'T KNOW, HONEY. SOMETIMES, WHEN I'M FEELING KIND OF BLAH, I THINK MAYBE THINGS JUST ARE. A LOT OF TIMES, RIGHT AND WRONG DON'T EVEN COME INTO IT.
A LOT OF TIMES, THERE'S JUST GOOD AND BAD.
LIKE, IT SEEMS THERE'S ALWAYS GOING TO BE POOR FOLKS. THAT'S BAD. I DON'T KNOW IF IT'S WRONG OR NOT. THAT'S JUST HOW IT IS. AND IT'S BAD TO BE POOR.
BUT IF YOU CAN HELP POOR FOLKS, THAT'S GOOD. DO YOU KNOW WHAT I MEAN?
I THINK I DO.
OH, LOOK AT YOUR FATHER THERE.
I LOVE YOU, MOM.

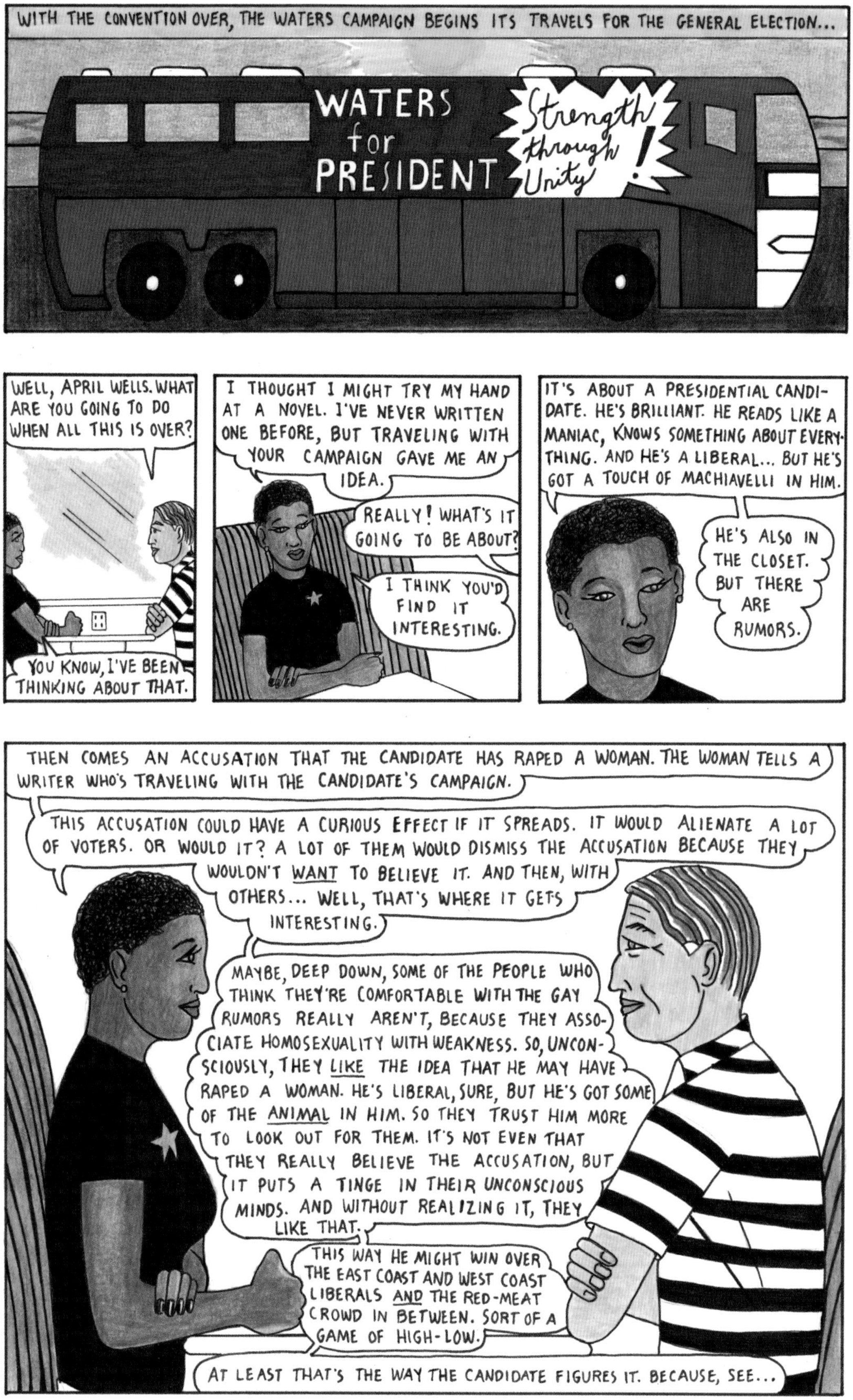
WITH THE CONVENTION OVER, THE WATERS CAMPAIGN BEGINS ITS TRAVELS FOR THE GENERAL ELECTION...
WATERS for PRESIDENT
Strength through Unity!
WELL, APRIL WELLS. WHAT ARE YOU GOING TO DO WHEN ALL THIS IS OVER?
YOU KNOW, I'VE BEEN THINKING ABOUT THAT.
I THOUGHT I MIGHT TRY MY HAND AT A NOVEL. I'VE NEVER WRITTEN ONE BEFORE, BUT TRAVELING WITH YOUR CAMPAIGN GAVE ME AN IDEA.
REALLY! WHAT'S IT GOING TO BE ABOUT?
I THINK YOU'D FIND IT INTERESTING.
IT'S ABOUT A PRESIDENTIAL CANDIDATE. HE'S BRILLIANT. HE READS LIKE A MANIAC, KNOWS SOMETHING ABOUT EVERYTHING. AND HE'S A LIBERAL... BUT HE'S GOT A TOUCH OF MACHIAVELLI IN HIM.
HE'S ALSO IN THE CLOSET. BUT THERE ARE RUMORS.
THEN COMES AN ACCUSATION THAT THE CANDIDATE HAS RAPED A WOMAN. THE WOMAN TELLS A WRITER WHO'S TRAVELING WITH THE CANDIDATE'S CAMPAIGN.
THIS ACCUSATION COULD HAVE A CURIOUS EFFECT IF IT SPREADS. IT WOULD ALIENATE A LOT OF VOTERS. OR WOULD IT? A LOT OF THEM WOULD DISMISS THE ACCUSATION BECAUSE THEY WOULDN'T WANT TO BELIEVE IT. AND THEN, WITH OTHERS... WELL, THAT'S WHERE IT GETS INTERESTING.
MAYBE, DEEP DOWN, SOME OF THE PEOPLE WHO THINK THEY'RE COMFORTABLE WITH THE GAY RUMORS REALLY AREN'T, BECAUSE THEY ASSOCIATE HOMOSEXUALITY WITH WEAKNESS. SO, UNCONSCIOUSLY, THEY LIKE THE IDEA THAT HE MAY HAVE RAPED A WOMAN. HE'S LIBERAL, SURE, BUT HE'S GOT SOME OF THE ANIMAL IN HIM. SO THEY TRUST HIM MORE TO LOOK OUT FOR THEM. IT'S NOT EVEN THAT THEY REALLY BELIEVE THE ACCUSATION, BUT IT PUTS A TINGE IN THEIR UNCONSCIOUS MINDS. AND WITHOUT REALIZING IT, THEY LIKE THAT.
THIS WAY HE MIGHT WIN OVER THE EAST COAST AND WEST COAST LIBERALS AND THE RED-MEAT CROWD IN BETWEEN. SORT OF A GAME OF HIGH-LOW.
AT LEAST THAT'S THE WAY THE CANDIDATE FIGURES IT. BECAUSE, SEE...

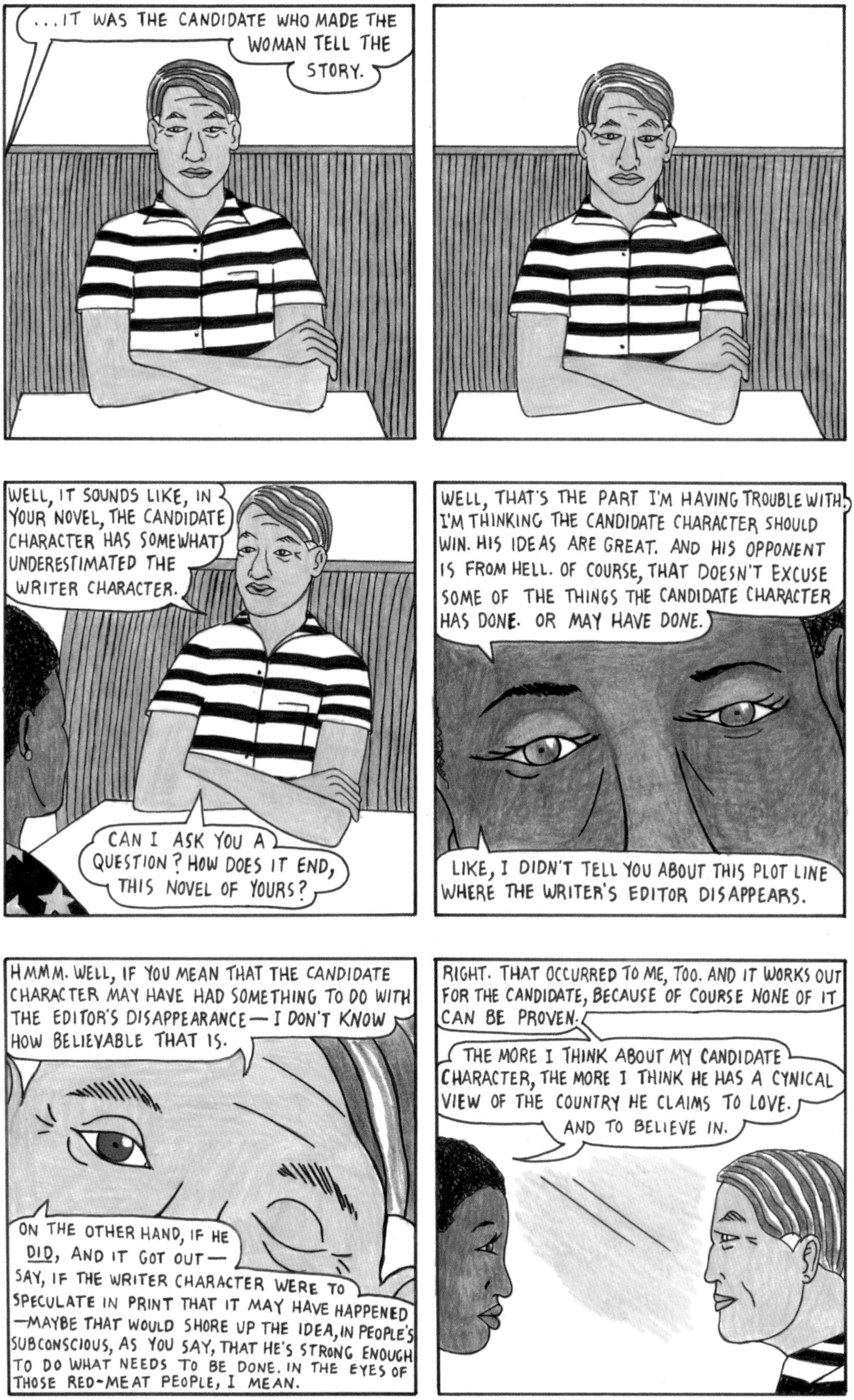
...IT WAS THE CANDIDATE WHO MADE THE WOMAN TELL THE STORY.
WELL, IT SOUNDS LIKE, IN YOUR NOVEL, THE CANDIDATE CHARACTER HAS SOMEWHAT UNDERESTIMATED THE WRITER CHARACTER.
CAN I ASK YOU A QUESTION? HOW DOES IT END, THIS NOVEL OF YOURS?
WELL, THAT'S THE PART I'M HAVING TROUBLE WITH. I'M THINKING THE CANDIDATE CHARACTER SHOULD WIN. HIS IDEAS ARE GREAT. AND HIS OPPONENT IS FROM HELL. OF COURSE, THAT DOESN'T EXCUSE SOME OF THE THINGS THE CANDIDATE CHARACTER HAS DONE. OR MAY HAVE DONE.
LIKE, I DIDN'T TELL YOU ABOUT THIS PLOT LINE WHERE THE WRITER'S EDITOR DISAPPEARS.
HMMM. WELL, IF YOU MEAN THAT THE CANDIDATE CHARACTER MAY HAVE HAD SOMETHING TO DO WITH THE EDITOR'S DISAPPEARANCE — I DON'T KNOW HOW BELIEVABLE THAT IS.
ON THE OTHER HAND, IF HE DID, AND IT GOT OUT — SAY, IF THE WRITER CHARACTER WERE TO SPECULATE IN PRINT THAT IT MAY HAVE HAPPENED — MAYBE THAT WOULD SHORE UP THE IDEA, IN PEOPLE'S SUBCONSCIOUS, AS YOU SAY, THAT HE'S STRONG ENOUGH TO DO WHAT NEEDS TO BE DONE. IN THE EYES OF THOSE RED-MEAT PEOPLE, I MEAN.
RIGHT. THAT OCCURRED TO ME, TOO. AND IT WORKS OUT FOR THE CANDIDATE, BECAUSE OF COURSE NONE OF IT CAN BE PROVEN.
THE MORE I THINK ABOUT MY CANDIDATE CHARACTER, THE MORE I THINK HE HAS A CYNICAL VIEW OF THE COUNTRY HE CLAIMS TO LOVE. AND TO BELIEVE IN.

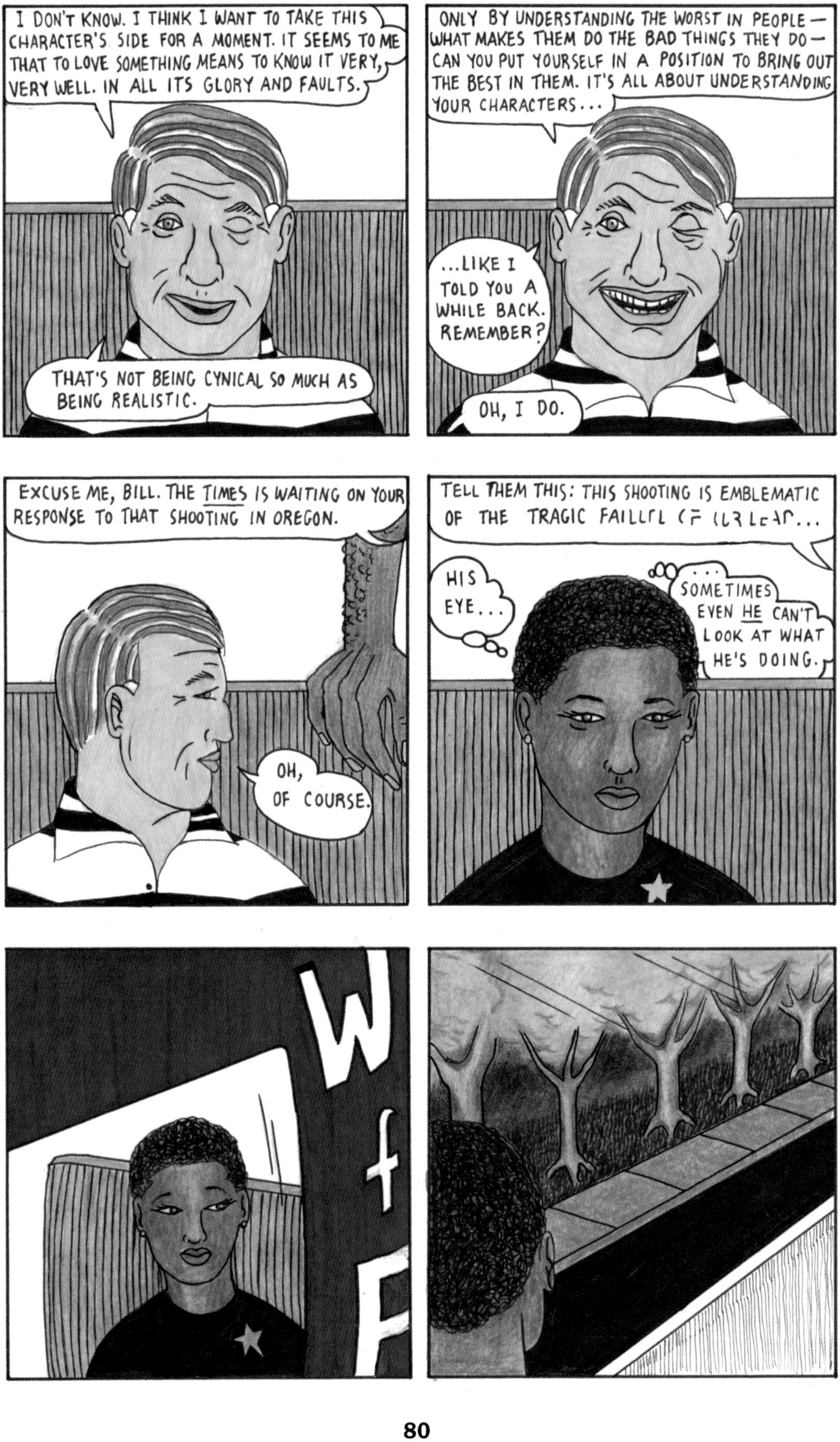
I DON'T KNOW. I THINK I WANT TO TAKE THIS CHARACTER'S SIDE FOR A MOMENT. IT SEEMS TO ME THAT TO LOVE SOMETHING MEANS TO KNOW IT VERY, VERY WELL. IN ALL ITS GLORY AND FAULTS.
THAT'S NOT BEING CYNICAL SO MUCH AS BEING REALISTIC.
ONLY BY UNDERSTANDING THE WORST IN PEOPLE — WHAT MAKES THEM DO THE BAD THINGS THEY DO — CAN YOU PUT YOURSELF IN A POSITION TO BRING OUT THE BEST IN THEM. IT'S ALL ABOUT UNDERSTANDING YOUR CHARACTERS...
...LIKE I TOLD YOU A WHILE BACK. REMEMBER?
OH, I DO.
EXCUSE ME, BILL. THE TIMES IS WAITING ON YOUR RESPONSE TO THAT SHOOTING IN OREGON.
OH, OF COURSE.
TELL THEM THIS: THIS SHOOTING IS EMBLEMATIC OF THE TRAGIC
HIS EYE...
...SOMETIMES EVEN HE CAN'T LOOK AT WHAT HE'S DOING.

WEEKS LATER...

PRICE $8.99   SEP. 1

METROPOLIS

GENERAL INTEREST

APRIL WELLS ON WILLIAM

NEW RELEASES IN

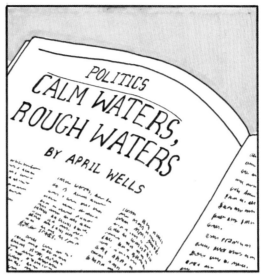

POLITICS

CALM WATERS, ROUGH WATERS

BY APRIL WELLS

Imagine an office, a workplace of fifteen or so people, situated on a bus. Some of the people appear to outrank others, though no one is clearly in charge. Most of the workers are men, and most are white, but the brown-skinned folks and the women, while outnumbered, seem to have jobs as important as the others.' No one looks to be older than mid-thirties.

There is one exception: a somewhat older man, white, late forties maybe. He seems at first to be the office assistant, because the others continually ask him to do things, and he agrees, with almost unfailing graciousness.

The odd thing, you begin to notice, is that this assistant—if that's what he is—never goes anywhere. His various bosses come to him, looking mildly anxious, then leave again, their calm restored.

This middle-aged assistant, it turns out, is running the office. He is the boss, the wheels on the bus. He is William Waters, and he is the Democratic nominee for president of the United States.

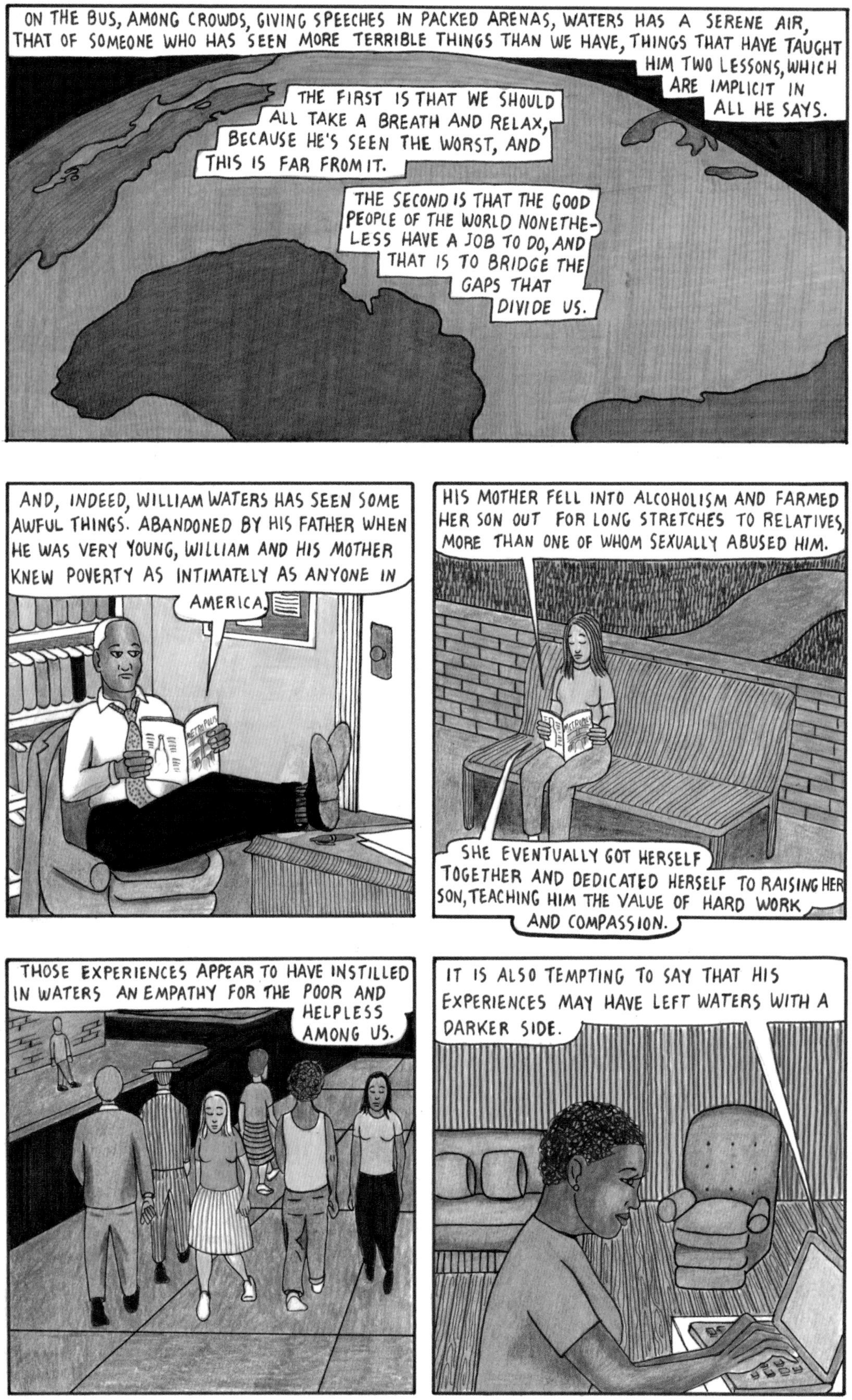
ON THE BUS, AMONG CROWDS, GIVING SPEECHES IN PACKED ARENAS, WATERS HAS A SERENE AIR, THAT OF SOMEONE WHO HAS SEEN MORE TERRIBLE THINGS THAN WE HAVE, THINGS THAT HAVE TAUGHT HIM TWO LESSONS, WHICH ARE IMPLICIT IN ALL HE SAYS.
THE FIRST IS THAT WE SHOULD ALL TAKE A BREATH AND RELAX, BECAUSE HE'S SEEN THE WORST, AND THIS IS FAR FROM IT.
THE SECOND IS THAT THE GOOD PEOPLE OF THE WORLD NONETHELESS HAVE A JOB TO DO, AND THAT IS TO BRIDGE THE GAPS THAT DIVIDE US.
AND, INDEED, WILLIAM WATERS HAS SEEN SOME AWFUL THINGS. ABANDONED BY HIS FATHER WHEN HE WAS VERY YOUNG, WILLIAM AND HIS MOTHER KNEW POVERTY AS INTIMATELY AS ANYONE IN AMERICA.
METROPOLIS
HIS MOTHER FELL INTO ALCOHOLISM AND FARMED HER SON OUT FOR LONG STRETCHES TO RELATIVES, MORE THAN ONE OF WHOM SEXUALLY ABUSED HIM.
SHE EVENTUALLY GOT HERSELF TOGETHER AND DEDICATED HERSELF TO RAISING HER SON, TEACHING HIM THE VALUE OF HARD WORK AND COMPASSION.
THOSE EXPERIENCES APPEAR TO HAVE INSTILLED IN WATERS AN EMPATHY FOR THE POOR AND HELPLESS AMONG US.
IT IS ALSO TEMPTING TO SAY THAT HIS EXPERIENCES MAY HAVE LEFT WATERS WITH A DARKER SIDE.

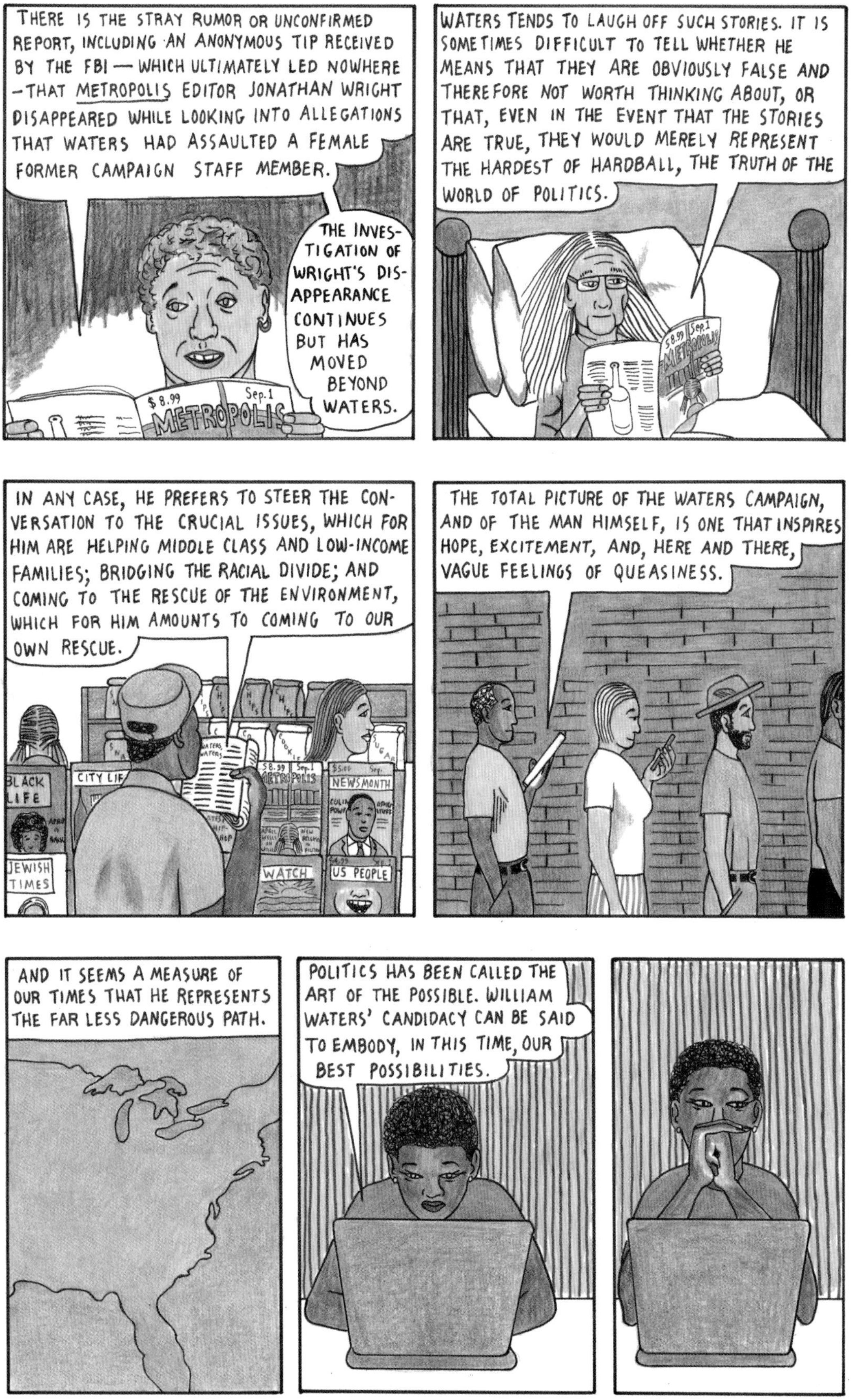
THERE IS THE STRAY RUMOR OR UNCONFIRMED REPORT, INCLUDING AN ANONYMOUS TIP RECEIVED BY THE FBI — WHICH ULTIMATELY LED NOWHERE —THAT METROPOLIS EDITOR JONATHAN WRIGHT DISAPPEARED WHILE LOOKING INTO ALLEGATIONS THAT WATERS HAD ASSAULTED A FEMALE FORMER CAMPAIGN STAFF MEMBER.
THE INVESTIGATION OF WRIGHT'S DISAPPEARANCE CONTINUES BUT HAS MOVED BEYOND WATERS.
$ 8.99
Sep.1
METROPOLIS
WATERS TENDS TO LAUGH OFF SUCH STORIES. IT IS SOMETIMES DIFFICULT TO TELL WHETHER HE MEANS THAT THEY ARE OBVIOUSLY FALSE AND THEREFORE NOT WORTH THINKING ABOUT, OR THAT, EVEN IN THE EVENT THAT THE STORIES ARE TRUE, THEY WOULD MERELY REPRESENT THE HARDEST OF HARDBALL, THE TRUTH OF THE WORLD OF POLITICS.
IN ANY CASE, HE PREFERS TO STEER THE CONVERSATION TO THE CRUCIAL ISSUES, WHICH FOR HIM ARE HELPING MIDDLE CLASS AND LOW-INCOME FAMILIES; BRIDGING THE RACIAL DIVIDE; AND COMING TO THE RESCUE OF THE ENVIRONMENT, WHICH FOR HIM AMOUNTS TO COMING TO OUR OWN RESCUE.
BLACK LIFE
CITY LIFE
JEWISH TIMES
METROPOLIS
NEWSMONTH
WATCH
US PEOPLE
THE TOTAL PICTURE OF THE WATERS CAMPAIGN, AND OF THE MAN HIMSELF, IS ONE THAT INSPIRES HOPE, EXCITEMENT, AND, HERE AND THERE, VAGUE FEELINGS OF QUEASINESS.
AND IT SEEMS A MEASURE OF OUR TIMES THAT HE REPRESENTS THE FAR LESS DANGEROUS PATH.
POLITICS HAS BEEN CALLED THE ART OF THE POSSIBLE. WILLIAM WATERS' CANDIDACY CAN BE SAID TO EMBODY, IN THIS TIME, OUR BEST POSSIBILITIES.

EPILOGUE

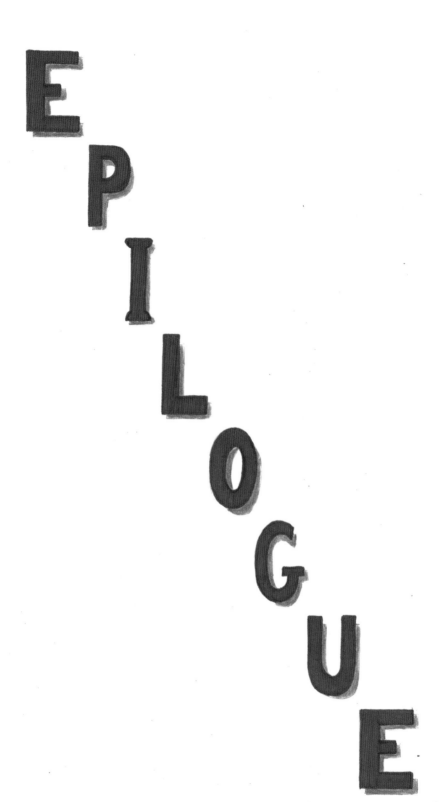

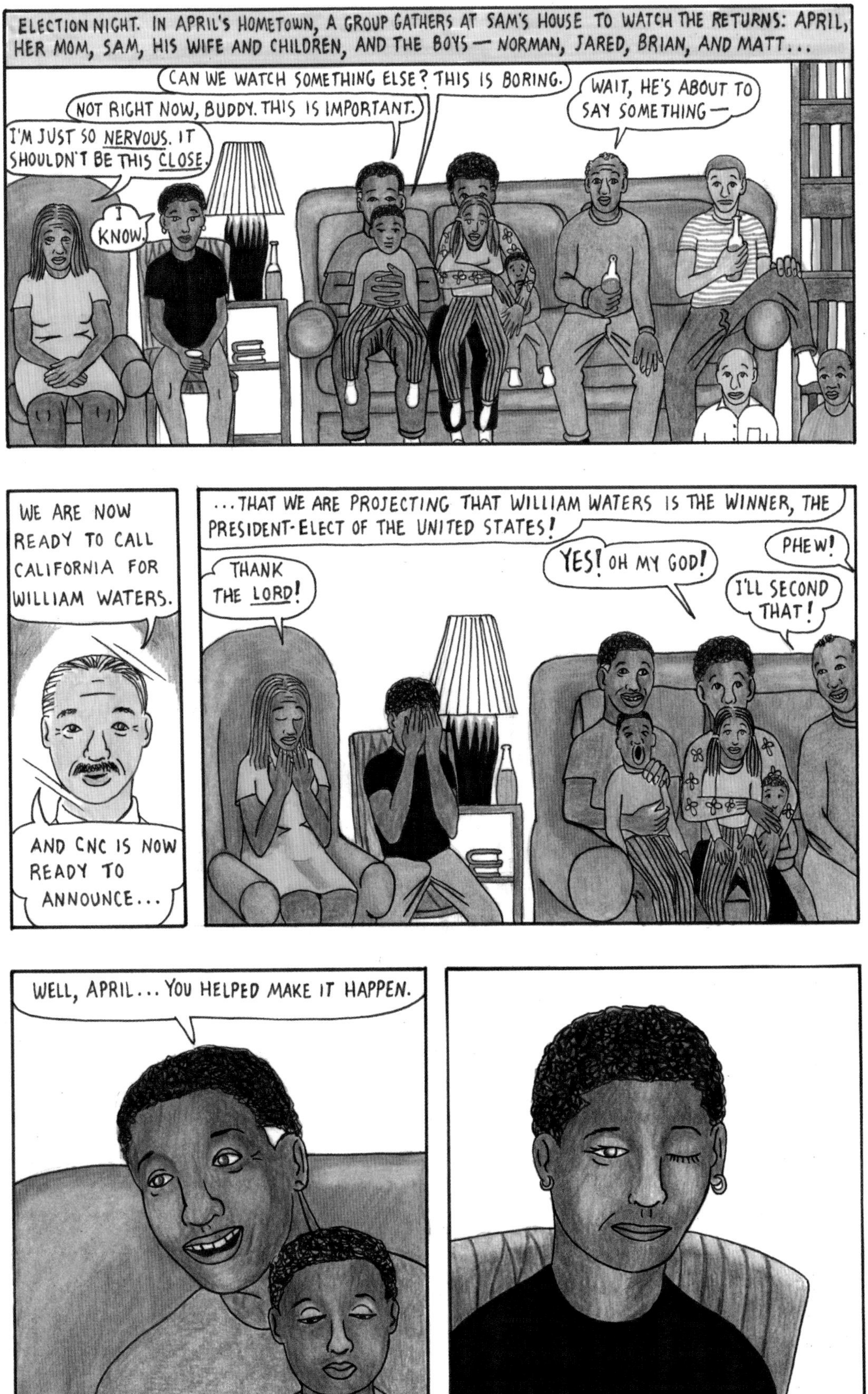
ELECTION NIGHT. IN APRIL'S HOMETOWN, A GROUP GATHERS AT SAM'S HOUSE TO WATCH THE RETURNS: APRIL, HER MOM, SAM, HIS WIFE AND CHILDREN, AND THE BOYS — NORMAN, JARED, BRIAN, AND MATT...
I'M JUST SO NERVOUS. IT SHOULDN'T BE THIS CLOSE.
I KNOW.
NOT RIGHT NOW, BUDDY. THIS IS IMPORTANT.
CAN WE WATCH SOMETHING ELSE? THIS IS BORING.
WAIT, HE'S ABOUT TO SAY SOMETHING —
WE ARE NOW READY TO CALL CALIFORNIA FOR WILLIAM WATERS.
AND CNC IS NOW READY TO ANNOUNCE...
...THAT WE ARE PROJECTING THAT WILLIAM WATERS IS THE WINNER, THE PRESIDENT-ELECT OF THE UNITED STATES!
THANK THE LORD!
YES! OH MY GOD!
PHEW!
I'LL SECOND THAT!
WELL, APRIL... YOU HELPED MAKE IT HAPPEN.

Acknowledgments

One of the sparks for this book was a conversation I had in a Park Slope watering hole, on an early August night in 2019, with my good friend David Ochshorn. "Part of me wants to make a film," I told David, "but I'm too old." He said, "I can see that. You're a writer and you do visual art." That itself was like a moment from an old movie — *Wait a second, say that again!* — because the next thing I said was, "I *can* make a film. But in the form of a graphic novel." And that is what I set out to do. So thank you, David, for jarring something loose in me.

As fat a cliché as "eternal gratitude" is, that is what I feel toward my publisher, Judith Gurewich, who believed in and championed this book from the beginning. I also greatly appreciate the hard work and insights of the staff at Other Press, including Yvonne Cárdenas, Janice Goldklang, Alexandra Poreda, Gage Desser, Mona Bismuth, Iisha Stevens, and Jessica Greer. I tip my old black homburg to my capable agent, Andrew Blauner. And quite a few people deserve thanks for giving me their support, ranging from constructive criticism to practical advice to generously shared expertise to well-timed words of encouragement. Those people include Kevin Harris, my old back-in-the-day cartooning partner in crime; Amadou Diallo; Tom Rayfiel; Wendy Weitzner Wasman; Chip Kidd; Jim Buckley; Tom Carling; Ian Belknap; Amy Worden; Chris Ware; Elinor T. Vanderburg; Andrew Neisler; Alan Bradshaw; Adam Shatz; Diane Mehta; Greg Varner; V. Hansmann; Alexandra Horowitz; Amy Steingart; Susan Kaufman; Murdo McGrath; Megan Culhane Galbraith; Maria Mutch; Alice Mattison; Ben Anastas; Susan Cheever; Jonathan Lethem; Phillip Lopate; Louie and The Pie; Nicholas Chimienti; and my darling wife, Amy Peck — Amy, who was there for all of it, occasionally giving an offhand suggestion that turned out to be invaluable. A special thanks goes to my longtime friend Charles Hawley, who helped me think through aspects of the story and asked key questions. This is a better work thanks to you, old pal.

Finally, I want to thank Charles M. Schulz and Stan Lee, who, half a century ago, planted seeds in the mind of a young Black boy.

About the Author

Clifford Thompson's work has appeared in *The Best American Essays 2018*, as well as the *Washington Post*, *Wall Street Journal*, *Threepenny Review*, and *Village Voice*. He is the recipient of a Whiting Award for nonfiction and teaches at New York University, Sarah Lawrence College, and the Bennington Writing Seminars. His previous book, *What It Is: Race, Family, and One Thinking Black Man's Blues*, was published by Other Press in 2019. He lives in Brooklyn, New York.

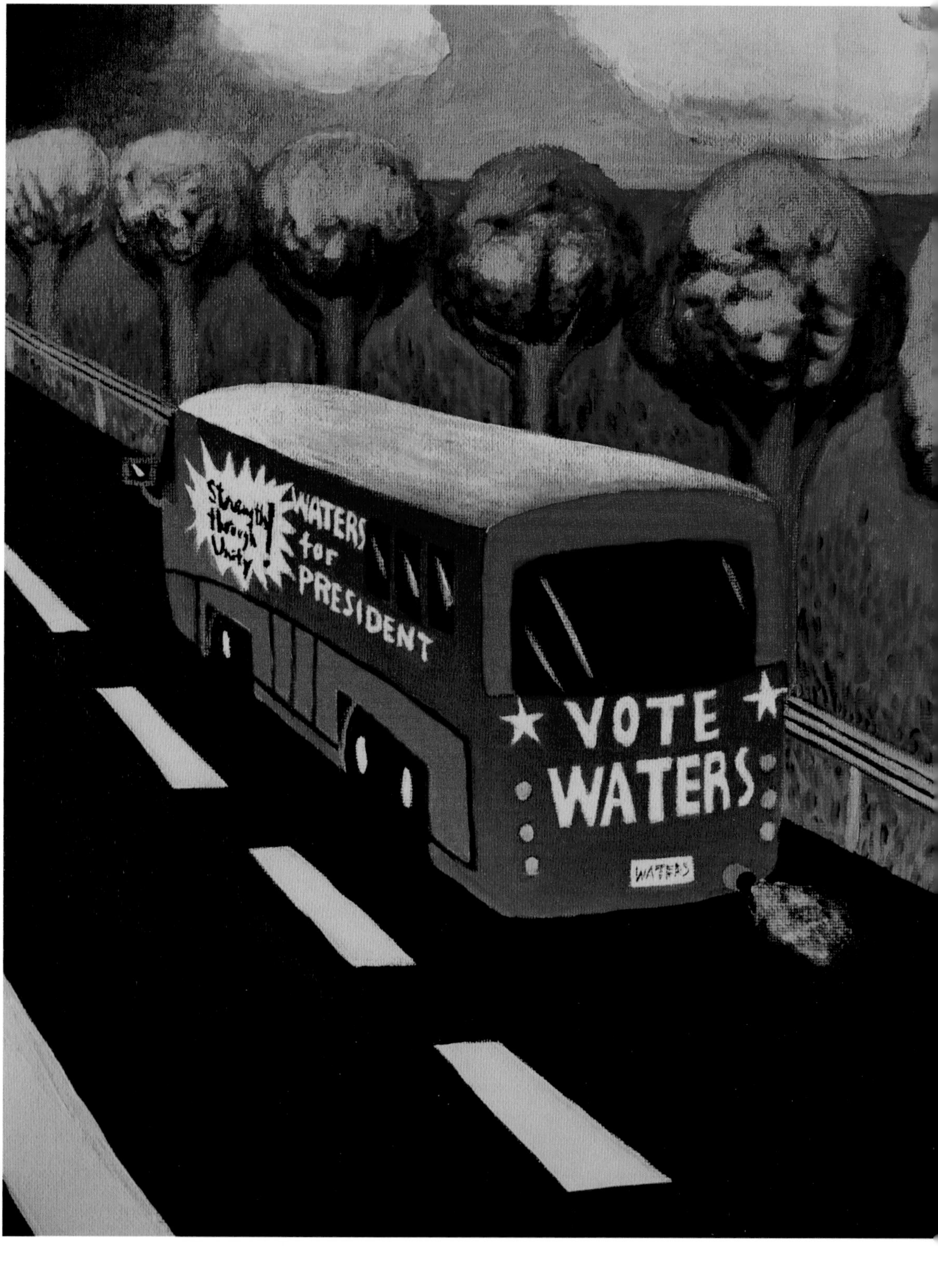
Strength through Unity!
WATERS for PRESIDENT
VOTE WATERS
WATERS